PRAISE FOR *THE* NORAH BOW

"*The Last Tale of Norah Bow* is a thrilling story—a roller-coaster ride with unforgettable characters and suspenseful life-and-death moments on the wild waves of Lake Erie. Like brave Norah herself, it is full of heart. I loved every page of it."

— Mary Logue, author of *The Streel*

"Like Homer's *Odyssey*, *The Last Tale of Norah Bow* is a voyage—ultimately, a voyage home. Through storms and calm, night sailing a great lake in a small boat, Norah is on a quest for answers to dangerous questions. There's a wonderfully vivid sense of place in this book: Lake Erie, its islands and inlets and its treacherous weather, the seedy dockyards of Prohibition-era Detroit, its whiskey river roaring with deadly opportunity. *The Last Tale of Norah Bow* is unfailingly eventful (buildings are destroyed, weapons wound and kill, death by drowning threatens more than once), but the story's real drama lies in Norah's heart, torn with suspicion, driven by love."

— Lon Otto, author of *A Man in Trouble*

"Norah Bow, the narrator of the novel by her name, is a dream of a character—a storyteller as clear-eyed and canny as the most memorable protagonists in the rich history of the American coming-of-age canon.

Capturing the reader instantly, Norah's vibrant, precocious voice carries us into the world, and the historical moment of *The Last Tale of Norah Bow*, where the tender, heartbreaking, and utterly believable story unfolds on the whiskey river of Detroit. With a setting so vivid it nearly breathes, a storyline propelled by the fearless, hopeful curiosity and wonderment of youth, and a narrator as captivating and compelling as any I've read, this novel is already a joy to read; but the language of the book makes it infinitely more than the sum of its parts.

White's lyrical mastery and exacting eye for what Nabokov called 'the divine detail' are evident not just in the glorious sentence-level prose but in their creation of a world and a story that envelops the reader from the first page to the last."

– Marya Hornbacher, author of *Wasted* and *Center of Winter & Madness*

THE LAST TALE OF NORAH BOW

J. P. White

Regal House Publishing

Published by
Regal House Publishing, LLC
Raleigh, NC 27605
All rights reserved

ISBN -13 (paperback): 9781646034604
ISBN -13 (epub): 9781646034611
Library of Congress Control Number: 2023943389

Cover images and design by © C. B. Royal

Regal House Publishing, LLC
https://regalhousepublishing.com

The following is a work of fiction created by the author. All names, individuals, characters, places, items, brands, events, etc. were either the product of the author or were used fictitiously. Any name, place, event, person, brand, or item, current or past, is entirely coincidental.

Printed in the United States of America

For Lynne Armstrong
and the many ancestors
who made of Rye Beach
a summer cottage home

"Secrecy flows through you, a different kind of blood."

    - Margaret Atwood, from *Secrecy*

"The future is long gone by and the past will never happen."

    - Kenneth Rexroth, from *This Night Only*

1

You can reach only so far into the cloud that anyone is and then that cloud travels on without you. Sometimes when I close my eyes, I can still feel the sway of the porch swing in that leeway between dusk and dark when the failing light is reluctant to lay down its truss. Daddy and I are sitting next to each other, speaking in low tones, careful that Momma is out of earshot. The upward notch of the swing is followed by the backward creak reminding me that Lake Erie is forever heaving itself on Rye Beach, then pulling back, always close and far away. I can hear again Daddy telling me about the one thing he and I shared. He called it our "demon switch." He said if you weren't born with this hidden fuse, you couldn't ever get it, no matter if you walked on your hands or ate steak and eggs every morning. The womb gave you the demon switch. Only the grave could take it back.

"Do I have it? This switch?"

"No question about it," he said, gripping my shoulders like he wanted me to know the full burden of my strength and brokenness.

"How does this demon go about its work?"

"When everything else breaks down, the demon in you takes charge."

"What do you mean?"

"Remember when that toddler fell into the lagoon and he sank like a stone? You and I were out taking a walk. You couldn't have been more than ten or eleven. I was looking out at the lake when it happened and I didn't even see the boy. The parents screamed. No one could think, but you didn't need to."

"I've tried to forget that day," I said.

"You dove into the water beside the breakwater with the waves pounding the rocks and somehow, Norah Bow, you brought that boy back. The father and mother looked at you like you were both an angel and a devil for doing something they couldn't imagine being done in this life. They thanked you many times, but they walked away from you faster than you could dry yourself off. Remember that?"

"Are you saying the parents of that boy thought I was…?"

"It scared them to be in your presence, even though they wept with joy at the return of their son. They thought you were a wild animal. Not of this world. I'm also saying you've known about this demon switch all your life. That you are different from other girls."

"And you have this demon, Daddy?"

"Top dead center," he said, drawing the heel of his right hand across his forehead like he was taking aim on a stubborn crease.

"How come I've never seen it?"

Daddy didn't answer me as we rocked on the porch swing watching fireflies gin up holes in the dark. He gave me his answer on another night, when I saw his demon change roles with the man I loved. I guess you could say most of my life has been about talking to my demons and angels, but for decades, I believed only my father was given to such spirited confessions in this land of bones and unbelief. Vigil and verse-reading have shown me otherwise. No matter how pretty we talk or how little we sulk, no one I've ever met is unfamiliar with the gates of the netherworld, and few in my wake have refused the help of a warrior angel. Even if you don't cotton to the Bible, you have to admit there are some lines there so riddled with the wild dark flame they can't be lit any better. Like this one from Psalm 141, *Let the wicked fall into their own nets while I alone escape.* That one verse peppers my blood and wings me back to the summer of 1926 when I was fourteen and I went after Daddy who'd been kidnapped by rumrunners on Lake Erie.

Just to be clear, my going after Daddy was not about serving justice or making sure my two brothers had a father or even about trying to assuage Momma's tears. No, my need to retrieve him was more fierce and elemental like some message staunch-writ on the tablet of my soul. Daddy never took counsel from an angel, never for one day believed in God's legion, but he did believe in me. For that reason alone, I wasn't about to quit on him because if I did, it would be like quitting on my own dream of a sailing life. The second reason was more like a sack of pig iron. I believed I was to blame for his being taken at gunpoint.

Because I don't sleep much anymore, I have the night's long middle to tell you how my Lake Erie net was cast long ago, or was it yesterday when the light and dark strands fell around me and I could do nothing more than set forth into a quadrant of great unsettling?

My beach hound, Bob, and I went down to the beach cove to polish off a slab of peach pie when we saw this lap-straked cruiser ghosting in without her red and greens showing. We heard the *blub blub* of the inboard idling, the kick of backwash, then the skipper cut the engine and this night boat slid into the dock like jelly off a knife.

Bob and I squinted to make the shapes emerge amid a cluster of fireflies peppering the dark. Before we saw faces, we heard voices scratched with smoke and long hours running. Bob wanted to sniff up close, but we talked it over, eyeball to eyeball, and decided to scoot back in the dune grass and let these men flesh out their intentions. We saw three men unloading wooden crates onto the dock, no wider than a pencil. Head-cocked and baffled, Bob and I looked at each other thinking these men were not hauling milk bottles for the Sandusky school district.

"Hard to believe water weighs more than whiskey," one man said, his voice kinking Bob's tail.

"Would you shut the hell up," another man said, his voice cut down to a rasp.

"This hooch is killing my stones," the first man said.

"Don't give a damn what's killing you," the second man croaked. "You'll get your money same as the Mexican Export."

"Who's buying these shipments?" the second man asked.

"Some local big," the throaty man said.

"How can one man quaff it all?"

"Far as I know, whiskey never goes bad."

What Bob didn't know about the sweaty tang of evil-bearing people was not worth knowing, so I guess what happened next was just a way to spotlight his own instincts. He flashed his yellow teeth at the low-slung moon and peeled over the top of the dune faster than a man-of-war. He ran straight for the three runners bent over their whiskey cases like he needed a jolt himself. I was fast on my feet, but Bob was the uncomplicated wind itself. Before I got off one shout, he'd already jumped toward the third silent man whose face I couldn't make out. The man with a sandpaper voice pulled out a gun. I figured I had about two seconds to jab into the gunner's spine and make his shot kick wide.

The third man barked, "Put your goddamn gun away."

"The dog was aiming for my throat," the man said, waving his gun in the air like a sparkler.

"It's my daughter's dog."

"What?" the gun-waving man said.

"You heard me," the third man said.

I grabbed Bob by the collar, dragged him away from Daddy, and tucked him behind my knees. Blood thumped my temples and every hair on my head tingled fire. I couldn't believe Daddy was with these men. He had even less patience with booze than he did with God so why was he crabbing sideways with these smugglers? Why? That's all Bob and I wanted to know.

"What the hell?" the man with the gun said.

Daddy said, "Leave her alone."

"Spies don't live long," the gunman said, then spat.

"I'm no spy," I said. "Bob and I were sitting over there in the dune eating a piece of pie when you come in and he smelled Daddy out. If I was a spy, do you think I would make it so easy for you to catch me?"

"Don't get smart with me, missy," the man said, his eyes sticking me.

"Smart has nothing to do with it. Just saying what happened."

"Let her be," Daddy said. "She'll be no trouble."

"What are you doing here?" I asked Daddy with as much scold as I could muster while pressing my thumb into Bob's collar to keep him from gnawing holes in these men.

"I can explain later," Daddy said, holding his palms up like he wanted to place them square on my shoulders and reason his wrong away.

"You better," I said, my eyes wet at the corners.

"If she says anything to anybody about seeing us here," the gunman said to Daddy, "you're going to end up face down in the drink. Then, I'll go after her."

"She won't talk to anybody. Will you, Norah?"

I took a long look at Daddy hoping he'd show me what to do next, but he fought to hold my gaze. Scanning the beach beyond, Daddy shouted, "Get out of here and don't come back."

Bent down over my dog, I backed away. Bob was a whimpering handful, miffed with me for cuffing him just for picking Daddy out of the whiskey dark.

That night, I tossed like I was lit up with a three-day fever. Bob was none too happy with my restless legs which kept spilling him off my bed. And I was none too happy that Daddy made no attempt over the next four days to seek me out and explain what he was doing on that dock with rumrunners. The absence of any explanation chewed on me real good.

I dragged myself to our regular Sunday night cottage dinner with enough questions and doubt to fill another Bible. Lots of folks, including Uncle Bill and Aunt Cora, had come over for fried perch, corn on the cob, home fries, tomatoes, cukes, lemonade, and peach pie with vanilla ice cream hand-cranked in an ice bucket. No beer, no whiskey, no wine. Daddy was a teetotaler—or so he boasted—and he wouldn't allow one thimble of booze in our Rye Beach cottage.

Daddy sold life insurance, which was a funny thing because he never believed in it and he never inked a policy for himself. He said nothing can insure a man against the darkness waiting at either end of the line. I asked him what he meant by that and he said, at birth we come out of darkness and at death we return, and there's just a patch of light, no thicker than a saltine, flickering between the two. All we ever get here is a chance.

Was the same man who helped me build my own sailboat a whiskey rogue? Whenever I needed money for wood, bolts, screws, halyards, sheets, paint, you name it, Daddy gave me coin. Since I was a happy drain on his wallet, maybe I'm the one who drove him to run booze across Lake Erie, but he wouldn't even look at me, let alone tell me how he came to be there. My head hurt from trying to unlock the chance my father had come to. More than food, more than sleep, I wanted answers.

What made this hurt hard to bear was a simple fact: Rye Beach was our paradise. It was a sandy splice of land set downwind from the Bass Islands. It came with a fishing pier, a park shaded with red and white oaks, a marshy lagoon perfect for launching toy boats, a penny candy store, and an ice cream stand with the three dependable flavors: chocolate, strawberry, and vanilla. Time itself, in 1926, had left long ago, so nothing ever changed except the wind's direction. Even Prohibition, six years old and counting, didn't seem to jigger the pulse of our beachy place. Yes, I had heard men and women whispering the allure of liquid escape like they were necessary stops on a rosary bead: *tipple, toddy, giggle water, flutter juice,* but those whispers seemed harmless. More unsettling were the descriptions of being drunk. I'd find them casually delivered by teachers, storekeepers, and sprinkled in cartoons and sermons. The words always spoke of sudden breakdown: *plastered, buckled, clobbered, hammered, shredded, crooked, four to the floor.* It was hard for me to imagine the appeal of such chaos and escape and so I never laughed when those descriptions were throttled as punch lines.

Occasionally, a crime story, connected to booze smuggling, would creep into the newspaper, but never on the front page of the *Sandusky Register*. Men still gabbed more about the Cleveland Indians winning the World Series in 1920, and when they might do it again, than they did about gangsters in Detroit and Chicago.

Others still prattled about the influenza epidemic of 1918 like it was a coming disaster instead of a freak storm already blown through. I nearly died of that flu when I was six, but Daddy wouldn't let me cross over into the bye and bye. I remember Doc Williams shaking his head, saying, *Good God Almighty, here today, gone tomorrow.* Both my lungs were packed with gunk. My fever jumped to the moon. I saw grackles in a swarm outside my window. Like they were coming for me with a shroud. Daddy told the doc, "God has nothing to do with it." In my delirium, I didn't know who I was, but somehow Daddy brought me back to our namesake. The doc left my bedside soon enough. Daddy never did.

Weeks later, when I did manage to find a slouch, I peered again out my window at the world I nearly lost and saw bodies stacked up at the end of our street like cordwood. I tried to stand, and I fell over. I had cracked most of my ribs from all-night coughing fits and I had no use of my legs. Daddy didn't even bother to consult with Doc Williams. Instead, he found every ladder-back chair we had and a pair of curtain rods and he brought them up to my bedroom. Like he was shaping a piano, Daddy set the chairs in two rows, then ran the rod through the open gaps and made me my own set of parallel bars. Every hour for four weeks, he fed me what he called "vital broth" and he made me stagger and thrash my way along those bars until some life returned to my legs. He wouldn't let me die and then he wouldn't let my legs fail. Grief was delivered that year in small, untidy bundles set out by the road, but I was not among them.

Mostly we talked perch and walleye. God, we loved to gab about this false god. *Where were they biting? What were they biting? Who was catching more fish?* For all the nursing and cursing of that fish, you'd think walleye would be the name of our church. I went fishing a couple of times with Uncle Bill and even caught a stringer, but I thought trolling for walleye was about as exciting as snagging a dead man's boot off the lake bottom. No bigger than a peach pit, my Lake Erie beach town was hard to find even if you lived in Sandusky, but once you were there, you never wanted to leave.

One street off the beach, our cottage sat wide and low with porches slung across the front and back. The front screened porch had a sleeping room on the right side and that's where I slept with my head full of Lake Erie surf knocking against the boulder pier and the long bramble spit running toward the amusement park known as Cedar Point. In paradise, you have no need for secrets crowding your blood. All you do is get a burn. Get your feet wet. Get an ice cream. Do it all over again and again like you know in your bones that the rhythm of such days will outlive you. I once heard Momma claim to a neighbor woman that she and Vital had no secrets and that was the secret to their marriage. Seems Momma got it wrong.

The night was hotter than a penny run over by a train.

Aunt Cora wore a short, scooped-neck white dress with green buttons in front like a military jacket along with gold hoop earrings, a matching bangle, and scarlet lipstick. She was a flirt with a nice shape and Daddy had trouble not throwing her a second glance. Momma wore a full-length blue-flowered dress with matching flats. She parted her chestnut-colored hair in the middle, pulled it back in a bun and held it in place with a mother-of-pearl clip that her momma had given her. Despite the cheerful hum of her kitchen, her own pale complexion stood out with a shadow of fatigue tucked under deep-set hazel eyes. Her one false tooth in front made her self-conscious about smiling so her thin lips vanished beneath the sheer of her nose. Momma wanted me to wear a dress when we had company. She rolled her eyes at my navy blue shorts, then softened her look when she saw the cream-colored blouse with hand smocking at the yoke she'd made for me last winter. I thought it was too girly, but I knew the blouse would please her.

"You look nice," she said, sensing my agitation.

Normally, I didn't linger in the kitchen, but that evening I stood near Momma like I wanted her kitchen smells to tell me tomorrow was coming right on time. I looked at her kerosene stove fed with two glass oil bottles. Saw the grease-stained doors of the tin oven. The crowded wood box. The black matchbox on the wall from West Virginia. The sink with the cast iron worn through the porcelain. The jar of wooden spoons. The teakettle, the rolling pins, the Flower of the Month calendar. Her life cut and peeled and scrubbed and served from this poorly lit stronghold.

"What's got into you?" she asked. "Take Bob upstairs so he won't bother our guests."

"You mean, Aunt Cora. She's never liked my dog."

Momma nodded. "Go on."

When he wasn't with me, Bob never strayed far from the backdoor near the kitchen. He had flattened himself from the heat like a fat squirrel does in August. He looked at me with hurt and baleful sorrow, a look he had mastered as a pup.

"Not a chance," I told him as I dragged him upstairs to Momma's bedroom. I stopped and looked at myself in Momma's vanity mirror and Bob looked too, his nose crinkling with faint hope for some culinary reward.

"What do you think?" I asked him. He tipped his head like maybe I had struck upon a new game. The face I saw there was veined with light and shadow. I had Momma's hazel eyes, chestnut hair, high forehead, thin, worried lips. Like her, I could be pretty enough if I smiled some. My square chin and big ears didn't do me any favors. Instead of smiling, I opened my mouth to check if any food was jammed in my teeth. I shook out my ponytail, but my hair looked greasy so I bunched it again, tied it off with a band, then I undid the knot, and let my hair hang long. I told Bob to get some sleep. Sunday supper could take a while.

That night Daddy was a sheepish spit of a man parked in a ladder-back chair. He didn't weigh much over a hundred and twenty-five pounds. If he turned sideways, he could disappear in a shadow thrown off a doorway. He had ears big enough to flag down a garbage scow, but he had no wiggle in them that night. At five foot five, I was every inch as tall as he was and just as strong. He kept a chin-up bar in his study and no matter how many pull-ups he did, I matched his strength followed by a skin-the-cat. He and I never failed to make each other laugh with our derring-do, but there was no laugh in him that Sunday night. Momma and I seldom laughed because she was always after me to be more like her even though I told her I was not like anybody else and I was certainly not keen on sewing, cooking, and keeping things clean and tidy.

"Hey, Vital," Uncle Bill said, "you hear about the boat they found off Huron all shot up with holes? Two men, dead. Rum-runners, I guess."

Daddy scratched an eyebrow with a pinkie. I saw a bead of sweat on his upper lip. A little hint of rain curtain traveled across his face.

"Yeah, I did hear something about that."

"Right here, in our own backyard. Second time this month," Uncle Bill said. "What kind of whiskey's worth dying for?"

Never at a loss for words, Daddy surveyed the room like he wanted to make the shape and feel of it stick in his memory. Then he said in a hoarse whisper, "Money's never worth dying for."

We gathered round our oval table draped with a flowered oil cloth. When Daddy pulled out his chair, we took our cue to sit down, boy-girl, boy-girl, everyone laughing except Daddy and me and Momma. If there ever was a Sunday dinner at the cottage when I wanted to offer a blessing, it was that one because I figured Daddy needed all the help he could get. Since Daddy was an atheist and Momma seldom attended church except on Christmas and Easter, no one had ever heard more than a mumbled blessing at our cottage, and that night we didn't even manage that. Momma brought out a platter of fried perch and a bowl of steaming corn. The corn got passed, then the butter and salt followed, then a plate of tomatoes thick as steaks, then a bowl of string beans, snap peas, and cukes brushed with salt and vinegar. Everyone started grinning like there was a photographer on hand. I had to hand it to Momma—she knew how to lay out a spread that brought everyone together. Each perch filet no bigger than the palm of your hand and not as thick. The white flaky meat so sweet I can still taste it even though that savoring was a thousand years ago yesterday.

My two brothers wobbled in a day crib I had made out of a grocer's pallet and fish net I'd found on the beach. The crib worked pretty good except it didn't muzzle their fussing and whining. They could have invented the word crybabies for those two snot-nosed boys. Momma looked at me like it was my job to make them happy, and I shot her back a look saying, *Forget it.* You'd have thought because they were boys, Daddy would have been eager to spend time with them, but he seldom did. Momma and Daddy tried for more than a decade to have more children, but I guess it took so long that Daddy's enthusiasm for fatherhood wore out. That night he never looked at his boys, not once.

I sat to Daddy's right, close enough to brush the back of his hand. His jaw bulged while he tapped his right foot. His whole body twitched and flexed like a hoisted sail fresh out of wind. I extended my fingers and wrapped them around his. He smiled, surprised at my reach, and nodded like maybe he knew I sensed the full measure of his discomfiture. Our eyes worked out some code of hope and confusion. In that one shared moment, I felt shiny new and old as dirt all at the same time. I squeezed harder and he squeezed back. I thought, *Daddy is still here. That's all that matters.* Everyone leaned into the table, eager to dig into Momma's food, and everyone was temporarily frozen, suspended, waiting for Daddy to begin. I could hear the breathing of the table, the licking of lips, the scraping of chairs, the men loosening their belts, and Aunt Cora running her hands through her hair and smacking her tongue against the back of her teeth like she was sucking hard candy. One blue bottle fly with orange eyes as big as headlights circled the table like it was aiming to return to the source of some animal remains that had spawned it. Daddy picked up his knife and fork and that prompted a creaking in the sashes and a rattle of window glass.

The cottage door burst open and the three candles strung along the length of the table all bent down their flames. One blew out. Three men in long coats and bandanas over their mouths poured across the threshold like a sheet of burning oil. Aunt Cora dropped her hands against her plate. Her fat ear of unbuttered corn cartwheeled off the table and hit the floor like a cannon ball.

Uncle Bill muttered, "What the hell?"

One of the men conked Uncle Bill with the butt of his gun. Bill slumped and fell out of his chair, blood gushing from his forehead. A moan trickled out of my uncle's chest. The man in the middle whipped out a black sack and cinched it over Daddy's head. The man held a gun to the black sack covering Daddy's head. I looked at the head in the black sack. I didn't hear a sound from Daddy.

The gunman said, "If anyone screams, I'll pull the trigger and scatter his brains inside this bag, eh."

Momma's face turned white as the butter dish. Her eyes spun in her head before she fainted, which made the man holding the gun to Daddy's head twitch his ears like a roadside rabbit. I studied the men for height and build, clothing, shoes, anything I might use to recognize them in some other place at another time. The man on the left was bald and stocky and he had a beard bulging from under his bandana. The man in the middle was a spoon over six feet. His thin, calloused hands hung at his sides. His middle index nail was swollen black, the rest of them were cracked and jagged. The man on the right had a ropey gut. He made a two-footed hop like a roadside crow guarding a kill. He was the one who scared me the most. I was glad I'd left Bob in Momma's room. It flipped my stomach to think of him lunging at the gunman and getting himself shot up full of holes. I blinked once, maybe twice, and the men poured out of the house as fast as they had come in, the smell and stain of them lingering like a foul gas.

No one knew what to say. They stared at the front door like maybe Daddy would return on his own accord. I knew better. I ran outside. Momma called out, "Norah Bow, get back in here." I looked out into the night, wet my finger to feel the wind and the hole those men had slipped through. I backed myself into the cottage knowing I had to tell everyone what I had seen on the beach.

"Those rumrunners took Daddy to Canada," I whispered. "We've got to follow them."

"They have guns," Momma squawked.

"Don't care what they have," I said, rushing toward the door, but Aunt Cora blocked my path.

"You can't do that," Aunt Cora shouted. "You're just a—"

I tried to push Aunt Cora aside, but she threw her whole weight against me and I sputtered sideways and collided with the dry sink. Uncle Bill pulled himself up off the floor, pressing one hand against the gash in his head. Blood and all, he had the clarity of mind to reach for the telephone on the wall and ring the sheriff.

"It's my fault," I blurted out.

"What are you saying?" Uncle Bill asked.

"I saw Daddy on the beach and—"

"We're all upset Norah, but now is not the time to—" my uncle said.

"Let me tell you what—"

"Not now," Aunt Cora said. "We have to figure out what to say?"

"What do you mean?"

"What are we going to tell the sheriff and the neighbors?"

"You're worried about the neighbors?"

"Norah," Momma called out. "For once can you hold your tongue?"

One long hour passed after Uncle Bill rang up Sheriff Kelly and he came over to our cottage. The sheriff was an imposing figure, but not in a way you could lean into. So much sweat poured off his forehead, you'd think he was stoking a train. He had a gut you'd need to carry in a wheelbarrow. Before any of us could say anything, he asked for a glass of water and killed it in two gulps.

"Do you know who took him?" he asked, wiping his brow with his forearm.

"Rumrunners from Canada," I piped up.

The sheriff held out his glass to Aunt Cora for a refill.

"How do you know this?"

"I could smell their breath and the engine oil on their clothes," I said. "The gunman rounded his Os, flattened his As, and finished his sentence with, eh."

The sheriff smiled weakly like he should have known to ask about the sounds and smells the men brought with them.

"You might be right, Norah Bow."

"I know I'm right."

Those three men plucked Daddy right out of our paradise and they meant him no good. When the full force of this crime hit me, a terrible loneliness ran me over because I knew this kidnapping was my fault. I didn't say a word to anyone about what I saw on the beach, but the three men must have figured I would. They came back to make sure it didn't matter what I said.

Sheriff Kelly said no man had ever before been abducted from Rye Beach. He looked lost when he said this, like maybe we would scotch our story and replace it with some other version. I figured whatever chance we had to follow the three rumrunners was nearly gone. They were probably speeding back to Canada with Daddy knocked out, bleeding or already dead. I got madder and madder just watching our dim-witted sheriff puzzle out the obvious coordinates.

"If those men took Vital to Canada, I've got no jurisdiction there."

"That's no excuse," I said. "Everyone knows you get seasick just looking at the water."

"Norah, that's enough," Momma said, her voice more of a whimper than a command. With each passing minute I knew it was up to me to bring Daddy home because our sheriff had no intention of going to Canada to fetch him. Best our sheriff would do would be to get the story on the front page of the *Sandusky Daily Register.* Daddy would get some ink, but that wouldn't bring him back from the green-black swells of Erie.

From early on, I remembered Daddy telling me, "There's nothing you can't do when you're sailing on Lake Erie, Norah Bow. When everyone else is afraid of storms, you stand strong. You are the bow of the world." When he first said this to me, I smiled because he was making a play on our name spelled the same way as the word that means the front end of a boat, the bow.

Why did Daddy have to call me the bow of the world like he was singling me out now to go bring him back from some unnamed torment? Why did three men, hauling my daddy away with a black bag over his head, make me feel like I was already dead, but never more alive? I don't like to swear, but goddamn tomorrow and send it back to running fire, but these men, whoever they were, would not get away with this crime. Even if Daddy had brought this on himself, I still believed in him the way he believed in my legs, *You will walk again, Norah Bow.*

Uncle Bill and Aunt Cora and even a few nosy neighbors eventually cleared off, all shaking their heads, some crying, some pledging to return in the morning, some saying they would help find Daddy. I knew better. They would all talk themselves into a corner while they nursed a cup of coffee, but they would never make a move, because all of them, like the sheriff, were mostly afraid of Lake Erie and the thin men who knew how to zigzag across it with hooch from Canada.

2

Momma curled on her bed. She wept past midnight, her sobs like something wrung out of a trapped animal. I went to my room with Bob following close like he knew what I was up to and didn't like it, so he let out a whine every thirty seconds just to show me how smart he was about the trespass that hung in the air. I changed out of my navy shorts into cut-off jeans. I pulled off the Sunday smock Momma had threaded and slipped on a T-shirt that read, *Little Sal's Bait & Tackle*. Bob led the way back to Momma's room. I sat beside her in silence, then I squeezed her arm, her hands. Her head hung from the stalk of her neck. Saliva dribbled from her bottom lip. When she closed her eyes, I scribbled a note, left it on her pillow.

Gone to bring him back.

I took the stairs two at a time and found Momma's blue canvas duffel in the closet. Half thinking Momma would stir, I ran to the kitchen. I flung open the pantry door and grabbed a jar of peanut butter, a loaf of bread, three big wedges of peach pie, and a sack of apples. I found a gallon jug of milk in the icebox, took a swig, and shoved the jug into the duffel. Before I left the kitchen, I sunk my hand into the cookie jar and took fifty dollars in crumpled bills. I hurried back to the living room, my head swimming with what else I might need. I went back to the closet and peeled my foul weather gear from a hanger. I eyed Momma's favorite wool blankets on the back shelf and took two of those and a towel. On a lower shelf, I found Daddy's binoculars, his pocketknife, his box of lures, his flashlight, and his chart of the Middle Bass Islands and the Detroit River. I thought twice about taking my fishing pole, standing in the corner behind the broom, then grabbed it too.

I couldn't look at Bob looking at me so I glanced at the folded chart. I figured there was only one place where Daddy might be still alive and that was Pelee Island, the southernmost tip of Canada, some twenty miles west of north. I ignored Bob's brush against my legs and crammed everything into Momma's blue duffel, tiptoed to the screen door, stepped out into the night, and locked the door.

I stood there, frozen with the weight of what I was about to do, and flicked tears. The thought of sailing alone to Canada raised a cold sweat along my neck. I cried because I remembered a proverb that says whoever digs a pit will fall into it and Daddy had surely fallen into a pit with no bottom. I couldn't stand to think of finding Daddy bobbing facedown in Erie with gulls anchored on his spine. I cried because I didn't want to live with Momma and two blubbering brothers with her telling me how I had to clean bottoms, wipe noses, fix a peanut butter and jelly. I cried because Bob couldn't come with me and because I was fourteen and everyone on this tipsy earth knows that fourteen is not yet an age when you can bend the world to your will.

I put my tears away and returned to our cottage because I forgot one important thing: a picture of Daddy. I removed the key from under the slate of the front walk and opened the door. Bob sat inside, nose to the door, like a priest in a confessional wondering what I was doing in the night's skinny without him. I stroked his head, then went to the mantel above the stone hearth. The picture was of Daddy and me fishing off the Rye Beach pier. I held a stringer of perch and he stood behind me looking like I just won a new car at the Sandusky Firemen's Annual $5 Raffle. I lifted the tacks from the cardboard back, slipped the picture out and stuck it under my shirt. I shuffled back to the door. I stood inside the screen door, flickering like a caught moth, and told Bob I had to do something hard. I got down on my knees, held his face to my face and told him I needed his help.

"Going to be gone a while and I need you to look after Momma." He shook his head, slumped over, got up, sat back down, listened to another dog somewhere.

"Don't let any strangers in. Save a piece of pie for me."

After a string of whines, Bob nuzzled my face. He leapt forward when I turned the knob, and I waved him off. When he pressed his nose against the screen, I couldn't blink back any more tears. I wanted to take him with me in the worst way, but I couldn't imagine losing him overboard. He didn't have sea legs. I backed away all the while wondering how I was going to keep my spirits up without Bob beside me. The night was cut with a silver dust but it offered no spotlight and gave no quarter. I tried to focus the dark without stumbling. I walked beside beach cottages I'd seen a thousand times, but I felt then like I was leaving the far borders of the known world and there was no telling what beasts and seraphim lay ahead.

I came up on *Odyssey* at neighbor Chuck Wilson's dock. She looked like what she was, a homemade boat tied off with fenders and spring lines and too small to accomplish what I needed from her—sail after three men in a speedboat bound for Canada. As I untied the cockpit tarp, my legs trembled and my brain went soft with doubt: *I can't do this. I can. I can't. I must.* I repeated the phrases until my seesaw chant turned into the slam of a gate in my head. A smallmouth leapt out of the water not five feet from the dock and thwacked the surface. I jumped back, rattled, angry at myself for getting spooked by a lunker with a nimble jaw in the slow and dark.

I stowed my gear and supplies in the cabin, hanked the jib on the headstay, untied the dock lines, grabbed my paddle and sank it into the ink of Lake Erie. A hundred feet out, I looked back and saw the twinkle of cottage lights tucked behind the cottonwood trees and heard the bark of Wilson's dog. That one solitary voice made me want to return home, all the way back to better times, but I paddled into the dark until I felt the wind freshen. I clipped the halyard onto the mainsail and hoisted the sail up the track. As *Odyssey* pulled forward out beyond my summer cottage town, the mainsail filled like a white shadow over my head. I told my heart to quit banging so hard so I could get my bearings, keep a close eye on the channel markers off Cedar Point, and make good for Kelly's Island.

I cast out a prayer. *Heaven help me bring Daddy home.* I knew my boat could make this happen because Daddy and I built her stout. *Odyssey* was a tough customer, and so was I. The men who took my daddy at gunpoint better know I was more than a match for them because I'd tasted more violence at the lee rail of a Lake Erie squall than those men in a speedboat would ever know. And then there were the spoils of the demon switch Daddy said were only mine and his. Surely, I could use those spoils now.

Daddy and I had spent more than a year building *Odyssey*. I needed a boat no bigger than sixteen feet so I could take her out single-handed with no trouble. I'd found a design in a boating magazine at the library with a sleek cabin so Bob could hunker down when the lightning jigged. The plan cost me ten dollars, but even with the cabin for cover, Bob howled at the first clap of thunder. Daddy and I figured the design would cost nearly a hundred dollars in wood and other materials, which was a pile of dough back then when a brand new Model T roadster cost only three hundred and change. He said he'd fork over the money for my boat as long as I helped him repair his cars at night and on weekends.

Daddy loved cars and engines and knew just about everything that could go wrong with carburetors, spark plugs, fan belts, clutches, brake shoes, transmissions, you name it. I could never figure out why he became an insurance salesman when he was born to have engine grease under his fingernails. Daddy asked me why I needed to build such a seafaring craft.

"I want to stay out on the lake after everyone else comes in."

"Why?"

"I want to know about storms."

He winked like maybe he should have known I'd say that. Daddy and I ordered the best wood we could find. White oak for the keel, mast step, and stern post. Virginia white cedar for the planking. Spruce for the spar, boom, and deck ribs. All of it slow-dried and rich with the smell of the lumber yards in Vickery, Ohio. Then, I got to work, first spreading out the design on big sheets of drawing paper to see how the white oak frames would lay out on six-inch centers.

Everything I'd built before then, I'd cobbled out of scrap timber washed up on the beach, so you can imagine my boats were not much for water-tight. I didn't know the first thing about steam-fitting, but Tom Mullins, who milled heartland pine in Rye Beach and repaired wooden sailboats, showed me how to use his steam bender. Daddy helped hold the planking while I edge-nailed with hot glue. It was the hardest work I'd ever done but with each plank hugging the frames, I could feel a boat with backbone and clean lines coming forth, sweet to gaze upon even when she wasn't holding a bone in her teeth.

With fear wetting my eyes, I saw what my year of hard work had been all about. I built the *Odyssey*, with my own knuckle-busted hands so I could trim and test her on a night like this, when Sheriff Kelly wouldn't even look at a chart of Canadian waters. Then again, the man couldn't even swim.

3

Once I pushed off from shore, I stopped shaking and regained the familiar comfort of leaving the land behind. Just me and *Odyssey*, heading out, the wind leaving no more than a cat's paw on the water as the mainsail and jib filled to starboard. I found some lift and speed and more than enough moon to smooth the edge of my jangle. I passed the outer entrance to Cedar Point in less than an hour.

I pictured myself wandering the deserted midway, past the blinking neon Ferris wheel and two roller coasters, the entire amusement park closed to the world but opened to me. You can't live anywhere in Ohio without visiting Cedar Point at the end of a spit running just west of Rye Beach. We didn't go often because of the cost, but right then I would have paid dearly to be at Cedar Point with Daddy, waiting for the dawn to greet us so we could be the first to ride the Blue Ghost.

I felt the wind flex the rigging and kick up whitecaps through South Passage below Kelly's Island and everything in the night slapped my face. I sheeted the main and jib, and reached below for my sweater and flashlight because my red compass light was on the fritz. I clicked on the flashlight, cupped the beam to dull the glare, and held it over the compass, flush-mounted on the cabin bulkhead. My heading was just west of north at 340 degrees.

With the steady southwesterly wind, I thought I could make Pelee Island on a single tack. I cracked the sheets just so I could feel the wind in my left hand like a living flame drawing me out of the dark pocket I'd left behind. In my tiller hand, I felt the long pull of Erie as she ran out deeper and wider, the occasional crack of a wave on my port side reminding me not to nod off. The moon was so close, no matter how I steered, it held me in the fold of its track. I couldn't fashion into a consolation what

I planned to do once I got to Pelee Island, but that didn't stop me from letting the wind tickle my backbone. I settled in for the night reach to Pelee when I saw about twenty degrees off to port what appeared to be a dinghy, aimlessly adrift from its owner and destination. I put the binoculars on the ghostly rig and saw what looked like a frayed coat dangling from a carnival ride.

I would have been happy to retrieve such a boat, under any other circumstances, with the thought I might be able to sell her. But that night I had no business doing salvage as I had done on other occasions. Still, I had to honor the sea-faring obligation and find out if someone was on board and needed help. Early on, Daddy told me you never turn your back on a boat in distress because you never know when that boat might be your own. I pointed upwind as high as *Odyssey* could go, then flopped so I could run alongside this moon-drenched craft catching air with a drape of cloth. Even from a distance, I could see the boat was no piece of junk. It made me sick to think I couldn't tow the smartly lap-straked boat and convert her to sail. I saw a woman, legs propped on the gunwale, the wind billowing her dress and turning it into a miniature sail.

"Ahoy, there," I called out.

I repeated my greeting, flinching some when I did so, thinking this time the woman might be dead and I would be bound to haul her with me and make her death known. As I jibed, a tousled head of red hair fell inside a vein of moonlight. The woman was just as surprised to see me as I was to see her. Both of us slack-jawed, we said nothing, but stared after each other like we'd never seen another living, breathing female before. I jibed again, aiming to find the right tack to drift down on her without bringing harm to either craft. Something had gone very wrong and there was no telling what that was.

"What are you doing out here?" I shouted.

"Might ask the same of you," the woman said.

I came into the wind, not two yards from the craft and lowered sail.

"Grab a line," I said.

The red-headed woman reached out and caught the line. With her arms outstretched, I saw she wore a silver-beaded flapper dress, low cut in the front, the hem torn away and blackened from smoke. Her kiss-curl hair didn't cover the bruises on her face. Her left ear was puffed out like a water balloon. I wondered if this once-fancy woman, sprung from a fire, might be a ghost, invisible to all in this life but me who had fished her out of my own unspoken need for crew.

"I've got no fenders so we can't raft up," I said.

The woman reached out and drew my boat closer. As she pulled, I had a notion to hoist sail and veer away because there was no way of knowing whether she would offer me more muscle or mischief than I already had. She had heft on me and looked as if she could cast me overboard, take my boat. She read my thin smile.

"I mean you no harm," she said, her eyeballs burning me.

"You didn't answer my question," I said, grabbing the paddle.

"I was knocked on the head and set adrift by the captain of a fishing boat called the *Purple Goose*."

"Why'd he do such a thing?"

"Need to ask him," she said. Something about the way she said this rang true like maybe this was not the first time she'd found herself keeping time with an agitated man. Moonlight caught the silver beads on her dress as she talked and they made her skin look like a living thing. The shimmer made me want to look at her more and look away so I wouldn't be blinded.

"When I come alongside, I'll steady the boats so you can step into the center of my boat."

"Sounds easy enough," she said.

"One more thing," I added. "You can't bring anything with you."

"I've got a traveling bag," the woman said.

"What's in it?"

"Just a few necessities."

"Guess so," I said.

The woman looked into the green heave of Lake Erie and sighed, the relief on her face more visible than the moonlight. As the two boats nudged and bounced, I pulled her dinghy toward me with my paddle.

"Time the swell," I said, looking her straight in the eye so she knew I meant what I said. "When the two boats touch again, step over. If you jump, you'll land in the drink."

She eyed the waves, then stepped over briskly. In an instant, my once roomy *Odyssey* seemed crammed for space.

"Ruby Francoeur," she said, with a smoky voice. "Lately, from Toledo."

"What sort of a name is that?" I asked.

"Mother's English. Father's French. My name plays in both camps."

There was more rough than tender with this woman, a hard shine to her skin and a shrouded depth, her hair red as sundown, a beauty spilling out of a dress that would turn a priest into an eyeball sinner. Red hair, green eyes, something of the martyr turned gypsy. Her fingers trolled over her lips like she was looking to snag the right words to win me over to her cause. The only other time I'd seen a woman like this was at Cedar Point, a blond on the midway hawking the bottle-throw. Men lined up, besotted by her long legs, loose-fitting dress, and a bold array of teasing head angles, followed by a giddy, revealing stance while she called out, "Come on, sunshine. Try your luck with me. There's a winner every time. Anytime you want. Try your luck with me. Only a dime. Any time is summertime. Only a dime. Anytime you want."

"Norah Bow," I said. I matched Ruby's formality by giving my port of origin. "From Sandusky, Ohio. Actually, Rye Beach, four miles east of Sandusky."

"Never been to either place," Ruby said, straightening herself out, "but I've heard of Sandusky."

"It's just behind us." I pointed into the low black swells behind us.

"So you got some trouble too?" Ruby asked, as she eased back into the cockpit combing.

"Three men burst into my house in Rye Beach and took my daddy. I aim to bring him back."

She laughed from her belly and threw me a crinkly-eyed smile that made her look broke and beautiful at the same time.

"How do you know where to look for these three men who took your daddy?"

"They're rumrunners," I said, with more than a spark of defiance. "And whiskey comes from Canada and the southernmost point in all of Canada is Pelee Island. If you're going to stay on my boat, that's where we're headed now."

"Are you sprung from a farm or something?"

"How many farmers sail their own boat?"

"You look like you've been toting bales."

"Wouldn't know the first thing about that."

For one recently adrift, Ruby spoke with an ease and assurance that pointed to a dim appraisal of her situation or a complete acceptance of it, but she wasn't letting on which might be the true account she wanted me to grasp.

"Nothing has a claim on me," I said defiantly, "but my own conscience."

Ruby rolled her thumb over her first two fingers like she was trying to kick out a spark from her own skin.

"Spoken like a soldier. Whose war you fighting?"

The French woman twanged my head. Whose war was I fighting? What hot mustard was that? Plain and simple, I was going after my daddy because no one else would. I opened my mouth to spit conviction. I tasted something less.

"Don't really know how to answer that."

She smiled a lot, this time from some faraway place like she knew she had me looped, snagged, swallowing hard. A spate of foam-licked waves smacked the hull and carried us over into a lulling silence she took advantage of.

"Always loved chestnut brown hair and straight at that."

"What?"

"Your hair. It's a pretty color. You'll want to ditch the cap and wear it below your shoulders."

"Why is that?"

Ruby pondered my question about as long as it took to blow air through a straw.

"Two ways to answer that," Ruby said, her words teasing me out of my retreat.

"Give me one and leave it at that," I said.

"You've got the strength part figured out, but what's the point of saying no to beauty."

The animal boldness in Ruby slinked into me. She was hard boiled and soft at the same time. I wanted to take off my cap and run my hands through my hair the way she did. I resisted the impulse because what did the color of my hair have to do with a man stolen in the night from the stronghold of his family?

"How old are you, Norah Bow?"

"Fourteen."

"Old enough to know better."

"Nothing I can't do on this lake," I said, gripping down on the tiller and staring off toward Kelly's Island. My tongue swished cotton inside my mouth and I did have trouble swallowing.

"These men have guns?"

I said nothing.

"You have a gun?"

"Don't need one," I said. "I have the truth and the North Star," I boasted, pointing straight north to the star glowing like the tip of a knife blade.

"Crazy as a two-headed goose," Ruby said, clutching her traveling bag to her chest. I now saw her face more clearly. Her cheekbones were smudged with engine oil and her eyes were like loose buttons that matched the frayed hem of her dress. She added with a start, "Men with guns like to use them."

"So what," I said.

I looked straight into her blood-rimmed eyes, thinking who

better to help me navigate the world of vultures than a worldly woman like this one. Ruby shook her head like maybe she would have been better off drifting until dawn.

"I could use a little bounce and lipstick," I said, wondering if this woman's ample curves might help me draw a straighter line to my father.

"Not so fast, girl—"

"When you come aboard my boat, you sign on as crew."

"I don't think your odds are much better than spit, so—" I cut her off.

"I can take you back to the shit middle of nowhere and you can sit in that dinghy of yours with no oars until the next fishing captain comes along and takes a fancy to that torn dress of yours."

"At fourteen you already know something about being mean."

"Just sizing up the facts," I said, feeling an uptick of wind in the pull of the tiller.

She gathered some argument into her eyes, but again I stopped her.

"You look like a woman accustomed to getting her own way," I said, pausing long enough to shore up my courage to show her both strength and need. "I could use crew and you could use a ride."

"Where in the hell did you come from?"

"I'll get you back to dry land, but first you have to help me."

"You don't want much."

"My daddy taught me about skin in the game."

"Your daddy's a gambler?"

"I heard him say it once."

"You've got some spunk."

"I've got more than that," I snapped.

"Damn, it's dark out here."

"Get used to it," I said, like this was my hundredth dark crossing of Lake Erie instead of my first. Truth be told: Ruby looked like someone practiced in the art of the big gamble and

with her on board, the loneliness of the world's harm weighed
a little less or that's what I told myself just then. Ruby slowly
unclenched her fist from her leather traveling bag, then ducked
her head into my doghouse cabin.

"Just scrunch your bag anywhere in there," I directed.

"I've got some clothes I want to keep—"

"You won't be needing any clothes," I said.

Ruby chuckled as she wiggled below with her duffel.

"What I mean is—"

"I know what you meant," Ruby said. "You wouldn't have a
smoke?" she asked, rubbing her hands together like it was the
middle of January instead of July.

"I don't smoke or drink and I don't swear all that much," I
said.

"Give me time and I'll change that," Ruby said.

"Tell me again how you came to be floating out in the middle of Lake Erie?"

Ruby leaned back against the combing, resting her bare feet
up on the port side as if she had just sailed from one end of
Erie to the other and had dropped hook in a safe harbor. In a
voice both slow and husky, she described her nights working
in a Toledo speakeasy, waiting tables, working for tips, making
men feel happy enough to spend down a wallet. Her words,
zigzag a plenty, and easy off the tongue like their own brand of
odyssey cut loose from a long war.

"Been on my own since I was thirteen," she said. "Married
twice to dead-beats. Worked nights mostly. I'm a friend of good
luck and bad. Know how to trade them both for a rope and a
shovel."

I figured Ruby to be twice my age, and so unlike my mother
they couldn't stand in the same room without that space holding its breath in wonder that both these creatures were women.
Momma had long ago retreated from the world of pretty, come
hither, what's your name, where this woman was full of that fast
world fed with bourbon and torn dresses.

"You wait tables?"

"More or less," she said, pulling a strand of red hair off her face.

"How'd you end up on that dinghy?"

"I'm getting there," she said, "but where do you pee on this boat?"

"Hang your butt over the side at the shrouds or use the fisherman's bucket," I said, pointing to a plastic bucket. "Or try it both ways to see what suits you."

Ruby crabbed to the lee, hiked her dress, parked her bottom at the side stays.

"This how you do it?" she asked, her bottom skimming Erie like a white stone.

"I use the fisherman's bucket myself."

Ruby pinched off a smile and wrapped her arms around her chest, her eyes streaked with restless flashing. It occurred to me, as I watched her shiver, that Ruby was just as backed up in her mistakes as Daddy was.

"Have anything to drink?" she asked.

"Milk."

She laughed again. "Nothing stronger?"

"What'd you expect?"

"Coffee?"

"Milk or lake water. Take your pick."

"Milk, it is."

I pointed to Momma's blue duffel at my feet. She uncorked the jug, tilted back her head, and the milk cascaded into her mouth, her gulps nearly as loud as the splashing against the hull. She passed me the milk jug. I wiped off the glass lip with my T-shirt, took a drink. She eyed me just then, so I passed the bottle back. Like that, our first ritual on board.

"Polish it off," I said.

Ruby guzzled on and tossed the bottle overboard.

"Don't throw bottles in the lake," I said.

"That right?"

"When you're on my boat, you do things my way."

Ruby shrugged. There was plenty of kick and fire in this

woman to match her name and it made me wonder how long I could keep her on board or whether she would try to toss me over.

"Getting tired," she said.

"No sleep tonight for either one of us."

"You run a tough ship."

"Who else is going to steer?"

Our beam reach was all tender lift and ride. *Odyssey* was so perfectly balanced, I needed only to keep one finger on the tiller. There was no sting to the waves, no bite, no threat, no balancing on the forward edge of a wind shift. I took some comfort from the soft pull of sailcloth. The green pour of water off the hull. The distance of God from everything. Ruby looked almost happy watching the trailing foam of our wake. My comfort didn't last. How could I find Daddy taken at gunpoint? I hoped Ruby could help me, but she seemed content only to help herself.

"You were saying about how you came to be here?"

I just stared at her pretty mouth and wondered if she would lie to me through omission or some other means.

"Have anything to eat?"

"Give me something first, then I'll give you some food."

Ruby grimaced and said, "I met this guy named Marvin Shots, nice enough, not bad looking, said he had a big boat and asked me if I'd like to see it. I told him after closing time I'd go with him." Ruby knotted and unknotted her fingers, and fiddled a spool of hair.

"All ears," I said.

"I didn't figure he wanted to make flapjacks, but I had no idea he had two friends. They were hidden down below. I didn't see them until we left the dock." Her smudged face wrinkled the moonlight. "Sure you want to hear all this?"

"Keep talking."

"My daddy said pussy makes a man crazy," Ruby said, throwing water on her face.

"Maybe you don't need to tell me the rest," I interrupted.

Ruby palmed her eyes like she was trying to quit seeing what happened to her.

"Come on, girl, you wanted to know what happened."

"Changed my mind."

Ruby was now liking the squirm she saw in me.

"After the men fell down drunk and laughing like hyenas with their pants still around their knees, I found a gas can, poured it on the engine hatch and threw down a match. I grabbed a knife, jumped in the dinghy trailing off the back, and cut the boat loose before the explosion. I don't figure they ever knew what happened."

"You said you were knocked on the head and set adrift."

"I lied."

"Why?"

"Thought maybe you wouldn't pick me up if you'd known all that."

I couldn't wrap my tongue around what to say next except that it seemed like bad men came in threes. It wasn't like her bad men didn't deserve punishment for what they did to her, but blown to smithereens, up in smoke, gone? She was right. Maybe I wouldn't have stopped had I known what she had done. Someone would come looking for the men she killed or someone would come looking for her, but at that moment flying north, all I knew was this: *I needed her as much as she needed me.*

"You telling truth?"

"Stone-cold," Ruby said.

"Well, then, I guess we both have more trouble than we really need."

"Amen," she smirked.

"What will you do?"

"I hope to be way up in the Klondike by fall or maybe in British Columbia. I've heard about pretty country up there, worth the ticket."

"I'll get you back to Canada if you help me get Daddy back."

"You want my two cents?"

"Don't know."

"Been my experience most men stumble from one self-delivered wound to another," Ruby said, like she'd tangled in the limbs of every man since Adam.

"You saying Daddy brought down his own trouble?"

"You go far enough back in any family line and they say you'll find a king and a thief, and most times you don't have to look back too damn far. Better than even chance you can't tell from your daddy's tracks whether he's coming or going."

"Why are you saying that?"

"The eyes don't lie, sweet pea."

After she said that, I knew it would be hard to hide anything from this woman. She'd already wandered a long time in a back forty of pleasure and deception and she knew more than I did about wrong turns and dead ends. Maybe it was the snap of the wind in my ear telling me weather could be gathering, but I started talking.

"A week before Daddy was kidnapped," I said, with some contrite in my throat, "I caught him on the beach smuggling booze with the three men who took him."

"I could have written that postcard," Ruby said, which I didn't appreciate hearing. Her remark was just one step removed from, *I told you so.*

I concealed my hurt with a lashing out. "You going to help me or not?"

"What else am I going to do out in the middle of Lake Erie?"

Ruby and I shook on the proposition. Call me old-fashioned or foolish, but I believed what Momma told me. Even criminals in the Bible carry a crooked spark way down in the hierarchy of their soul. No matter who she was and where she had been with her red hair, I had every intention of getting Ruby to light my way into a world I knew nothing about and that scared me more than I let on.

Ruby didn't know the bow from the stern, so I gave her a quick lesson in the points of sail, handling the sheets, and keeping her head down so she didn't get conked by the boom. Most people who fall overboard are not swept over by a wave, but by an accidental jibe. On a downwind run, the wind can sneak behind the mainsail and whip the boom from one side to the other, clearing out a skull in its path. Ruby nodded, asked the occasional question, but it was unclear whether what I said about sailing downwind, pointing upwind, coming about, and jibing really stuck.

"Show me," she said.

I pulled the mainsheet out of the traveler and drew the boom and main closer to the cockpit. I told Ruby to sheet the jib and she almost looked like she knew what I meant.

"She's going to heel," I told her. "Stay on the high side."

I pulled the tiller into my belly and nearly kissed the lee rail.

"This is as close to the wind as she can point. About forty-five degrees off the wind."

I pointed to the southwest wind, sculpting my hand in the air like it was a force easily seen and even more easily understood. Ruby nodded like maybe she was game to know more.

"Next, we'll come about or tack. When I push the tiller all the way to starboard and say, 'Coming about,' you release the jib on the starboard side and bring it in on the port side." I took a flop, then ran downwind, jibed, and then returned to our original heading, all in about three minutes.

"Got that?"

"Clear as mud," Ruby said.

"Your life could depend on this," I said. "Let's run through the points of sail one more time."

We hardened up, came about, laid off to a beam reach, ran downwind, jibed, then hardened up again close to the wind. Ruby ducked on cue and sheeted in and out on the tacks. She didn't have much snap, but she wasn't bad, and she didn't look queasy lost. She would have been no good to me seasick and I would have put her ashore first chance I got. Lastly, I reminded her who was boss.

"Out here, my word is law. Understood?"

Ruby offered a toothy grin. I smiled back, wondering if I was doing the right thing taking her with me. I told her to grab

my Pelee Passage chart from down below. She returned with the
chart and with the photo of my father which I'd left inside the
folds of the chart. She held the photo in a shard of moonlight.
"This your father?"
"That's the one."
"See the resemblance," she said, her eyes washing over me.
"How so?"
"The chin. The ears."
"Daddy says we both have a demon switch."
"What's that?"
"We can do hard things others can't."
"Like what?"
"Good in a pinch, I guess."
Ruby looked again at the photo and I saw a shiver of wonder
or worry run through her like an old hurt talking back from a
knot in her spine. She handed back the photo. I snapped on the
flashlight to look at the northeast thumb of Kelly's Island on
the chart.
"We should be seeing the flashing green of Kelly's Island
shoal. I need for you to clue your eyeballs at about ten o'clock
and tell me when you see it."
"Aye-aye, captain." Ruby winked.
"Skip the aye-aye part."
I retreated as far to the stern as I could while Ruby leaned
forward on the cabin top, her eyeballs scanning the green-black
shadows. I didn't like playing back her story because Toledo
was a long way from where I found her, and there was no good
reason why the *Purple Goose* would come so far east. I was not
even sure a powerboat could travel that far on a single tank of
gas. Something about her tale didn't take me to market, but I
would have laid a five-dollar gold piece at the good shepherd's
door that she and I hadn't met by accident, so what little I really
knew about Ruby would have to ride. I held the tiller with my
right foot and threw back my head to swim in the clover of
unnumbered stars. Always a previous source of marvel and
nourishment, those flecks of light now made my lips quiver

when I considered how much distance lay between Daddy and me.

I had sailed alone at night before, but never this far, never for such a purpose, never less clear on what I might find. I heard a thump against the hull, turned my head, and saw how we had scraped an upended log called a *deadman*. I pictured all the wrecks hidden beneath Lake Erie, and I feared *Odyssey* might become another set of sister ribs rotting on the Lake Erie floor. But what else could I do? I'd rather collide with a deadman than turn back without putting my demon switch to good use. Ruby raised me by pointing off to port.

"There's your green flasher like you said it would be."

"A mile beyond that flasher, we'll enter Canadian waters," I said.

"Then what?"

"We'll keep on the same northerly heading till we leave Chickanola Reef to port and go ashore on Pelee Island at Mill Point."

Ruby grabbed the folded square of the chart and sized up the island.

"You'd be better off running up to Windsor," Ruby said.

"Why's that?"

"All the action is between Detroit and Windsor. On the whiskey river as they like to call it."

"That so."

"There's nothing on Pelee."

"How would you know?"

"Never heard anyone say Pelee was made of gold."

There was something prickly in her reply, like I hit a nerve with an invisible needle.

"Pelee is where I'd go if I was running mule kick into Ohio."

"Detroit is a better bet."

"Now I know what you think."

The pit in my stomach dropped like a trapdoor as we drew closer to land. In less than an hour, I glimpsed the dark thread outline of Pelee Island looking like a man laid out on a slab. I rolled my tongue over my teeth, trying to find moisture to make a sound I could recognize.

"Got an idea," Ruby said, her face saying she was in love with it.

"What is it?"

"Still working out the fine points," she said.

"Don't get shy on me."

"All in good time."

I couldn't stop thinking about the rough upending both she and Daddy had come to. How the dark, unstoppable blew into each of them like spirit. How they each had met up with the flood of three men who swept them off. One of them had been found, the other was still missing. Both held something back.

"You think you'll have to pay for what you did?"

"They had it coming."

"Who will come looking for you?"

"No way of telling."

"That's not much to tie a ribbon around."

"Most stories don't come with happy endings. Mine will be no different."

With her husky voice wrapped around a conclusion, Ruby didn't give me running room to feel good about my chances. Still, I meant for this first night with Ruby Francoeur, fugitive from an exploding ship, to be the start of my return to Rye Beach. The barometer could plummet. The waves could reach higher than a house. All hell could come calling my name while God held his tongue, but no matter that. I reached over the gunwale, dipped my right hand into Lake Erie to sign the water's covenant to fetch me home with the cargo I set out to haul back. *Shake me, Lake Erie, if you must but hold me steady.*

4

The waves out of the southwest slid hard toward Pelee like they were being reeled in on a silver spinner. I didn't like coming into land with no channel markers, but there was no way I wanted to sail around to West Dock where the ferry hove to and people might be about. Better to arrive in the spill of the after dark. No one around. Nothing familiar. No welcome wagon.

"Ruby, you may have to walk us in."

"You know what you're doing?"

I didn't answer. As we kept close to the wind in the pale rose light, I saw the ghost of docks, some busted down to only creosote pilings and wrapped in a seaweed skirt of beer bottles, fish line, tin cans, the tangle of things thrown down in a hurry.

"Where is this place?" Ruby asked.

"Mill Point," I said.

"You figure they cut wood here?"

"Good a guess as any."

I guided *Odyssey* into a finger cove until she ran out of wind and depth. Ruby lowered the main and jib and paddled us into shore from a perch on the bow. For a fancy lady given to rouge, she was nimble enough on a foredeck. When we touched bottom, she slipped overboard, grabbed the bow line, and walked us the last twenty feet into shore. I climbed out as well and guided the stern while she held the bow.

"We'll need to haul up on shore and camouflage her."

"Whatever you say," she replied.

We worked fast, our feet numb from the cold press of bottom stones. *Odyssey* weighed nearly five hundred pounds and it took all we had to nuzzle her into the bank. We tore down leafed branches, layered them over the cabin, neither of us talking. The exhaustion from the long night setting in fast.

"Okay if I leave my bag here?" Ruby asked, after pulling out a skirt from her bag.

"Suit yourself."

I grabbed my ditty bag from the stern lazarette, then emptied the bag of its needles, thread, thimble, and scraps of sailcloth. Daddy had given it to me when we launched *Odyssey*. Said every skipper needed a "housewife." I put his pocketknife into the bag, then tied it to my waist, and we started walking. Hunger and ache soon brought us to a stop. We turned back, made a fire, hoping it wouldn't attract attention from an early morning fisherman, woodsman, or rumrunner scouting the shoreline. I wanted to eat, then grab thirty winks. No, the brave in me was all but spent and I thought more about home than food or sleep.

"Thinking about friends?" Ruby asked, glancing into the first sparks.

"One," I said, not revealing that my one good friend was Bob.

"That's it?"

"Can't figure other girls out," I said, pulling a blanket over my shoulders.

"How so?"

"They don't say what they really mean."

"Like what? It's been a while."

"If a boy asks another boy if he's got a pimple on the end of his nose, his friend will say, 'You better get yourself to a mirror and pop that ugly, god-forsaken thing.' If a girl asks another girl the same question, her friend will say, 'That's just a tiny blemish. I can hardly see it.' Then, her friend will trot over to another girl and say, 'You should see that pimple on the end of her nose. It's so big and ugly I can't believe she came to school.'"

"Two-faced?"

"They keep lists. Little rules. About everything."

"Some of that never goes away," Ruby said, stirring the fire with a stick to spark the flames.

"I see just as much monkey-business with my aunt Cora."

"Sounds like a boy's complaint."

"Sometimes I feel like one. The other girls say I act like one. Maybe some part of me is one."

"You have a boy on your tail?"

"There's another chunk of the human race I can't figure," I said, picturing Daddy again on the beach unloading crates of whiskey.

Ruby said, "If women keep company with whispers, men get jacked on secrets."

"Bible says we're all fallen creatures," I said, like I had seen the light fall and fail to rise on every creature. "And we can use this life to better ourselves."

"Who sold you that promise?"

"Everyone knows it's the truth," I said, not admitting that the business of being fallen creatures was from Momma, not me. Ruby poked the crossed branches with a forked stick until the embers kicked out an orange pulse. She wrapped herself up in her arms, knees pressed together, her right resting on top of her left.

"That's the book almost any jackass can use to prove a case," Ruby said.

"Daddy don't believe a word of it," I replied, "but Momma and me read it some."

"That's homespun for you," Ruby said.

"You were saying about men?"

"Mermaids, cash, porkchops, and lipstick. In that order. Easy creatures to understand, if you can track the far reach of their hungers."

"You make it sound like they are cave dwellers."

"Haven't crawled but one inch. There's a part of every man," Ruby said as much to the fire as to me, "that hopes for the hour when there's blood in the dirt so he can return to his true animal nature. At birth we have no clothes. At death our clothes are stripped away. In between, the lamb bleats just once then the lion takes it down."

"Is it the lion that keeps you moving?" I asked, frightened

suddenly by the half shadows lingering outside the spark-lit tunnel of our two bodies set out in the island dark.

"I'd like to believe otherwise."

"God fixes what man breaks."

"Tell that to the worms," Ruby scoffed, her mouth now ugly twisted.

"I guess those three men on the boat are busy doing that."

"Touché."

I tried to picture what happened to Ruby off Kelly's Island and what she did to get free of the *Purple Goose,* but I couldn't make sense of it and mostly I just wanted to think she cooked it up. If not, then how strange and unsettling was this invisible chain between us. She could be on the dodge from bad men while I was trying to locate bad men so I could grab one good one in their midst. Maybe she was right about there being something broken and unreachable in men, but still I believed then and now almost everything you regard as evil has some good, worth digging out.

"Still waiting on your big idea."

"There must be a bar on Pelee."

"I didn't come to Canada to see you get cozy with drunks," I said, squinting to make myself look both fierce and disappointed.

"Hear me out now," Ruby said, rising to her feet, her hands square on her hips the way Momma stood when she aimed to point me back to a book. "If you want to find out what really goes on in a place like this, you go to a bar. If there are whiskey runners here, they're not going to hide out under a rock waiting for the next shipment. They look for a quick grab at a watering hole."

"That's not an idea. That's an opportunity for you to land back on your feet."

"What's your big idea, Norah Bow?"

"What am I going do in a liquor establishment?"

"Wash glasses. Push broom. Put on some elephant ears. Listen up," Ruby said, shaking out her hair like it was some kind of trophy I should take notice of.

"I can do better than that," I scoffed, kicking at a stuck stone in the dirt.

"You want to ride into this island with your six shooter blazing," Ruby said, with her two hands cocked, "but you don't have a gun."

"He's here. He must be," I said, throwing a crooked piece of driftwood on the fire to make the embers leap out at Ruby. I took the last wedge of peach pie for myself. I laid down close to the fire, hoping I could calm down enough to catch some shut eye. When I awoke, I didn't see Ruby at first and some part of me imagined she had cleared off. Then, I saw her at the shore's edge. She peeled off her clothes faster than I could swat a horse fly and pranced like a freshly painted carousel pony. Momma had never let me see her without her clothes on and she would not have looked favorably on this woman lingering over a bath. Momma thought nakedness was best left to a locked bathroom door and the quick shine of a scrub cloth. She avoided talking about being a woman as if the whole business was too complicated and messy for anything but the occasional whisper, then hush.

Fact was, I had never before seen another woman naked and I couldn't take my eyes off Ruby's body, all curvy and spacious, her freckled breasts in a pendular dance. Ruby turned around, saw me watching her. I turned away. When she returned to our make-shift camp, she was still naked as the day she was born, her nipples apple-hard, shiny red, things of wonder. She carried her dress bunched in her arms, looking like nothing showing should cause a spectacle.

"Don't suppose you brought a towel?"

"You're in luck," I said, reaching to grab Momma's pink beach towel.

"You going to clean up?" Ruby asked.

"Hadn't given it much thought."

"Nice private cove. No one about. Might help the cause."

"How so?"

"Someone might be more willing to talk to you if you didn't smell like a dog's mattress."

Ruby knew how to twist a rope. I stomped off to the water's edge and pulled off my wet jean shorts and T-shirt. She followed.

"You forget something?" she asked, tossing me the soap.

"Don't look," I cried. I made a grab for the bar of soap and it back flipped out of my hand and dove for the bottom. I fell over sideways trying to fish it out. Ruby snorted, then turned away while I soaped up and swam out, the water rushing between my legs and tingling my skin, the tension of the last twelve hours draining from my arms and shoulders and making me feel weightless. I laughed while I treaded water, realizing this was the first time I had ever skinny-dipped. Why had I never tried this before? I laughed again when it occurred to me that Ruby made me feel reckless and safe in the same torn moment.

"Not so bad, was it?" Ruby asked from a distance when I returned to shore.

"Got the stink off," I said.

"Progress," Ruby said.

Ruby looked chipper and refreshed as if she had not a single worry to slow her down. After I dried off, my old fears returned like a series of doors clicking behind me. *Could I find Daddy? What if he was dead? How would I bring him back?* I had thrown my lot in with a killer with red hair, a slender waist, and an ample bosom. There was no telling how our first day together on land might unfold.

5

Once dry, I dug into my vanishing rations and tossed Ruby an apple. She shined it on her hem until the apple found a blush, then she sank her teeth into the skin. The juice dripped from her chin. She closed her eyes as if to let the greed and complication in her mouth take her over. Tooth and tongue welcomed ivory flesh. I'd never seen anyone roll their tongue over an apple, holding a bite until all the puckering had been released so the softer flavors might follow.

"Nothing like a good apple," Ruby said.

"Can't beat a Macintosh," I said, making conversation.

From my ditty, I pulled out Daddy's pocketknife, a loaf of bread, the jar of peanut butter and made four sandwiches, two for now, two for later. I took huge bites of my sandwich, then handed one to Ruby who nibbled the crust like a mouse.

"What's wrong?"

"Nothing," Ruby said.

"If you don't want it, give it back."

"I'll eat anything."

"Not your idea of food?"

"I'm French."

"Sweet Jesus. You want a menu?"

I put the other two sandwiches and the two apples into my ditty and we set off looking for a tavern. I took one last look at *Odyssey* under brush. It stung my eyes to leave her. Ruby let a bluebird whistle work through her lips as if this day of unknown roads and libations was just like any other. I couldn't keep from thinking any minute she would bolt and I'd have to go on alone. Even with this nagging fear, how could I not warm to her brisk gait, her easy smile, her casual defiance of her own troubles? Ruby stopped her smooth animal glide, held me by the arm, pivoted toward the marsh and caught a whiff from a smokehouse, the fat abiding in the wet wood.

"What do they catch around here?" Ruby asked, her eyes scanning over marsh grass and sapling woods.

"Sturgeon, whitefish, and walleye, most likely. Me and Daddy used to..." I stopped myself. What was the point of digging another hole for my sadness?

"I could sure use some smoked whitefish," Ruby said.

"You already had a peanut butter sandwich."

"Still hungry as daybreak," she said, looking to skirt the marsh for drier ground. "About that tavern?"

"We can't go too far with nothing more to eat."

I wanted to call the shots, but she had a stride I couldn't match. We pushed on with whitefish in the wind.

"You got money?" I asked.

"I lost what little I had," Ruby said, with hesitation, "in the explosion."

"How you planning to pay for your hunger?"

"IOU."

"Fishermen trade in cash," I said.

"Maybe so," she said, licking her lips like maybe she's already sunk her teeth into a rich, flaky fish. We walked along the edge of cattail marsh, our shoes squishing muck. The tang of smokehouse fat coated the air, made me queasy.

"You look like a dog in a duck boat," Ruby said, glancing back.

"Better on water than on land."

I saw a rickety building about twelve-feet square with a sharply pitched roof. Smoke squeezed out the cracks of clapboard. Ruby blew the air from her lungs, glided forward, swan in the making. My feet got sinkhole stuck.

"You can miss every shoal in Lake Erie, but you can't sidestep a pothole the size of a tennis racket," she said, her right hand gripping firm against my own.

"I'll get the hang of this place," I said.

"Your daddy's counting on it," Ruby said.

Her innocent remark gave me a stab for I thought he might be dead and beyond counting on anything in this world. Ruby must have seen some doubt parceled in my face.

"Your daddy ever have women problems?"

"What do you mean?"

"What do you think I mean?"

"Daddy has a wife."

"That don't mean a thing," she scoffed.

"Means something to me," I protested.

As I slogged through duck grass, I remembered lying on my back tightening the lock nut on the oil pan of Daddy's Austin 20 and seeing a woman come near him. I saw only red shoes and black silk stockings and Daddy sidling toward her. I scooted on my back toward the rear axle so I could keep their feet in view. I saw the woman step forward with one leg in between his straddled legs and I heard the sound of something more than a kitchen kiss. Curiosity craned my neck. I turned sideways and conked my head on the car's underbelly before I could shimmy out and see who this woman was. She left as quickly as she arrived and Daddy found his voice.

"You all right, Norah?"

"Who was that woman?" I snipped, still on my back, the blood pulsing my ears.

Daddy's silence clamped down tighter than a wrench on a rusted oil pan nut. He finally said, "Just a friend."

In the shadow of that car's underbelly, I could not see enough that day, but I knew there was no point asking him again about the woman. What seemed clear enough was Daddy held back at least two cards: the woman in red shoes and black stockings and a whiskey sideline. It made me wonder how many other secrets Daddy cloaked behind cheerful patter and a marriage he praised to the stars. Wondering, as I have learned with age, is not the same as knowing. Even at this late hour in the actuary tables, I can hardly discern what stalls and flutters in my own heart, so why would I imagine I could ever know what drew him forward? Ignorance has encouraged me to trust curiosity.

When in doubt, I put my hands over my heart and ask a question, then pray that I have the common sense of a house fly to listen for an answer. With this one hand-over-heart ritual, I've made a life of small astonishments to soften the many mistakes and misadventures I can lay claim to. I can't say this observance has always worked when I consider the follies of others who I have loved and squandered.

"Hey, Ruby, what is it with men and whiskey?"

She was ten steps ahead of me in a full food-driven stride. She turned sideways, cocked her head, smiled like I had thrown her a funny bone.

"A thousand reasons for a man to drink," she said.

"Give me two."

"With a full bottle in hand, you can twist the truth and make it your servant. With an empty, you can rule the fallen world from the floor and damn near forget anything."

"Daddy's view of things is almost as dim as yours. You two might get along."

Ruby glared, then bit off another verse of dark sermon.

"Men live in a hell made from their own seclusions."

I looked toward the Bass Islands scattered to the south, the home of a hundred shipwrecks, and I thought if Ruby had it right, maybe there was nothing glowing inside a reef half as cruel as what can happen inside the rough water of a bottle. We walked up to the smokehouse and Ruby knocked on the splintered pine door slung low enough for a troll. The door was warped outward from the bulge of heat and vented smoke. She knocked again, but didn't wait for an answer.

She opened the door, stepped inside. I followed because I figured she knew what she was doing and maybe I could use more nourishment. The smokehouse was as dark as an axe head and drenched in the stink of fish guts and gamy smoke. There was a firebox in the middle of the floor piled with green wood waiting to be lit. The walls were lined with curing racks, but there were no fish. Up in the collar beams, I saw pegs, nails, hooks, and chains for hanging filets.

"Smell the apple wood?" Ruby asked.

"Kind of sweet," I said.

"Burns hot without giving off flame."

The studs and walls were shiny black with creosote. Light angled through a window the size of a lunch pail, fell on the floor in thin stripes. Ruby inspected the smokehouse by sniffing. In the pinched light, I couldn't navigate worth spit. I stumbled over a two-by-four covered by a skein of sawdust.

"You do have trouble on land." Ruby laughed, peering up into the blackened rafters and joists, looking maybe for some hidden meat dangling from a hook. I got up and brushed off the sawdust, thinking whoever owned this place was coming back soon to lay out his pickerel or herring onto racks, light the apple dust in the cast-iron pan, and start the slow cooking of fillets.

"Let's get out of here," I said, my throat tightening with the acrid air trapped in this dim, narrow place. I turned to leave and choked back a cry when I saw a man leaning against the door jamb, the whites of his eyes slanted upward, his hands in a flutter.

"What brings you ladies to Blind Danny's smokehouse?"

The man wore overalls, duck boots, and a blue denim shirt older than the Civil War. He smelled of fish guts and kerosene. He was so small I could have almost leapt over him, but there was one obstacle. He carried a hickory cane with an ivory grip.

"Haven't eaten anything in two days," Ruby said.

"Don't need to steal just to prove you're hungry," the blind man said, turning sideways in the doorway like a spoke of shadow.

"We're not thieves," I said. "I'm here on Pelee looking for my daddy. He was kidnapped two nights ago in Rye Beach. That's in Ohio near Cedar Point. I've come here looking to fetch him home because our sheriff has no backbone."

"I didn't ask you for heartache," the blind man said, scratching his balls.

"Food is not why I'm here," I said.

Ruby winced like maybe I was a fool to discount the value of a meal.

"One dime and a kiss," the blind man said, "and I might believe you."

"I wouldn't sail all this way to snitch a bucket of smelly fish." The blind man pondered what I said, turning sideways twice as if to consult an invisible companion. The sunlight trembled behind his slumped shoulders as he turned back to face Ruby.

"What do they call you? Goddess of the Golden Thighs?"

"Ruby will do."

"What say you, Ruby?"

"Girl told me the same story. No reason to believe otherwise."

I didn't much care for the cold flavor of her answer. This was the first of many times when I saw how Ruby always looked after herself before any other consideration, a trait I learned to both envy and distrust in equal measure.

"One of you wants food. The other wants answers. That it?"

"We'd take both if you're offering," I said, inching toward Blind Danny to see if I could catch a better look at his eyes flaring up and dying down in a circle roam. His own odor reeked like flowers gone off. He wedged himself in the doorway to snort and unload a gob of spit.

"Just 'cause I'm blind, don't mean I can't see."

"What I told you is God's unvarnished," I said.

Ruby looked at him, her eyes measuring the length of cane. Then, the blind man unleashed a smile. "Let's talk outside in the light. It's one hell of a day to be alive." Blind Danny stepped back out of the door frame, twirling his cane once as he lifted his pixie gum boots.

"What can I offer you two ladies?" he said as if he were now a maître d'.

"Rumrunners took Daddy and I figure he might be here. He's got a ruddy face and wiry frame. Big elephant ears, not much hair. No taller than I am. If he turns sideways, you could trade him out for a toothpick."

"What does he like for trouble?" Blind Danny muttered.

"Whiskey," Ruby said.

"He's a good man," I said.

"A good man," Danny said, waiting to finish chewing tobacco, "is anybody's guess."

"Good enough to be brought home," I said.

"The only way to find a man is to figure out if he's lost," Danny said, casting his eyes downward.

"That's riddle talk," I said.

Danny stuck me with a grin the devil would be eager to take back.

"I'm just saying, dying can take forever and living takes no time at all."

"That clears things up," Ruby said, raising her eyebrows.

"He was taken at gun point from Sunday dinner," I said. "Can you help me find him or are you just going to waste my time?"

"Ain't seen this bantam."

"Who have you seen lately?" I asked, losing patience with this unblinking, pint-size geezer.

"I've seen the beast with seven heads and ten horns," Danny said in a hoarse whisper, "rising from a sea of blood."

"Saw him the other night myself," Ruby said with a smirk.

As I turned to leave the man, he put his hand on my shoulder.

"Can I give you a fish bone?"

Ruby sighed through a clenched jaw.

"Go home," he said to me.

"Can't do that," I snapped.

"I hear that in your voice."

"Hear what?"

"Your heart beating down the door in your throat."

"Too bad," Ruby said, "you don't have any fish in this smokehouse."

"Come back another time," Danny said, twirling his cane as

if strangely lightened by hearing of troubles greater than his own.

"Which way?" I asked, looking for some semblance of a road.

"That depends," he said, with an impish smile, "on what you hope to find."

"Work," Ruby said, cracking the knuckles of her right hand.

"You'll want to steer clear of the Custom's House at West Dock. Somebody there might want to know why such a girl is traveling with an older woman. You know that song, 'Who is who? What is what? Where you from, pretty Polly?'"

I shrugged, then crossed my hands at the wrist and pointed in different directions.

"Walk on the Eastside Road. Head up to the North Bay store or to the Pelee Hotel or—"

Ruby interrupted. "Where's your nearest watering hole?"

"There's the Irish Rose Tavern. See Jack Little. Maybe he can help. Jack's my brother. And, miss, you'll want to get yourself some other sort of outfit. That torn dress of yours will turn some heads you don't want turned." Ruby glanced down her dress knowing what Blind Danny said was true enough, then she lifted her head with a lopsided grin, realizing that Danny was no more blind than a rock bass.

"Thanks," Ruby said. "I've got no need to make a fuss."

"I don't believe a word you say," Blind Danny said.

"Don't care what you believe."

Ruby swiveled her head toward me. "I like that name, the Irish Rose, don't you, Norah?"

"Gimme a pint of Rosie with a skirt," Danny sang. "You must at least know that song, darling?"

"Never heard it," Ruby said.

Blind Danny bowed with one hand thrown down in our path and we took our leave of him. Ruby held her breath when she walked past him. I saw a crease in her forehead nearly as long as his cane. Each of them carried a live coal on the tongue. The talk of doom came easily to them and often.

6

We stayed snug to the lake road bordered with an irrigation ditch and pesky gnat bundles. The sun, wet hot sticky as a winter glove. Something about the muggy glare brought out snapping turtles intent on a crossing. A forty-pound granddaddy the size of a truck tire parked himself in the road. I grabbed a stick lying in the road to see if I could entice him to clamp down on my brand of religion.

"You think that snapper doesn't know how to take care of itself?"

"One horse and buggy could bust him up."

"Why do you need to rescue things?"

"I aim to keep him moving."

The big snapper wouldn't bite the stick, so I reached into my ditty for a sandwich, lifted up a corner, and smeared some peanut butter on my finger.

"What are you doing now?"

"Giving some smell to my stick," I said, wiping my peanut butter finger on the end of the stick. The snapper pulled in his head so only his eyes showed like two black marbles. I waved the stick like a wand under his earnest gaze.

"Seems he doesn't like peanut butter any more than I do." Ruby laughed.

The snapper pulled his head all the way in, then he lunged. Once he grabbed hold of the stick, he wouldn't let go out of some ancient need to prove his mettle, so I showed him how strong he was by dragging him off the road and shoving him into the ditch where he belonged.

"How do you know he won't just come back?"

"I don't."

"They'll be another one."

"Then I'll get another stick."

"God knows we've got more peanut butter," Ruby said, with regret stalling her voice. After an hour or so of walking, Ruby looked drained by the dust and the heat, ready to sit down, turn back, flag down anything moving faster than her own two dogs. Mile by mile, she always kept one eye over her shoulder for dark clouds. Dark clouds? I've never sorted out whether they are a good thing in disguise or just another name for death. No matter, I would take her as she was. As much as Ruby could annoy me, I wanted her on that road the way you want to hear someone else's breathing in a room.

"Anybody in particular you keep looking for?"

"You never know what you don't know."

"That's a deep thought for a fishing pole," I said.

"Detroit or Windsor is where you want to look for him," Ruby reported.

"And I told you," I said, with equal authority, "this is where we start."

"How much farther?" Ruby asked, her hands looking for some way to turn her dress into something other than a tarnished showpiece.

"My chart says Pelee is not more than nine miles long."

"Too damn far to walk. How come we didn't sail to the north end?"

"Wanted to make landfall."

"Maybe we should go back and get your boat," Ruby said, tired of hoofing a dirt road cut between stands of ash, cedar, and a chalk line of sandy beach.

"Too late for that," I said, not really knowing what to do, but also not wanting to backtrack, lose time, start over, let my doubts run me down like that hog snapper in the road. My throat was so parched my teeth itched. With every other step, I thought maybe I could still find a phone, reverse charges, tell Momma I'd be home by nightfall—then again, how could I tell her I hadn't found him? How could I let him go before I knew who he was? And beneath that question, another one like a stone in my shoe. How could I breathe the same air under the same roof and not know who he is any more than I knew a scarecrow in a tomato patch?

"Breeze feels good," Ruby said.

"We're in the lee of a real bite."

"Lee?"

"Wind's out of the southwest and the island itself is blocking the wind."

"How come you've got a special word for damn near everything?"

"No doubt, it's the same in your world."

"Have it your way," Ruby repeated, stopping a minute to stretch her back and take another hard look in all directions.

"No one coming yet," I said, hoping to tease her out so she would tell me something she didn't want me to know. I had stopped her from telling me what the men had done to her on the *Purple Goose*, but now I wanted to know how she knew such men or how exactly they had come to fetch her.

"Maybe we could borrow a couple of horses and ride to the north end?"

"Last I heard stealing horses was still frowned upon," I said.

"Not stealing, borrowing."

"You see any horses around here?"

"You don't give an inch," Ruby said.

We walked on, one escapee and one seeker of lost fathers, both of us partly open, partly closed to the other, like we were not walking but stuck in the same hospital room late at night. We pushed north so slowly, you'd think we were dragging a brick wagon. The sun broke across our necks while the dust nipped our ankles. Already I longed to hear the flap of sail-cloth, taste the smack of whitecaps, hear the wind taking charge of the land's complications. Walking on a dirt road banked by a stand of wind-bent cedars, I couldn't see out to Lake Erie and the water couldn't see me.

"Ever been with a boy?" Ruby set down in a minor key.

"What's it to you?"

"Just making conversation." Ruby frowned.

She bunched her lower lip in a pout which made me want to laugh, but then I wanted to cry or I wanted to go home, the confusion in me startled awake by her question.

"Something happened once," I said.

"Once it is, then."

"One night on the beach." I paused, my words hanging in the road.

"You can't tell me anything I haven't seen, done, or heard before," Ruby said.

"This boy, Jimmy Shade, he was sweet on lots of girls. He told me he was going to be a movie star and he might be right because he was not some beanpole. He had real muscles, a thick wave of black hair, smart green eyes."

"With a name like Jimmy Shade, you've got trouble right there."

"Jimmy said he wanted to kiss me real bad."

"They always say that," Ruby said.

"I let him kiss me because other girls had teased me I'd never kissed a boy. When he shoved his hand down my shorts, I jerked my right knee into his privates. He fell in the sand but he grabbed my shorts with both hands and shucked them down. I could feel the wind nipping my backside, and my first thought was I hoped no one was looking because then I'd have a lot of scrambling to do."

"Hope you hurt him good."

"Before Jimmy could knock me down and do what he'd come to do, Bob snapped at Jimmy's legs. Jimmy crawled away like the thug he was, saying, 'Norah, you'll pay for this,' and I shouted back, 'I already have.'"

"Bravo," Ruby said, with an exaggerated Italian accent.

"I ran home with tears staining my T-shirt, but I wasn't crying because of what had happened. I was crying because my momma never told me boys could be all smash and grab."

"Mothers don't always say the right thing," Ruby offered.

"When I told her, Momma shook her head with a moan that sounded worse than Bob when I haven't fed him. She kept saying she was sorry and she aimed to talk to Jimmy's father. I said it was no use. He'd grabbed other girls. Momma winced when I said this. She couldn't bargain on monsters and she couldn't stop whimpering like she was the one who got jumped."

"Sounds like Momma has her own story she ain't telling."

"I slammed my bedroom door so hard, the house shook on the hinges."

"You should have seen this coming," Ruby said, switching from warm concern to ice over easy.

"What's that supposed to mean?"

"I can't be looking after you."

"Can't what?" I fired off.

"There's always another Jimmy Shade."

"I can take care myself," I said.

"Even after I told you what happened to me, you have no idea what you're up against. The men in this game are something feral in this world. The fact you are young will only make their mouths water."

"You can't scare me."

"That's too bad," Ruby said.

Ruby and I stopped beside a pair of willows so grand their branches swept the ground. A pair of dragonflies riding piggyback circled her head, their fat emerald eyes pulsing. Daddy loved dragonflies. Said they were oldest insects on earth. Bringing their splash here even before the dinosaurs made an appearance. He said they could see forward and backward at the same time and their two sets of wings let them hover, change direction, cartwheel, all in a glide. Maybe since he was a thin man in a hurry, he wanted to be like them with more speed and agility at his disposal.

To hold off hunger, I closed my eyes and folded my arms over my stomach with my fingers pinching my sides. No sooner closed, I pictured sitting down at Momma's porch table spread with a tomato-cucumber salad, three-bean salad, a mess of fried perch, a pitcher of lemonade, and a tin of chocolate-chip cookies. I fell asleep beneath the spindly green branches of a willow that brushed my cheeks. I dreamt of better times with Bob and Daddy at Rye Beach, the three of us playing tag with each other and the waves, the day unaware of any mischief or misdirection. Then, I heard voices. I lifted my head expecting to see Bob and Daddy, and Rye Beach itself and Cedar Point beyond, but what I saw instead was Ruby climbing into a one-horse driven carriage just like she was a princess swept off to the ball.

"This here is Zane Hooper," Ruby said. Zane tipped a finger my direction. "He's taking me for a ride." Zane Hooper was a lug with high cheekbones, a square-set chin, and long black hair parted in the middle and swept back off his forehead. He struck a match on his sun dial belt buckle, lit a cigarette, dragged on it, then offered it to Ruby like it was a spark stolen from the first fire. She found a loose, easy smile inside the smoke. Just then, she was the moon. He, a baleful dog on a ledge, staring up. That said, it was the way she hoisted her chest and the way he wet his lips that prickled my neck hair.

Before I could soak up the full import of this encounter, Zane Hooper jumped up on his buggy and disappeared into the slipstream of fate and wonder governing all things seen and unseen and I wondered then if I was still sleeping or if I had been carried off by dragonflies to some terra incognita. I was so flummoxed by what I saw, I waved a happy little wave, thinking maybe Zane and Ruby were taking a spin around the block except there were no blocks, just this solitary north and south road with the occasional east and west rut spliced through pasture, marsh, grape fields, and stands of hickory and oak perched on high ground like sentinels. I climbed back up to the dirt road and started walking, but to where I couldn't say except now I was looking for two wayward souls, a red-headed woman in a cleaved party dress and my skinny father of the elephant ears.

I would like to say I took Ruby's vanishing in stride, but such was not the case.

I stood in the road with my hands over my head and spun

around like my dog snapping at a bug-eyed deer fly. I considered retracing my steps back to *Odyssey*, but I walked on to the north where Ruby and Zane Hooper slipped away with a whip crack. So, this is what it meant to search for your father, I said to myself: *walk hard, get nowhere, lose your only crew member on the first piece of land you come to.* I felt like a wrong-way snapper that just got spun sideways and mangled in the sunbaked road. Weather bore down from the west, but more heat was needed before the pillow clouds would sag black and break open. In the gathering swell, I wondered if Pelee had a sheriff and if it made any sense asking him of the whereabouts of Vital Bow. Talking to myself, I figured he might be just as likely to stick me on the Pelee Island mail boat bound for Sandusky. I tabled the thought, and started walking again with more finesse, like I knew where I was going and how to get there.

I came to a cluster of mulberry trees and picked a bunch swinging from a slender stalk while I listened to the orioles in the trapeze of the upper branches. Momma and I transplanted a mulberry tree. I thought the tree was dead or diseased, but she talked to the tree, ordered it to live because she loved mulberry jam. She even blessed that tree with a reading from Solomon and prayed for it. Stunted and spindly, the tree never thrived, but it did live on. From day one, Daddy wanted to chop it down. He said the juice stained his wheel rims. He told her the droppings from birds that feasted on the mulberries stained the carport. Daddy did eventually cut the tree down, but she took a cutting and it rooted nicely where she originally found the sick tree. I licked the juice from my fingertips and wondered if Daddy ever regretted putting the axe to that mulberry tree given how much Momma loved it or did he regret anything?

I passed open marsh edged in cattails and tall grass rippling like short stacked waves and saw the white heads of two bald eagles glinting in the sun. "Lucky devils," I said, believing no matter how high they soared, they were still closer to their next meal than I was. I entered a string of vineyards with row after row of grape clusters baking in the sun, none quite ripe enough to forage. Daddy once took me to Catawba Island as he weighed the risks and rewards of getting into the wine-making business. He let me taste a couple of dark purple wines, but I preferred the jams made from those grapes spread on crackers and left beside the tasting tables. I couldn't tell a Catawba from a Concord grape, but the ones in front of me were green. Still, I dropped off the road and ran my fingers over the bunches, picturing them filling with juice and sugar and all the good things God puts into a grape that he doesn't put into spinach, cauliflower, or the swell of the human heart. I held a bunch in both hands like it was the face of a baby when an elderly woman appeared. She wore a blue head scarf over a thinning bob of white hair. Her eyes pored over me. She smelled like old boot.

"What's your name, girl?"

I didn't expect such directness from a woman no bigger than a tomato vine.

"What's it to you?"

"You look like you could use some food."

"You look like you could use a bath," I said. The woman almost smiled.

"Tobacco gum is hard to scrub off," she said.

"Tobacco? Here on Pelee?"

"Hooper ships well over a million pounds to Leamington every year."

"You're joking, right?"

"Picking suckers is the only way to get to the bank."

"What's that," I asked, "some kind of green-eyed worm?"

The woman released a breathy snort, then sucked in air between her teeth.

"Suckers are tobacco shoots. You've got to top them off for ten to twelve weeks or you get nothing for your trouble."

"What's that pay being a sucker picker?"

"Five dollars a week and a whiskey jug."

"Think I'll look for other work."

"You don't strike me as a girl looking for work," the woman said, her face its own wrinkled grape that drew me down into confession.

"Looking for my daddy."

"Running hooch, is he?"

"Need to bring him back."

"Heard that one before," the woman said, the sweat clinging to her face. "You won't find out much on Pelee," she said, nibbling her lower lip.

"How so?" I asked, our faces no more than inches from each other, like maybe we've been sucker pickers together but just didn't know each other's name or how much more the tobacco rows would ask of us.

"Tobacco and wine," she said. "That's what we have to sell, and most of it goes elsewhere, unseen and untaxed."

"You're saying the islanders are cozy with rumrunners?"

"And then some," the old woman said, scratching the tip of her veined nose flecked with black hairs. "We can't get too worked up about whiskey when we're busy peddling wine."

"I see what you mean," I said, wondering if there was an honest person left on Lake Erie who would tell me how to draw a bead on the rumrunners who took Daddy.

"Not much comes our way," she added, reading my chagrin. "Islanders have to reach into a lot of pockets to put anything into their own."

I walked with the old tobacco woman to a one-bedroom house set on a bluff of quince trees.

"I can pay you for a meal," I said.

"I know something about being on my own," she said.

She fixed oatmeal and corn fritters sprinkled with wild raspberries and honey from her garden, and I was grateful her plain food was hot and plentiful. I kept my head bent over my bowl because if I spent any time looking at her fierce green eyes laced with purple veins, I got more than a little jumpy. If I listened to reason, I told myself this was just a lonely sucker-picker living in a wind-tossed place and she meant me no harm, no mischief, no help. With no encouragement from me, she jabbered on about one fatal indiscretion after another.

Her name was Betsy Dobbins and she'd floated to Pelee as a mail-order bride. Her husband got drunk one February and drove his roadster across the frozen lake to Leamington only to hit a Canadian train. Betsy never remarried, never went back to Kentucky, never really went anywhere but into the stronghold of a roof cellar or up on the roof to track the clock of a storm. She said she'd only been hitched for two years and didn't really know her husband that well, but recognized he was not a man cut out for the ordinary deprivations of an island winter. Betsy said she knew he would leave her because the November before his death, twelve crows came to roost in her quince trees. No matter how she tried to scatter them with pots and pans and even buckshot, she told me, they circled, swooped, and lingered like a dark-lit candelabra. Then, not long after such an omen, a neighbor took a smudge of pneumonia deep into both lungs and no doctor could reach down in time, and still another went down in a storm that sprung out of Erie in ten minutes and another met up with a rattlesnake. Like that. Island living, pretty as a postcard and a scorpion that devours its young. After my belly was full, I plied Betsy with questions because that's what Daddy told me you do when you're looking for more than you've got to hand out.

"What do you know about Zane Hooper?"

"That would be Roy's boy. Living high, wide, and handsome off the old man's tobacco money. Smart enough, but oh my, lazy as a daisy. Even though he's got a blue-blood wife from back East somewhere, nearly every woman here, even married ones, are sweet on him and they have paid dearly for all that."

"My crew, Ruby Francouer, went off with this Zane fellow for a buggy ride."

"You won't be seeing her any time soon," Betsy said, clutching the back of a chair with both hands and thrusting her hips forward.

"I don't believe that."

"Most people tell themselves a mess of little lies so they can work up the courage to swallow the big ones. You struck me as different."

"Speak plain or don't speak at all," I rattled.

"Better than decent chance, your daddy's parked on the bottom of Lake Erie. And this Ruby woman? Any way you salt the dumpling, she's curled up with Hooper. You'll just be slipping sideways if you stay on. Best go home before something bad happens and you don't have enough strength left to change your name."

"Thanks for the porridge."

"You're welcome to stay," Betsy said. I wanted to leave, but there couldn't be more than a few hours of daylight left. After picking suckers all day, I figured Betsy had little strength left to boil me in a pot.

"Any place will do," I said.

"There's a cot upstairs."

"That'll do fine," I said, relieved to have a place to lay down my head and not think about what was ahead, what was behind. "Thanks," I added. "Very kind of you."

The night was long and hot with a strangled wind from the south. The mosquitoes slipped through a tear in the screen, and soon enough, they found me. I woke with a start from a dream, the air chafing my throat. I thought *Odyssey* was taking on more water than I could bail, her mainsail shredded, her jib hanks torn off the headstay. I couldn't sleep so I crept downstairs. The air in the house hung close with the tang of vinegar and tobacco leaves. With each step into someone else's darkness, I heard the house creaking on its rough-cut stone foundation, the windows flustering in their rotted casings. I squinted into the kitchen and jumped back when I saw Betsy looking straight at me like she was waiting for me to make off with her butter knife.

"Going somewhere?"

"Couldn't sleep."

"That makes two of us," she said.

"Have any milk?"

"Goat is all."

"That'll do."

Betsy opened a squat ice box, no bigger than a foot locker stood on its end, and snatched a jug and set it on the counter. She wiped a cup with a sleeve from her nightshirt, poured a cup, and handed it to me through the ropey shadows left by the moon over her kitchen sink window.

"Much obliged," I said, taking the cup from her and putting it to my lips.

"Probably won't help," she said. "Not with this heat."

"You believe in love?" I asked her as she rocked on the balls of her feet.

"What?"

"That love is possible?"

"Anything's possible."

"That doesn't tell me much."

"Love left early on."

"Where did it go?"

"Someone always cheats."

"That's sad," I said, sipping from my cup and feeling the goat's milk slide down my throat.

"Most things are."

"But you don't seem—"

"Nobody is what they seem."

"Goodnight then," I said, as much to the uncurtained darkness as to her.

"You'll be leaving early, no doubt," Betsy said.

"Thanks for the milk."

I left two dollars on Betsy's kitchen table, uncertain whether the old woman was friend or foe. She had fed me and given me a place to stay and I was grateful for the kindness but the bitter drape of her words hung on me. I scrambled off her bluff as fast as I could and grabbed a golden quince from one of her trees. My thoughts came after me hard and fast and didn't let me peel the fruit.

Ruby might have already feathered a love nest.

Daddy might be the new master of the dead man's float.

Momma was no doubt locked inside a Bible grief.

I knew nothing more about rum running than I did the day before.

The green grapes were still hard as cat's eye marbles.

Still, it was a good day to be walking on, if only my mouth weren't dry as beach sand and fear wasn't slithering my limbs, making me shiver even though the sun was already hot. And then I heard it again, the sound of my feet, a familiar string of notes rising over the dust, a music old enough to not sound like music, my old friends returning for another session, my feet saying, *We've got places to go, girl.* Then also, another voice wanting to pipe up again. *Love left early on,* she said. I was hoping with each step that Betsy, the sucker picker in the shade of the golden quince, had that wrong. Love never fails, the book says. Love takes no delight in evil. Love does not quit. Love girds truth. Finds a way home. Saying that to myself, without knowing if I believed it, is what kept me going just then. Love and truth, those old school companions, were my anchors that morning. I seek them out still, such as they are. Fashioned from dread and longing.

7

I walked north at a brisk pace. A blister on my right heel reminded me I had signed on for one of the strangest of all occupations: looking for a father who everyone said was parked on the bottom of Lake Erie, his pockets full of stones. I couldn't tell if Betsy wanted me to believe that story because then I'd go home or if she really thought it was true. Some people trust in fortune-telling cards. Some trust in vultures and the world collapsing to a jumble of bones. Some only trust what shines. I trusted Daddy was still on this earth and only I could bring him back home.

The east side road ended, but I walked on by gravel path to Lighthouse Point and sat amid the ruins of a former lighthouse, wondering why the islanders let this stone beauty fall down upon its cornerstones. The spit was still a dagger thrust a mile into Lake Erie and no friend to freighters bound for Detroit or Cleveland. The open water, cut with whitecaps, lifted my spirits. At a glance, I read all the angles I would have to lay down and follow. I saw the scratched horizon of Leamington, Ontario, fifteen miles to the north and figured I could lay up there, work my way west to Kingsville, then reach over to Detroit where all rum running was said to begin and end with a pot of gold.

I took my sneakers off, followed the shoreline west, taking comfort from the sand between my toes until I came to the Scudder Docks where a sign told me the mail boat tied up once a week on Fridays. I couldn't remember what day it was, but in any case, I had no need to post a letter. The harbor sloshed with the smell of carp and bluegills starting to go off. I saw a man using a long-handled brush and a bucket of suds to clean the hull of a wooden boat. A young girl with him was eager to help. I stared at them, thinking of better times with Daddy, but they didn't look at me. On the dock, I met a young boy, no more than ten years of age, and we talked weather and fishing while a lone gull decided to weigh in with a chuckle cry.

"Perch biting?" I asked.

"Not yet," he said, not looking at me.

"What you using?"

"Night crawlers, what else?"

"Ever try crawdads?"

"Perch will damn near eat anything," the blond boy said, squinting into sunlight. "My brother says they love baby German roaches, but who needs to spend time with those bug eyes?"

"Big shiner minnows do some good," I said.

"You from around here?" the boy asked, holding one eye on his bobber.

"Yes and no," I answered. "I live near Sandusky."

"Ohio?"

I nodded while I slipped my shoes back on.

"You a far piece from a fishing pole," he said, looking me over twice like I might be somebody fished out of the drink.

"Suppose so," I said.

"What are you doing way up here?"

"Looking for somebody," I said, aiming to lay down my own bait.

"I know everybody on Pelee," the boy said.

"Everybody?"

"I'm always fishing here on Scudder. I talk to the mail boat captain every Friday. He tells me who's got mail coming and going. I see who leaves on that boat, who gets off. I'm telling you, what I don't know ain't worth church spit," the boy said with a swagger I was banking on.

"Then you're the only one who can make me smile."

"What kind of help you need?"

"Don't know a soul on this island except you." Even as I said this, I realized I was fishing with too much splash. I had never before put on airs like this but I needed his help a lot more than he could ever use mine.

"What do you need to know?" he asked, now glancing away from his bobber more than watching it.

I pulled out my Daddy picture and stuck it under his nose.

"Ever see this man with three other men?"

The boy looked hard at the photo like the man in question might be somebody he could trade something for.

"Those funny ears look familiar. Yeah, I believe I've seen this one over at the Irish Rose."

"Was he standing up and breathing?" I asked, almost knocking the boy down with a breach.

"He was drinking a cold one with another man."

"Never seen Daddy drink a beer."

"This daddy does."

I wanted to give him a kiss on the cheek or a hug but I thought better of it.

"What's your name?"

"Everybody calls me Wink. That's not my real name, but Wink will do."

"I owe you one."

"Maybe you do. Maybe you don't. But don't come looking for me if the man you turn up is a dead one. One of those washed up here last week. When they hauled him up, one arm jiggled loose out of the socket and seagulls had pecked away his eyes. No wink left in him." The boy smiled when he said this like he wanted me to know how clever he stood in the land of the living.

"A rumrunner?"

"He didn't have a face no more so I couldn't tell you what he was."

"How far to the Irish Rose?"

"Far enough to get thirsty," Wink said.

I thanked the boy, then waved, but he had already returned to eyeing his bobber. I walked out to the North Bay road, turned right, and picked up my pace for the Irish Rose, but stopped to watch a knot of crows hectoring a daylight owl through a stand of oaks. With each rising of the owl, the crows swooped, their long curved beaks snapping air as they careened after the barrel-chested bird. The rise and fall of their screeching made me think no one—least of all Christ—ever stands a chance against all the mischief let loose upon this world.

In another hour, I stood before the Irish Rose. I walked around back and waited for someone to come out. Parked on the stoop, I tried out a half dozen opening lines on a pair of chipmunks who had set up shop beneath the rim joist. A bald man wearing a bloodstained apron over a white T-shirt popped open the screen door with a sack of trash in hand. I saw him before he saw me.

"Excuse me, good sir, I was wondering if I might trade work for food?"

The pudgy man sprung back and nearly dropped his sack of empty bottles. His nose was as fat as a baby's fist. His brown eyes sunk above his flabby, unshaven cheeks. He had stubby fingers that looked like uncooked dough with grease under the nails.

"What have we got here?"

"Just passing through," I said, raising myself to my full height with the intention of representing myself as a rugged veteran of the wayward life.

"Damned raccoons," he said, talking more to himself than to me. "I've seen a big-ass momma coon the size of a basketball squeeze herself through a four-inch chimney hole. You have any idea how much trouble a coon can cause?"

"Can't say I've crossed paths with many of them," I said.

"Nasty, unmerciful creatures," he said, stuffing a trash bag into an empty oil drum. "The females will stop at nothing to find a nursery. The males hunt and kill their young. God made a fat mistake making a critter as ornery as all that."

"With all due respect, from what you described, sounds like the raccoon is just a worthy adversary."

"I like them belly up or face down."

I thought to argue some because I favor animals over people but I held my tongue.

"Not every day I see a girl on her own. You be headed from where to where?" he asked, peeling me back like I was a filet lifted from a spinal bone.

"From Sandusky."

"That so," he said. "What kind of work you do?"

"Sweep floors, wash dishes, fix about anything, good with my hands."

"Bet you are," the man said, showing the blackened stems of his bottom teeth.

"You must have a broom around here," I said, my mouth puckered, my hands clenched. As he lashed the lid of the oil drum with a chain, I saw the sweat running from his armpits all the way to the belt loops on his trousers.

"Okay, little lady, let's see what you can do," he said with a half-eaten smile circling me like a moat. The stubs of his fingers rolled the knob of the door. I wanted out. I wanted in. I dusted myself off, and stepped through the door of the Irish Rose.

Looking back, I can tell you this much, it's almost always a good thing to step into a bar, even if you hate booze, even if the smell of bargain perfume and cigarettes makes you gag, even if the clink of the bottle darkness makes you jittery, even if someone you know or love has entered the maw of a bottle and never returned from all the swallowing that follows. A bar is one of the few places on earth where you can gather up the pale stories of this life and use them to help you shine somewhere else. You don't have to look tough, sexy, or sad to get a little help. All you have to do is squint into the darkness, then listen and remember some of what you heard. I read somewhere it's the hollow where a hand disappears that makes a pot work. You might say the same about a bar.

8

On the other hand, a bar is always a shrine just off the road that's forever obscured by difficulty and longing. Every halfwit girl of a certain age knows you don't enter such a hiding place with a strange man, so I told myself there must be other people inside the Irish Rose and I would be safe enough. I would be able to read the room. I would be strong enough, brave enough, smart enough. What was I thinking? I sensed right away from the hollow, I was alone with a man whittled out of slippery, countersunk eyes. We walked into a kitchen stacked with wooden trays of glasses, empty bottles, coffee cups, plates. Light angled across a sink and settled on the face of dirty water there. The wide-planked floor scuffed with boot prints. A mouse scuttled behind a mop and bucket. The Irish Rose, something of a fallen beauty. With a glance over the shoulder, I measured the distance between myself and the doorway.

"The broom's in the corner," he said. "You can start in the bar and finish with a mop in the kitchen. Name's Jack Little, what's yours?"

Before I could answer, I realized I'd been holding my breath ever since I walked inside the Rose. Out of air, I nearly fell over my feet.

"I forgot to mention," I said. "I met Blind Danny."

"He's no more blind than a smallmouth nibbling a bacon strip."

"He told me to look you up."

"Why would that be?" Jack asked.

"I'm looking for somebody."

"Aren't we all?" Jack said, with a repeated flick of his wrist. Like the sucker picker I'd stayed with, Jack Little didn't need much daylight to loosen his tongue.

"My wife left me for a sailor who breezed in from Georgian Bay. She was a party girl with a pair of hips like two battleships, if you know that song. My God, she was a looker in a black sleeveless. Every man who walked in here wanted to walk out with her, but she was mine until she wasn't and that's how it goes here. Men and women fight like hell to get to Pelee, then they decide that heaven must be elsewhere."

From the rank, unwashed look of his unkempt bar, Jack no longer felt obliged to polish up his own bones. How he ever convinced a battleship girl to give him a second look was beyond my scope. By almost any ink on a ledger, Jack Little was not a catch, or if you did snag his lip, you'd make a point of throwing him back.

I wasted no time trying to steer the conversation in another direction.

"Wink over at Scudder Dock told me he'd seen my father here drinking a cold one."

"Wink, that fingerling. He'd sell skunk meat and call it flank steak."

"Look, I don't know who to believe, but I do know in my heart that my daddy is still alive. Can I work here for a spell and see if he shows up?"

"Okay, so now your story is not just food, but food, lodging, and a missing person thrown in."

"I can't do what I've come to do on my own."

"Don't want any trouble," Jack said, dragging a knuckle across his forehead.

"No trouble."

"Who's looking for you?"

"Nobody," I said, not knowing if that was truth or not, but hoping Momma hadn't sent anyone after me.

"How did you get here?"

"By water," I said.

I crossed my arms over my chest, not knowing what I could do or say to make this man give me work.

"How old are you?"

"Seventeen."

"Yeah," he scoffed, "and I used to be hitched to the queen of Sheba."

"Sounds like you were." I smiled.

Jack laughed and pointed a finger at me. "Can't have an under-aged girl working here."

"Must be worse things that go on."

"I run a clean establishment."

"I'll stay anywhere."

"There's a tent in the barn."

"Hoping for inside."

"Take it or leave it."

I nodded my approval, but after Jack's description of the raccoons, I had no desire to tread on their pathways.

"Work hard and stay as long as you want, under one condition. I don't want to lose a single customer because you've got a burning need to find a daddy who's run off."

I took the broom from Jack Little. I left the kitchen and entered the seating area of the bar thinking I was a long way from Rye Beach now, even though I was only thirty miles north. The horseshoe bar was fancy, built out of mahogany with a brass foot rail. A dozen tables had stacked chairs turned upside down, their legs nicked and splintered from hard use and long hours. Parts of the room, away from the windows, sat dark as an inkwell. I thought I would clean those sections last. The broom felt good in my hands. Gave me something to lean on. I was always more comfortable working than thinking, never more so than now. I swept up broken glass, cigarette butts, match sticks, a tube of lipstick, and a pack of condoms called *Midnight Glider*. Stamped on the foil pack was a picture of a man and woman slow dancing, her bare back showing, one leg kicked up, his hand on her backside lower than the rising moon.

Before the incident with Jimmy Shade, Momma told me sex was a mystery that your body came to when you were ready. My broom told another story. What happened between a man and woman was more about greedy hands not remembering what broke in the shadows. I put the *Midnight Glider* in my pocket and went back to the crumbs, bottlecaps, skeins of hair, and dirt. Seemed like hours melted into me. I felt faint from hunger, dim light, and Ruby gone before she could do me any good. Jack trundled in from the kitchen, saw me bent over the broom, nodded.

"Not bad," he said.

Once he left, I slumped in a chair, laid my head on the table. Everything hurt from my feet to my hands and there was a twitch at the base of my spine. Looking back now, I'm certain it was the worry, and not the work itself, that made me feel needled. How long I nodded off I can't say, but I jumped up when I heard Jack return.

"I'm sorry," I said, with a start. "That won't happen again."

Jack brought me a plate of hot dogs, chips, a pickle, lemonade.

"Pub food," he said. I sat at the table with my back to the wall wolfing what he had brought, thinking I could do this, I just had to stay awake.

"Take the chairs off the tables," Jack said, his bald head a lighthouse beam in the room. "Happy hour coming on quick."

"What's that?"

"Cheap drinks," Jack said.

Happy hour dragged in only a few customers that first night, but I made sure I was out front with a table towel and a smile. Sadly, none of the men looked like bootleggers peddling a whisper. No one drank more than a couple of beers. I looked into the eyes of one man stinking of whitefish as he gulped his dinner like he was desperate to start a fire in his throat and even more possessed to put it out. After washing glasses and pushing broom again, I staggered from the bar to the barn after midnight. I couldn't find the tent in the dark, but I nearly stepped on a pitchfork and ended my search early. I looked back at the bar and saw a room over the garage with an outside stairway.

In the room, I found a lumpy mattress on the floor with no sheets and fell into it like it understood who I was and what I needed more than I did. I wanted to sleep but couldn't after I heard a pattering on the roof. I looked out the screened window and saw nothing but the occasional firefly until a face swelled in front of me as big as my own, and I fell, ass over teakettle, every part of me shaking. A mother raccoon and a litter of five looked in at me, sprawled over the mattress, the yellow bars of their eyes glittering.

"Shoo. Get out of here. I'm living here now."

The mother coon raised up on her hind legs like a miniature bear. She must have weighed over thirty pounds and maybe it was the one Jack wanted to kill. She swung her paws at me like an aspiring pugilist, then led her litter back down the oak tree. After she had gone, I saw the tear in the screen and slammed the window shut. Better to get no air, than to have unwanted roommates, but when the air turned flat and stale, I cracked the window to sip air. I slept with my face in the wind and with one eye open for the return of the shadowboxing raccoon. Near dawn, I figured out why the mother wanted the room. It was loaded with mice. When one of them scampered across my arm, I thought again about trying to locate the tent. Instead, I laid there listening to mice scratching somewhere unseen like my own thoughts telling me to get out of there, get back on the water, and then again, don't go anywhere just yet, something as small as a mouse might just lead you to where you want to go.

9

After the first week of intrepid raccoons, scuttling mice, and no answers, my head hurt from a lack of sleep and from the uncertainty of what to do next. The only thing I learned was that Jack Little had his own whiskey pipeline. While looking again for the tent, I found a dozen cases of Canadian Club in the barn as well as in a cabinet behind the bar where he kept the hard stuff for a few select patrons.

After the second week at the Irish Rose, I wanted to leave, but I'd lost my courage to sail on to Detroit alone, and instead spent more time thinking about sailing back home. I mastered the late hours, but at least once a day I rushed to the head with a rumbling gut, my knees buckling, my hands shoved into my ribs like stones were grinding there. Standing over the toilet until my knuckles were as white as the porcelain bowl, I sputtered and heaved, but little came up. I bent over the sink, splashed cold water on my face, tried to smile back at the mirror, at the doubt I saw there, spread like a sprawling gray cloud. One night, after such a spell, the door to the Irish Rose swung open and a middle-aged woman with scraggly black hair climbed up on a bar stool.

"Who in the hell are you?"

"I work here," I said.

"If that's truth, fetch me a temperance ale."

Serving liquor was not part of my job description, but I thought this woman might be just the talker I hungered for to the point of sickness. I looked around for Jack, but he was over the sink, washing dishes. The woman's restless hands spiked the air.

"You going to get me a drink," the woman snapped, "or do I have to do it myself?"

I froze up.

"Jack," the woman shouted, "who is this nitwit under your thumb?"

Jack emerged from the kitchen drying his hands on an apron.

"Miss Kitty, long time no see. How you been keeping?"

"Been better, been worse."

"Glad you found your way back."

"I know you are always happy to take my money."

"How's that damn sciatica?"

"Don't go trying to get all cozy."

Jack shook his head.

"Whose your new mop?" the woman asked, looking me up, down, and sideways. Jack looked at me to answer the question. I looked at Miss Kitty thinking I didn't want this lush to know anything about me.

"Nor-ah," I said, half swallowing my own name.

"Noah? Where's your ark?"

"Norah," I said again.

"Well, Miss Norah, you should know Jack Little takes a shining to pigtails and ponytails, but I've never seen him make a play for anyone young as you. Times must be tough, Jack, for you to rob the cradle. Lord have mercy on the goat you are."

Miss Kitty yanked on my own fears about Jack, who winked at me, shook his head, and tilted a tall glass under a beer spigot. He slid the glass over to Miss Kitty.

"All you got is this 2 percent?" Miss Kitty said, biting off the head of foam.

"'Fraid so," Jack said, his hands anchored at his waist. "Hoping they repeal the law this year. Been six long years, but it can't go on forever."

"Told me the same damn thing last year, Jack. Don't know how you stay in business serving this swill."

"Should I run a tab?"

"It's criminal to take money for this piss," Miss Kitty said, taking another slug, then another.

Jack glared, frowned, smiled.

"Money makes the world."

"Jack, you've got so much coin, you wouldn't know how to spend it down. Maybe I could show you sometime."

Listening to these two was like listening to the gossip of two goats at our neighbor's fence line back in Rye Beach, each one picking, digging, and not letting go of some gnarly rind of unknown origin. I wondered who got up and died on Miss Kitty and left her stranded on Pelee. And no doubt Jack's battleship girl had more sense than both of them and was long bound for some other ocean.

"If you knew how little money I have," Miss Kitty said, polishing off her beer.

Jack rolled his eyes and left Miss Kitty in a snit.

"Miss Kitty," I asked, getting up into her face. "A woman like you must be friendly with rumrunners?"

She spun around on her stool faster than a snapper and knocked her purse off the bar with her elbow. Before the purse hit the floor, a pack of Midnight Gliders flew out which she didn't see.

"What are you doing, a school report?"

"It's summer break," I said.

"Give me one reason why I should tell you anything?"

"What are you drinking?"

"Got anything more ballsy than beer?" Miss Kitty said.

I looked around for Jack and didn't see him, but heard him outside dumping bottles into the trash. I slipped behind the bar and reached into the cabinet where he kept his private stash. I uncorked a fifth, and poured a good four ounces of Canadian Club into Miss Kitty's empty beer mug. She closed one eye when she put the mug to her mouth.

"What it is you want to know, sweet pea?"

"Who's running whiskey out of here?"

"You the new sheriff in town?"

"I gave you a healthy shot."

"You'll come to no good."

"That's my business."

"Aren't you something."

Jack returned from the kitchen with a tray of dripping-clean mugs. Miss Kitty hunched over her mug, then gulped half the whiskey. Jack turned on two corner lamps which gave the room a warm line of dusk inflowing. Business was off, but his pride in the Rose had not left him. While he gave each table an extra shine with the damp cloth he kept tied at his waist, I rushed off to the kitchen, cracked the ice box and took out a soup can packed with bacon grease. I opened the back door, buried the bacon can in the trash barrel, rushed back into the bar while he finished making his rounds.

"I've got some more glasses to clean up," Jack said. "You okay with Miss Kitty? I know she's a handful."

"Got it under control," I said, but I felt a long way from knowing how to open her up all the way.

"You smell funny, girl," Miss Kitty said, pinching her nose. "Don't you feel safe enough here to take a shower? Guess I don't blame you. Jack's as horny as a jack rabbit."

"I bathe in the lake," I said.

"That explains it. You smell fishy."

"Might say the same of you."

Miss Kitty threw me a lopsided grin.

"I like you," she said, slurring her words. "You got any money?"

"Some."

"Give me twenty-five. I'll tell you something."

"Don't have that much," I lied.

"Give me what you've got," she said, shaking her mug so the whiskey sloshed against the sides of the glass.

"How do I know I'll get something I can use?" I said, leaning close enough to Miss Kitty so our voices wouldn't reach back to the kitchen.

"Pays your money, takes your chances," Miss Kitty scoffed, the whiskey now sliding the words around in her mouth. I turned sideways to Miss Kitty, reached into my pocket and peeled off one of the five tens I'd taken from Momma's cookie jar. I put the ten in Miss Kitty's outstretched hand and she stuck the bill under her sweated glass.

Jack shouted from back, "Coons in the trash again. I'll be awhile."

I was not going to move one inch until Miss Kitty told me something. I was about to make a grab for my ten note, when she offered, "Who you looking for?"

"My father."

"Father in heaven. Father in hell. Father get your hands off my tits."

"Need to know where the rumrunners keep their boats."

Miss Kitty threw back her head with a wolfish howl.

"You are one silly slip of a girl."

I grabbed what was left of Miss Kitty's whiskey, gulped it down, and snatched my ten note back. The whiskey burned the back of my throat. My eyes teared up. I needed to show Miss Kitty I was not some schoolgirl. I slammed the mug down in front of her and waved the ten dollar bill in front of her pinched face.

"Girl's got a taste for the hard stuff."

"Don't have a lot of time."

"Who does?" Kitty asked, her eyes lit like embers fallen through the grate.

"I don't care if you've wasted your life."

"Know how to bite too, don't you?"

Miss Kitty's back stiffened. I tried another tack.

"I need your help."

"You want to get yourself killed?" Miss Kitty barked, holding out her hand for the ten note.

"Not afraid of dying," I said, after my shot of courage.

"What are you afraid of?"

"Not bringing Daddy home," I blurted out, the whiskey in me now like a buzz saw hitting a nail.

"I see where this is going." Miss Kitty smirked. "You're on

some kind of rescue mission. Your mother have any idea the company you keep?"

I slapped my hand over my mouth so I wouldn't laugh at Miss Kitty's motherly question about my mother. I said nothing because I needed this woman running in my favor or Jack would toss me out in the morning after he figured out I broke into his whiskey cabinet and threw a can of bacon grease in the trash. I tried coming at her from yet another angle. I dug into my pocket and put a second ten dollar bill into her palm. She straightened up at the sign of more cash. Like the last few minutes between us had never happened. Like we were sisters who had shared the lip of a glass. Like the corn would now be cut and buttered and served with big boy tomatoes.

"A half dozen men run hooch out of Pelee. They shoot back at anyone who shoots at them."

"Who do they work for?"

"All of them give up a piece to the boys in Detroit who give up a piece to Capone. It's a mule train up there and from what I hear, you don't want to get behind that mule."

For the first time since I had walked into the Irish Rose some hard facts feathered my way. It was such a relief to know I had not cooked up my theories about what happened to Daddy. I wanted to shout out what Miss Kitty had told me. Prohibition had turned men into foraging raccoons. The men went out at night and got into mischief. Many got fed, but some were plucked from the streets, docks, living rooms, and boats of their youth, and they were never seen again. Still others must survive and take the long way home, or at least that was the hope I found through Miss Kitty's revelation.

"Where do they keep themselves?"

"That'll cost you another fiver," she said, baring her stained yellow teeth and red, fleshy gums.

I pulled out more cash.

"You shouldn't look down at me like I'm some floozy."

"That's none of my business."

Miss Kitty took her time, spinning around to survey the

room, making sure empty was really empty, her face, a rumpled bed, her eyes flickering like a bulb on a chain.

"You never heard any of this from me, but between the Custom's House and the old stone dock, there's a farmhouse where they lay up."

"Anybody keep watch?"

"How would I know that?"

"Jack says you like men as much as whiskey." I lied about that. Jack had never said a word about Miss Kitty's means of livelihood, but at that moment, in that bar with the whiskey hot on my lips, I wanted to hurt her some for making me take a big chance.

"Ought to wring your neck," Miss Kitty said.

"That would not be your best idea," I said, digging my fingernails into my palms because something about her threat told me killing would not be all that hard for Miss Kitty. I'd like to say I took my expensive, hard-won information and cleared out fast, but before I could do just that, Ruby ambled into the Rose with her new heartthrob, Zane Hooper, in tow. How should I describe her face? Flushed and compliant with a hint of sadness riding shotgun. Hooper was all loose-jointed and aglow like a man who had just discovered why bumblebees seek the smear of clover even in a rainstorm. Ruby didn't see me right off and I didn't rush up into the smitten trance they had come to. Out of fear of driving her off, I didn't want to make a sound. Zane didn't see me either. My hesitation swung on a rusty hinge and I had no idea which way the door would creak next. I only knew I would have to step through, and there on the other side, the world of the Rose would be different.

"Norah Bow?" Ruby's smoky-edged voice found me skittering. "That you?"

I planned to keep walking into the kitchen, but I turned around, smiled thinly, not wanting to show how relieved I was to see her. "Where you been?" I asked, nonchalantly.

"Here and there," Ruby said.

"Mostly there, I reckon," I said, a burn flaring my throat

when I pictured being left by the side of the road and watching Hooper's horse and buggy vanish in a hoop of dust.

"Norah, it started to rain so we stopped. Then by the time it cleared it was dark, so—"

"I found my way."

"I knew you would."

"No thanks to you."

"We should talk."

"When would that be?"

Ruby looked at Zane, then at me, and I saw in the forlorn of his infatuation, how she had thrown herself at him and her allegiance now made it impossible for her to help me. I should have left her out in the drink because she was more unreliable than an outboard with no oil in the crankcase. Instead, I said the one thing that cast a shadow over the blush of her swelling breast.

"You agreed to help me find Daddy, and you'll honor your part of the deal or live to regret it."

Zane grabbed her by the arm. "Ruby, do we need to go?"

"Ruby's my crew and she owes me," I said straight up into the chiseled bounty of his face.

"Hey, Zane, how's your wife been feeling?" Miss Kitty asked. The mock concern raised her voice a note. "Heard the poor woman is under the weather again."

Zane pinched his mouth.

"Sickness that never leaves a wife must test the buttons on a man's trousers."

"Wife?" Ruby said to Zane with a glare.

"Thought you must have known," he said.

"'Course, I knew," Ruby said.

Ruby's face lost its April and some later month like November settled into her cheeks. Zane turned around and elbowed Miss Kitty in the right shoulder. She collided with me and I stumbled against a table and fell to the floor. Miss Kitty clapped her hands. "More, more," she yelled. Ruby lifted me up by the armpits.

"The bloom is off the rose," Ruby said to Zane and he failed to catch the play on words. After two weeks of staring down a momma raccoon, I was itching for a fight with a real person, but before I could tell Zane Hooper what I thought of him, two men slipped into the Rose like grizzled apparitions from my own patchy sleep. Both of them thin as a knife scar. The first bore angry red bumps across both cheeks. The second man smelled like deep-trolling bait. He wore blue jeans tucked inside duck boots. He carried a burlap bag cinched with clothesline. The one who smelled like bait lit a cigarette. The glow from the tip caught the jagged edge of a front tooth.

"Who might you ladies be?" he asked, with his eyeballs glued on Ruby like there was no yesterday, no tomorrow. I looked at Ruby, wondering if she ever got tired of being lusted after or if some part of her had just come to expect this maneuver and how she might use it to her advantage.

"None of your business," Ruby said.

Zane hung back, sizing up the odds.

The fisherman held the burlap bag by the throat and shook it.

"I'll give you girls a twenty dollar gold piece if you stick your hand in my bag and touch my monkey's paw."

"In a pig's ass," Ruby said.

The man looked at Ruby's bottom.

"Let me try," I said, half thinking if I did this, we could get rid of the man's fixation with us and replace the money I had shelled out.

"Don't do it," Ruby said as I reached for the burlap bag.

"Why not?"

"That's no monkey's paw in the bag," Ruby said.

"How do you know that?" the man said, all smugness glinting into the rise of his cheekbones.

"I'll give you thirty dollars, if you go first," Ruby offered.

I looked at Ruby like she must be an escapee from an asylum, but I reached into my pocket and pulled out the last of my money.

"Only twenty-five left," I said.

Ruby slapped two tens and a five on the table. The two men stomped the floor with laughter. The fisherman said, "How she'd know you had a rattler in need of some warmth and affection?" I grabbed the cash off the table, took two steps back, and kept one eye on the burlap bag dangling from the man's hand.

"We don't cotton to questions here."

Ruby squared up to the men. "What are you talking about?" I pictured Betsy sticking her hand through the long-necked tobacco leaves to grab a few bucks by telling these men there was someone looking for rumrunners or maybe Wink loosening his tongue for a bucket of minnows.

"Makes us feel hunted," the fisherman said, "when someone starts asking questions about our livelihood." He scratched the back of his neck and winced like he was lifting the bumpy edge of a stubborn scab.

The first man whose face was an angry splotch, said, "Grab the girl and stick her hand in the bag." I backed up, knocking over a chair, giving the fisherman time to punch me in the chest so hard I doubled over sputtering. Ruby picked up another chair, hurled it at a fisherman and hit him in the shin. Zane stepped between us and the two men. The fisherman threw a roundhouse that missed Zane's jaw. Zane rushed the fisherman and landed a fist at his throat and the man crumpled to the floor still clutching the bag. The man with the splotchy face pulled out a long knife and took at slash at Zane's face.

Miss Kitty shouted, "Always love a good knife fight with a cold beer."

Zane held a chair between himself and the knife. He circled the other man like a lion tamer using the chair to press forward and keep the knife at bay. Jack emerged from the backroom with a shotgun cradled in his arm. "Goddamnit, no one wrecks my bar," he shouted. "No one."

Ruby shoved me toward the door. "Run, girl, run." As we

lunged out the door of the Irish Rose, I heard a gun blast that deadened the thunk of my own running feet.

"We have to go back," I said. "What about Zane?"

"Can't help him now," Ruby said.

"What if he's been shot up?"

"Then he's got even more trouble than we have."

"Momma's blue canvas bag?"

"What?"

"I left it."

"You're lucky that's all you left back there."

I didn't need to meet up with a rattlesnake to know I was all of snakebit to find Vital Bow. So keen on this, I would have stayed at the Rose and had it out with those two men; then again, I was glad to have Ruby by my side again and the thought of running with her seemed like a better proposition.

Of all the things I miss about youth, it's the confidence that my legs could always find another gear above idle. Christ said all we need is a mustard seed to start scaling a mountain. One mustard seed and I might add, a ruby. Say what you want about a sapphire or an emerald, pretty as they are, but a ruby perks the blood, kindles the fire, lights the way forward, makes the night seem not so long. With a ruby, there's no need to reach out on a dare and touch a monkey's paw. With a ruby, you can run hard and not look down.

10

We ran from bramble into woods, then along the soggy edge of cattail marsh.

Everything hurt in my chest like maybe my clumsy fall had cracked a rib. I had less wind than I needed, no sense of balance, no onward push. I could feel my toes squish inside my tennis shoes and an old blister blooming. Ruby had a strong, sure stride like a deer. How did she know which way to turn in mid-air? How could she run so hard without getting tired? Then, I answered my own question. Ruby had been running a long time.

"Don't let up, Norah," Ruby said, at least a half-dozen steps ahead.

I looked up and saw a sliver of moon caught in the tangled cedar and ash branches, and in the time it took for my glance to return to the ground, I caught my left foot on a branch. I plunged downward and hit my nose on a mossy stone and blood trickled onto my lips.

Ruby turned back toward me, shaking her head.

"Good God, girl. You sure picked a poor time."

I felt the throb of my ankle all the way up my leg. I didn't think I could stand, but I did. I hobbled fifty paces into the brush and stopped in front of a rock outcropping.

Ruby said, "A bit of daylight."

"What do you mean?"

She found a slit in the outcropping, less than two feet wide. She wiggled into the crevice, disappeared for a moment, then returned.

"We're going underground."

"You're not serious?"

"Just to catch our breath."

She possessed an untroubled faith that the world, no matter

how darkly assembled and unavailable, was also cut with openings to slip through, and so we did. I came upon this confidence much later in life after many headwinds and much travail. Call it survival of the fittest if you want, but I prefer a shout out to the Psalms, help me to know your ways, O Lord, teach me your secret paths, detour by dead-end by unwanted interruption. I could never have joined the oldest of the old without a trust that every poor night on the run was also married to a better day of quiet in a safe harbor.

"Daddy worked as a child coal miner."

"Maybe he never left such a world."

I climbed down onto a ledge hating to admit Ruby might be right about him. No matter his distant origins, Daddy might still be working a vein of coal far below ground and I had been fool enough to follow. The wet dripping of the place made me turn all damp and soggy inside, then a shiver shot through me. Ruby slipped off her flats, handed them to me.

"Stay here. I need to go back to brush over our tracks and cover the entrance."

Through a sliver opening, I watched Ruby walk barefoot back the way we'd come. She tore off a branch from a bush, swept the ground. She yanked out marsh weed and grasses, and picked up fallen branches and handed me a bundle of sticks. She backed into the cave, then covered the mouth. We could not see out and we could not be seen.

"How did you know about this cave?"

"I have a nose for such places," Ruby said.

"I wished that made me feel better."

"Buys us time."

"Caves don't come with a lot of time," I said, thinking of Daddy's violent experiences in the coal mines of West Virginia, how a shaft could collapse for no reason and the men inside would never come out and those that did were never the same, their lungs the unspoken casualties.

"What's that supposed to mean?"

"I hate caves."

"You're a long way from a coal mine."

"Daddy must carry some memory of coal."

"That has nothing to do with you," Ruby said. Ruby was wrong about that. Daddy's below-ground life had long ago blocked his view of the upper spheres. Daddy quoted freely from the Bible, but he had no patience with a miner's favorite hymn, "How Great Thou Art." He said miners, regardless of age, size, or strength, got rat-faced drunk on Friday night, took all day Saturday to stagger to a toilet, then groused like hell on Sunday for having to shake off the poison and look sober. With each drink, they cursed the day of their descent, and on Sunday, they gave thanks to the Lord for the promise of his eventual rising. Blame him or love him, God has nothing to do with the creation of flammable coal dust, Daddy said with a glare. God can't stop a man from tearing a hole in his own heart. God can't start or stop a mine shaft explosion. God can't do anything because he, too, is trapped underground fighting for a shrinking air supply, and he, too, won't make it out alive. I can hear him now, his words an unbroken rumble from below. "A man can read the good book all day long, but the truth of his life is neither blest nor unblest, but only caught up in some blossom of dust unfolding."

We stood on a jagged landing inside the cave's mouth dripping and pinging with wet noise and I might as well have been in the bottom of a mine shaft with no air left in my lungs. I reached out and my hand slid against moss. Ruby listened like a cat tucked into a ledge. I couldn't tell what hurt most, my ribs or my foot or the thought of spending one more second underground thinking about my father who maybe never left such a world.

"Cold as hell in here," I croaked.

"Still have a pocket knife?"

"Yeah."

"Give it to me."

My hands shook too much to be any good at fishing out the knife.

"Reach in my pocket and get it."

Ruby pressed against me and dug into my pocket and pulled out the knife along with the Midnight Glider. She held the knife and packet up to a ray of moonlight that bounced through the cave.

"What do we have here?" she asked.

"Found it on the floor of the Rose."

"The beast is alive," she snickered.

"What's that supposed to mean?"

"My first time was thirteen, pinned down by an uncle."

"That explains a lot," I said, not knowing exactly what my words meant or what they left out. I couldn't imagine such a thing, the loss of control, the confusion. No wonder Ruby had such speed.

"Nothing is ever explained," she said.

We slid back toward the moonlight at the cave's opening. Instead of her silver-beaded flapper dress with burnt holes in it, I saw her floral dress with a ruffled neckline, cap sleeves, and blue cotton waist tie; it had a little too much kitchen to suit her curves. She flicked open the knife and cut a long strip from the hem.

She squatted and said, "Put your foot up in my lap."

She wrapped the cloth snugly around my ankle as if this was something she had done for herself. I could feel the pressure easing on my foot as she tied off the cloth.

"Zane said the dress belonged to his ex-wife, not a current one," she said into the cave's trickling light.

"I guess most of that sentence is true."

"What else is ailing you?" Ruby said, with some glint returning to her eyes.

"My ribs."

She put one hand under the shelf of my ribcage and pressed inward.

"That hurt?"

"You might say."

"Your ribs may be bruised, but that's not what's doubling you."

"What then?"

"You kinked your back in the fall."

"Sounds worse than a rib."

"A cracked rib can take weeks to heal. I can remedy your back in a few seconds."

Ruby turned me around so she was facing my back, then kneaded her hands into my spine. She thumbed down each bony lump of flesh until she found the knotted soreness. I cried out for her to ease up on the throttle.

"We're getting somewhere," she said. She turned me back around with my back against the cave wall. She folded my arms over my chest, found the knot again in my spine, then she found a flatness on the wall.

"Okay," she said. "Now, kiss the moon."

"What?"

In my distraction of looking up at the sparse light holding us there, she leaned against me so close I could feel her breath, then she popped me against the cave wall. I gasped when I heard the cracking. She stood away and I peeled myself off the wall with less pain burning a hole through me.

"Who taught you that trick?"

"Someone who gave me hope after I'd lost mine."

My spirits lifted in that dark, wet place. Ruby brushed her hair off her face and tidied her new floral dress as if she were ready to stroll again in search of another man's heartache.

"Speaking of hope, there's a farmhouse between the Custom's House and the old stone dock on the west side. That's where Miss Kitty says the rumrunners have set up shop."

"Miss Kitty?"

"The prostitute back at the Rose."

"Consorting with prostitutes now?"

"She was the only one who would talk."

"Nicely done," Ruby said, taking mincing steps out of the cave.

I wondered if we should enlist Zane's help before we set off. I looked back the way we had come. She read my mind.

"It's over between us."

"What if Zane did get himself shot up?"

"Let his wife pick up the pieces."

I climbed out of the cave and walked west through scraggly stands of birch and buckthorn, knowing from the kick of the southwesterly wind how to hold that heading on the nose. Ruby followed a few steps behind, glancing backward like a soldier scuttling a hostile border. Dusk sat upon us and the half-light cut our progress, but it felt good to swing my arms. I found an apple in my pocket, bit down hard, tossed it back to Ruby. I heard her teeth crunch against the apple and throw it aside.

"Peaches on this island, I heard Zane say. Sure could use one," Ruby said, her tongue clicking her mouth. No matter the circumstance, Ruby's appetite never wavered. Where I thought of food as fuel, Ruby talked about food the way you might talk about lingering in a bath or yielding to a sunset.

"Never met a stone fruit I didn't like. Apricots, cherries, plums, nectarines, peaches. Just like to say those words, but a peach, oh my, my kingdom for a peach."

"I would settle for a pump of cold water," I said, my ankle stinging with every third step and making me feel like a stone was rattling around inside of me. We crossed a trenched meadow of Holsteins scattered like so many black and white puzzle pieces on a tabletop. The swollen cows stared at the hitch in my step. We heard a rooster with the wrong hour caught in his throat. Then, a dog barked. A man called after it. The dog latched onto our scent and howled of its approach. We picked up the pace. Ruby read the rust of the late evening light, alert and ready to spring toward the canopy of oaks outside the rocky square of meadow.

"What should we do when we find the farmhouse?" I asked, my ankle wanting to drag me off to less danger.

"You tell me."

"I'm not afraid," I boasted, stopping at the field's edge to brake the pain in my foot.

"One unexplained death in a family is hard. Two is more than double."

"Momma and me are not the best of—"

Ruby interrupted. "She might never get out of bed again if you don't come home."

"You think I'm stupid for going on?"

"Selfish or stupid, don't know which," Ruby said, throwing a stone into a thatch of Queen Anne's Lace. "You think you're the only person on earth who has lost somebody?"

I didn't care for either selfish or stupid.

"For somebody who doesn't go to church, who doesn't believe in anything but her own sex glands, you sure like to preach," I said. "Least I don't run out on people," I spat out. "Least I know the difference between right and wrong. Least I can do more in this world than get men all hot and bothered."

Ruby threw down a thin, twitchy smile that would be hard to misread. "You done?"

"Done enough," I said, my mouth dry enough to hurt my lips.

"In that case," Ruby said, her pencil-thin smile replaced with a snarl, "you can track down these sons-of-bitches on your own. You've got such a high opinion of your own merit badge, why in hell do you need the likes of me?"

Ruby reversed course and walked back across the field toward the cave. Out of stubbornness and a dread of that wet place, I didn't follow. In minutes, the dark swallowed her. I heard crickets coming on like gospel while bats threaded the air. The darkness was nothing more than a meal to them. The dog barked again while a man's voice urged him on. I told myself to keep walking. I stopped and looked for her in the pitch of things coming on.

"You smell a human fox, don't you, boy?"

More bark and snarl. More bats in a gauzy tangle. The man

fired a shot while the rooster offered a salvo. I dropped to the ground, craned my head for a sightline. Saw nothing but stars like so many rivets in the hull of a faraway ship. I tried to picture this man and what I might shout that would make a difference. Heard a rustling inside the seed casings. Something or someone swung close to my patch of ground. I dug into earth with fingernails. My heart receding in the hollow I had become. The dog sent out another baleful sound, which I envied because I wanted to do the same. If I ran, the dog would outrun me. If I stayed, the man would find me. I didn't know what to do next. You might say, I froze up inside with the full empty of the situation pouring toward me.

"Come on, girl, let's not wait for a drunk shooting at stars to find us by accident," Ruby said, reaching down to pull me up. I unbolted myself from the earth, thrilled to see that Ruby had doubled back. I leapt up and put a snap in my step so as not to lose sight of her in the quickening. Soon we were out beyond the echo of man and dog.

"Sorry about what I said."

"Just tell me one thing, girl. Where exactly are the sex glands?"

The darkness hid my blush.

"That what my momma calls, you know—"

"Your momma calls the vagina your sex glands? No wonder you're all fuzzy in the head. Let's go find this farmhouse and hope some brilliant idea comes to you," she said, throwing her arm round my shoulder, as if to say maybe we could sort something out or maybe not, but walking that way through the dark kept us from breaking apart just then and I was grateful to be back in her company, not knowing when she would leave next.

Right about then, I thought I could use another jolt of the demon switch to come to my aid. The land had me all tied up with its muscle and rope. I couldn't read the strand of what to do next. The only thing I knew then was, as much as I was hunting

Vital Bow, all kinds of trouble was now hunting me. I had to think smart. Watch my feet. Like Ruby, I might need to run hard, run long, and keep at it until such running was all mine at any clip. Same time, I thought, all I want to do is find my boat, get off that island, and never touch ground again.

11

Whiskey is frisky, I heard Daddy say. I didn't know then what he meant by that, but that night I took a wild guess he meant whiskey could loosen a tongue, a pocketbook, a pair of pants, a zipper, or just about any other lock or clasp. No matter the meaning, I was glad whiskey helped me warm up Miss Kitty because she had been right as rain. Ruby and I found the farmhouse Miss Kitty mentioned backed up to a marsh with a front porch looking out toward Lake Erie. In a field of rye, I saw two small outbuildings, a hand plow canted in weeds, a couple of iron-strapped wood buckets, an abandoned car, all of it splashed with the light of a crescent moon. Most clear was a kerosene light lodged within, and the shapes of two men dividing the beam with their heft and shape. On some other night, on some other island, I would have thought this farmhouse deserved to be given a wide berth like some freighter in the hold of a shipping lane, but I had other plans. I wanted to storm it, sink it, run it aground, make it known to captain and crew I had been there. Tough talk from a bum ankle, but that's how I thought back then. Like I knew the price of a shiver.

"I have to get closer to listen in," I whispered.

"You don't have to do anything," Ruby muttered, "except live another day."

"What else am I going to do? Wait for one of these thugs to come out and relieve himself, then sit him down for a chat?"

We crept sideways to the northwest corner of the house, then slid along one wall toward an open window. I felt the scratch of sandpaper in my throat. The sweat ran down my shirt. Ruby crouched, then sat down with her back to the clapboard. She motioned for me to park myself beside her. I wanted to see faces, hear voices, draw a map in my mind of the interior. She pulled on me to sit down, but I kept standing to hear better.

"Three months ago," the first voice said, "I was making twenty bucks a week driving a milk truck."

"Now your wife thinks you're a big shot," the second voice said.

"Pulling down three hundred dollars a week, I think I am a big shot," the first man said.

"You'll piss it away," the second man said.

The second man piped up: "If we had a bigger boat, we could make bigger runs."

"If you had a bigger dick, you'd get more toss," the first man said with a laugh.

I peeked through glass at the two men. The two men caught in the kerosene smoke were the same size as two of the men who broke into our Rye Beach and took Daddy at gunpoint. One was short and bald with a stubble jaw, deep-set eyes, and crooked bottom teeth. He looked like a potato stuffed into a pair of pants. The other was tall and scraggly, all arms and legs. The tall man lit a cigarette, dragged hard, coughed, dragged again. He then poured himself a drink, tossed it back. He kicked at the door of a dry sink. He looked like the muscle and brains and wore a revolver holstered in black leather. When he talked, the other man stopped like he'd been gagged. When the tall man laughed, the short one followed. When he drank, the short man put his beer down and I saw how his fingers matched the bent track of his teeth.

"We need to spend some do-re-mi on a new engine," the short man said, scratching his nose. "We're coughing buckets of oil."

"She can still fly," the tall man said. "Half the time, I don't think the Coast Guard wants to give chase. Too much fucking trouble. Besides, don't you think the Feds are telling them to lay back? Everybody's making some jingle. No point killing the goose."

"You think that new guy could perk up the engine?" the short man asked.

"He said he could fix anything," the tall man said.

"Why do you think the casino boys roughed him up?"

"Beats me," the tall man said. "Not every day a mechanic comes along like that. Love to get him back here," the tall man continued, "but they sent him to Windsor or they dumped him in the lake."

Daddy was a mechanic, and a good one, but I couldn't believe they were gabbing about him. The two men passed a whiskey bottle between them. Some of the whiskey splashed off their chins onto the table. I hoped their tongues would loosen even more.

"What was his name?" the short man asked.

"It was one I'd never heard before," the tall man said.

"Something like Victor."

Victor was close enough to Vital to make me dig a fingernail. Ruby looked up at me from her patch of ground with a mix of fear and panic like maybe she knew we had stayed too long. I wanted to stay, but she tipped her head for us to back away from the farmhouse. As Ruby make an effort to stand she slipped. She caught herself before she fell against the house, but the heel of her hand smacked the clapboard. For once I wasn't the only one who was clumsy on land.

"What was that?" the short man asked.

"You're hearing things again," the tall man said.

"I'll take a look."

"Make yourself happy," the tall man scoffed.

Ruby and I wasted no butter.

For the second time that day, we ran hard, this time through the whipping rye but not hard enough to outdistance the eyes of the short man. He saw enough in the orange moon haze to call out, "Bix, we got trouble." We didn't look around, but headed back east, my ankle stinging with each step. We twisted and turned through the chaff and saplings. Ruby took long strides and I tried to match them and failed. My breath sounded like an animal panting beside me. We pushed on, throwing ourselves forward into rye. We stopped and used each other to stand up, then we ran again, this time with less speed, but with a greater pounding in my ears and so little air in my chest that I sputtered and wheezed.

"Got a cramp again in my foot," I cried out.

"Talk back to it," Ruby said.

"Cramps don't have ears," I said.

Ruby coughed once, then laughed. Every breath burned tight. We stopped at a field's edge to take stock and look back. Problem was we stopped for too long. I heard the men long before I saw them.

"Looking for somebody?" the tall man asked, as he nuzzled a rifle under my chin.

The short man jabbed a revolver toward Ruby's head. "We got a looker in a dress, Bix. Wait till Jerome and Sam come back from the Rose and see what we've turned up. Been some time since we had a party."

Ruby looked up at the short man, unfazed by his insinuation. The night surged toward us like a wave and made the two men loom large. The short one spit a long thread, then pulled some of it back. The tall one clicked his tongue. My whole body strumming from what I imagined these men might do.

"Get up," Bix said, scratching his scalp. "Keep a gun on the dress, Hank."

Ruby and I stood up. I could see a flash of lightning spidering her eyes. Like she was weighing the odds of running against the odds of returning to the farmhouse where no good could come of our captivity. I wanted to tell her I was sorry for getting her into this, but sorry was not what Ruby hungered for. She scanned the ground for a stone or a stick, anything sharp.

"We were just looking for food," I said to the man called Bix.

"What kind of food would that be?" Bix replied from the

smudged line of his mouth. Bix carried long strings of greasy hair that fell over his ears. Ruby rolled her eyes like she knew it was no good trying to reason. I studied these two men thinking it couldn't hurt to keep them talking.

"Listen up, shorty, the girl is telling some truth." Ruby smirked.

The man called Hank whacked Ruby in the face with his fist. Her knees buckled. She swiped at blood trickling from her nose. She didn't fall.

Bix said, "Let's try an old-fashioned march."

"What did you hear at the farmhouse?" the man named Hank said to me.

"Nothing," I said, my lips mostly pressed together.

"What are you after?" Bix asked, spitting in the meadow grass.

"We got caught in a storm and this is where we landed."

"Come again?" Bix said.

"I'm a sailor."

Bix looked at Ruby like fresh kill. "You've got a lot of bait in the water."

"Just hungry."

Now Bix looked at me. "Going to give you one more chance."

Ruby glanced at me, shook her head.

"Looking for my daddy."

"Sugar daddy?"

The two men threw their heads back, their cheeks shaking with laughter.

"This daddy have a name?"

Ruby shook her head. Hank smacked her a second time.

"Clarence Powers," I said, giving them the name of one of my uncles back in West Virginia so least ways they wouldn't know my name.

"The old sucker picker said you were asking about rumrunners," Bix said, "and I have to tell you, straight away, I have never liked anyone nosing in my business because what I do here is my own feeble attempt to climb the sugar mountain and it hurts when I think someone has a different plan for me."

"Don't care how you make your money," I said.

"Funny how we sent Sam and Jerome to scare a girl with a snake and now another girl has found us. How do you suppose that happened?"

Bix looked at Hank. He rolled his glazed eyes like he'd been stunned by a blow to the head.

"Miss Kitty must have told the girl, you candy ass."

Hank swallowed hard.

"Start walking," Bix said, holding a rifle to Ruby's back.

We walked in moonlight. The two men walked one step behind. Ruby dabbed at her bleeding nose, the look on her face split between panic and something like pleasure at the thought of testing herself in the zigzag of this new unstable moment. My right foot felt like it had been stuck with pins and needles. Through a stand of maples crowded tight as soldiers, the farmhouse flickered with kerosene and, just beyond it, Lake Erie quickened an open vein of silver. A southerly wind trembled the maple crowns and let me believe that if only I could get to water, I could find my powers again. I looked to my right and saw headlights bouncing through wheel dust and I thought our end was near because this must be the third man returning from the Rose. The driver pumped the brakes, skidding the car to a stop. The man slumped at the wheel, then got out, fell down, rolled in the dust, got up, staggered toward the farmhouse same as us, fell down again.

"Think Jerome has a drinking problem?" Bix asked.

Hank laughed. "What would give you that idea?"

"Never met a bottle he didn't want to kill," Bix said.

"Takes all the joy out of it," Hank replied, the two men keen on the lilt of their banter. "Think he might like a poke?"

"He'll be damn lucky if I let him see another day," Bix said, shaking his head.

"More for us," Hank laughed, waving me into the farmhouse with his revolver. Jerome lurched through the door, fell down, picked himself up, laughing with a thin squeak. His face was a chewed thumbnail hit with a ball-peen hammer. He wore blood smears on his chin and forehead. One of his eyes roamed sideways while the other didn't move.

"Didn't know…you boys…had company," Jerome said, blinking hard into the single bulb hanging from a wire, his head wanting to fall forward.

"Where's Sam?" Hank asked.

"Got his self all busted up real good," Jerome said. "Had to leave him. Seen the dress, somewheres."

"You say that about every skirt," Bix said.

Hank loosened his belt. Jerome slumped into a chair. Bix wet his lips. The room held its breath. I looked for some way out. This slow motion felt way too fast.

"This should be fun," Hank snorted.

I stood up in front of Bix. He spun me around.

"Being bootleggers and all, you must know about the demon switch?"

"Demon switch? Shut up. Bend over, schoolgirl," Hank said.

"Lots of men go into the switch. Few ever come out," I said.

"Never heard anything about no demon switch," Hank said.

"You boys must not be from round here," I said, trembling and tall where I stood like I was staring down a bear. Hank shoved Ruby and me onto a sofa. Bix left the room and returned with a chart folded cock-eyed like a road map.

"Show me," Bix said.

I unfolded the chart and ran my fingers down its ragged creases, my mind a mix of hope, doom, and one chance left.

"Here," I said, pointing first to Middle Island, then to Gull Island shoal due south. "When the wind kicks out of the northeast or northwest, you better keep watch between these two islands."

"What happens there?"

"Once the demon switch starts to swirl, it can suck down a boat like a goat swallowing a string."

"How do you know this?" Bix asked.

"Not much I don't know about the Middle Bass Islands. My family has fished and sailed these waters since long before the war. I know every shoal, every shortcut, every shipwreck, every hidey-hole, every demon switch. What I don't know about the waters between here and Ohio, ain't worth knowing. You boys look like you have some need of an education."

"She's talking shit," Hank said, spinning the chamber of his revolver.

"Did I ask your damn opinion?" Bix snapped.

Bix looked again at the tattered chart.

"Ever spend any time on power boats, missy?"

"Outboards, inboards, sailboats, I know them all."

"We could use her." Bix smiled. "Then you boys can do with her what you want."

"You out of your fucking mind?" Hank squawked.

"Shut your mouth," Bix said to Hank.

Hank waved his gun at Bix. "She's nothing but a pint. Show her who's boss."

"Don't care if she's a girl, boy, or chimpanzee. If she knows these islands, maybe she's worth more to us alive than dead. Maybe we wouldn't lose so many props if we had a local helping us out. We all know the charts don't tell us enough."

I saw the hint of a smile splitting Ruby's lips, but it didn't last long.

"Jerome, help me tie up the dress so she won't scratch out my eyeballs," Hank demanded of the drunk. Jerome got up from the table, staggered toward Hank, then spun around, and stopped in front of me.

"I know this piece of ass," he slurred. "She's a player..."

I looked at Jerome, then at Ruby, but her face didn't tell me anything about what to do next and I didn't know whether to run, kick, or scream. Bix glanced down again at the demon switch I pinpointed on the chart. Jerome spun back around, looked at Ruby. "She's the one who threw a chair," Jerome muttered, "at the Rose. More to her than you know."

"What are you saying?" Bix said.

"You want some?" Hank said to Jerome. Ruby leapt off the sofa. Hank caught the side of her head with the butt of his gun. In the speed of her crumpled falling, everything in the room slowed to the pace of a fly mincing off a pane of glass. A gust twisted and unfurled the lace curtains, caught a curl of smoke off the sinking wick of the kerosene lamp and spun it upward. Something like a page ripped from book of Revelation slipped into this sorry place. An orange ball of fire leapt outside the window, and for a moment I thought it was the sun itself flaming out and ending the world just in time so we wouldn't have to suffer what was destined to consume us. Then I imbibed a draft from a seeping lake of gasoline, heard the dry grass crackle with a gust, and in that upwelling of uncertain origin, how fiercely full this moment told me that Hank, Bix, and Jerome were the three men who had taken Daddy at gunpoint. As the three men turned toward the window like the tracing of one unholy shadow, I told myself the ferocious lamb was afoot and I would live another day.

Jerome said, "My goddamn car."

"What'd you do? Drop a cig in your gas tank?" Bix asked.

"He don't smoke," Hank said, watching the car roast with flame.

"What?" Bix asked, realizing too late that someone had set the car on fire.

The back door of the farmhouse burst open with Zane Hooper in suspension. Like a lawman practiced in the ways of surprise attack, he slid a revolver toward Ruby and me, then leveled a rifle at the three men framed by the commotion of the burning car.

"Gentlemen, I mean you no harm," Zane said, with a good deal more panache than he had shown back at the Rose.

"What do you call that?" Bix said, pointing to the car.

Ruby rolled off the sofa like she too had done this before, and swiped the gun off the floor. I had only known her for a few weeks, but already it was clear Ruby lived keenly on lust, courage, and an acceptance that life was nasty and short, and these three sisters gave her an unflappable bravado that would come in handy right about now. Not that I had a lot of time to appreciate her fine points just then because I followed her lead and dove behind the sofa, then duck-walked toward the door.

Zane held his rifle pointed at Bix's chest.

"What I propose, gentlemen," Zane said, "is you paddle back to the cesspool of Detroit where you came from."

I looked around the sofa and saw Hank take a step back from Bix.

"That's a generous offer," Bix said, "but we like it here. Island life agrees with us and we like schoolgirls and dresses."

Hank took another backward step and kicked the table that held the kerosene lamp. I peered around the sofa just as the lamp hit the floor and the flames caught the drape of the curtains. Hank flipped the table over and used it as a shield before he opened fire. Zane took cover with us behind the sofa.

"That gun's not for decoration," Zane said to Ruby.

"You didn't tell me you had a wife," Ruby said, holding the gun but not firing.

"Could you two talk about that later?" I shouted.

Zane stood away from the sofa and fired multiple rounds into the smoke. The shattering of glass and wood gave off a dull roar. Splinters and bits of cloth danced the air. Bix and Hank returned fire. The room spun over and beneath me like a Ferris wheel, the speed of the revolutions confused in my memory with a slowness, as if this violence were both stretched out and compressed, near and far, mine and someone else's. Weightlessly above the ground, I found a calm side pocket in the midst of smoke and gunfire.

Zane kept firing until Jerome slid down a wall, groaning and bleeding from the mouth. Another bullet from Ruby caught Bix in the chest. Hank had no quit in him until his bullets ran out and Zane took advantage of the lull to blast him through a window toward the flaming skeleton of Jerome's car. I looked over at Bix who had a hole in his heart the size of a corn cob. He leaned against a wall with his legs crooked beneath, his eyes sluggish and flickering, the blood pooling his waist and ankles. I hated to look at him and I couldn't look away. He was the first dead man I had ever seen. There would be more, but none with so bright a hole to see through to the other side of nothing.

Without a glance at the dead, Ruby rushed past me toward the kitchen. She opened the ice box and pulled out a wheel of cheese, a bag of apples, a loaf of bread, a ham bone, and a six-pack of Ace beer said to be favored by Al Capone himself for breakfast. She stacked the food and strode out of the burning house like she had done such things before with only the forgiving stars as witness.

"You could thank me for saving your life," Zane called after her.

"Took your damn time," Ruby said.

"Jackals," Zane said to her, as I stumbled outside coughing.

"Always more just like them," Ruby said, juggling her new stash of food.

"No more tonight," Zane said.

"What happens now?" I asked.

"Let it burn," Zane said.

The demon I had spoken of to these men swallowed them whole, not on water as I had invented, but on the very land the rumrunners trusted would be a haven for their escapades. Their last names were now forever separated from their first. Their wives and girlfriends would never learn what became of them. No one would know how their beautiful plans had been erased by fire and smoke. The pit in my stomach fell away and I stood on only air and saw what my search had come to, a farmhouse leaping into flame and falling down into ash. Zane saw my mind ruminating on the remains of their sudden earthly limit.

"Somebody had to clear out this nest."

"Whole world's going down in sauce," Ruby said.

"Can we talk?" Zane asked Ruby.

"Take it back home," Ruby said, stepping back from the heat.

"I'll leave her," Zane said.

"You're a kept man."

"I can leave with you and...the girl."

"Sounds good to me," I said, thinking a fast-action man might not be all bad in Detroit. Ruby twisted off a beer cap and turned around to face Zane.

"I'm grateful for what you did," Ruby said, taking a swig, not stopping till the bottle was half empty, "but I'm a traveling woman." Zane stepped back from her as if he knew she'd already left the island. Ruby finished her beer. He reached out and touched her face. She stepped back into shadow and finger waved, then she shoved the rumrunner's food into a firewood satchel, and we bolted from the reach of the farmhouse grounds. When I looked back from the meadow, I saw orange strings of fire snaking the roof. I only nibbled the cheese and bread Ruby stuck under my nose. I told her I had to grab some sleep, but she was lit up like she'd just come down off a rocket from another galaxy. Later that night, Ruby and I found a homesteader's cabin, long since abandoned to bramble and honeysuckle. We laid down on a warped wood floor. Rusted nails dimpled the spine. Sleep was all I wanted. Let mice and raccoons march on. Let Erie settle into its many shipwrecks. Let the wind nicker the trees. Let the ashes fall. Let nothing more be told of this. Let sleep come.

"You had enough?" Ruby asked, as the night drew down closer to my face. Shallow breaths raced my chest and sweat trickled off my forehead. I sat up in the dark when I saw again the splattered bodies and the fire that followed them to some ungathered place, reminding me how death is not some distant or erstwhile relative with bad breath and uncut toenails who lives in the far back room, but here right now, climbing the unlit stairs to keep my company.

"What happened back there?"

Ruby shifted her weight on the uneven boards, sat up, rubbed her eyes.

"I should have known Zane was hitched."

"The three men, Ruby?"

All I got for a reply was the pulse of crickets.

"You'll get over it or you won't," Ruby finally said.

"I made it happen," I said, my words muffled between my teeth.

"The men who took your father are dead and that's a good thing."

"Why doesn't it feel good?"

"Maybe some good will come of it," Ruby said, her voice a trill in the leaves.

"You afraid of dying?" Ruby took her time. I'd like to say she was busy parsing words, but that was not her style. While I waited for an answer, I looked for a lantern among the train of stars. It was a game Daddy and I used to play. Who could find the red lantern on the end of the caboose. I'd never seen a lantern at the end of a real train, but with him, I had seen one or two in the severed above. Once, while lingering on the heavens, he had said everything was decided before you were born and nothing can ever be known until you engage the next moment, and I couldn't then have said what he meant but he went on like a cipher speaking in riddles, saying between nothing and everything, a man could still find a sliver of wilderness in himself where the uncaptured might offer a way out or a way in from the story writ in his blood. None of that made sense then, but now after the dead I had left behind, I saw how little I really knew of who he was. Right this moment, he might be looking up for a lantern just like me or he might be bloated on the lake bottom with no glimpse of the sky. I had no linkage just then to where he was. No knowledge of who he was in this world between nothing and everything. No ground to stand on from which to see the above or the below of what he had come to.

"We all have to walk through the fire," Ruby finally said through a yawn. "Some sooner than others."

That's all Ruby said about a night singed by bullet holes and gasoline. Little comfort in that. Less when I thought Daddy might not be star-gazing or long drowned but rather elbowed in some Detroit engine room, clocking overtime for the big boys. Whether he went to the whiskey river of his own accord or with a hand tied behind his back, no one could say. One thing was clear enough: whatever those three men knew of my father was now gone to ash and I would have to go on if I was to see again that lantern at the end of the train. How could I do that? After all that fire, maybe I thought the devil himself had stolen Daddy and I needed another devil in my keep in order to bring him back.

12

We were so dragged out by all that had gone wrong, we stayed put for two more days. Given what had happened at the farmhouse, maybe it wasn't that smart to stop moving, but we found a sweet-tasting well, a couple of porcelain plates, even a drawer of knives, forks, and spoons tangled with spider webs. We divvied up the pickings from the rumrunner's ice box and made them last just long enough to not let our hunger dictate our departure. In between gnawing a ham bone and sipping her last Ace beer, Ruby looked like she had weighed and measured second and third thoughts about going on with me.

"Not easy eating their food," I said.

"You wouldn't make a good crow," Ruby said.

"What do crows have to do with it?"

"Without the dead, there's no hope for the living," Ruby said, tearing away a last shred of gristle.

"Nothing gets between you and your next meal," I said, captivated by the force of her bite.

"Learned that one early on."

"Why do you live this way?"

Ruby ignored my question, the happy animal in her still feeding.

"You're sailing back to Rye Beach, right?" Ruby asked from our ridge overlooking Lake Erie. Her question pushed me back within range of panic.

"Going to Detroit," I said, boldly. "He could be there."

"He could be anywhere," Ruby replied, sinking her teeth into a tart, juicy green apple the size of a door knob. "Or nowhere."

"Got to find him."

"Why?"

"Momma has two little boys at home."

"Seems like your daddy could be the third little boy."

"You don't know him."

"Do you?" she asked, smacking her lips.

Ruby spit downwind like cow pokes do in the movies, then wiped her chin and dried her hand on the grass. I looked out and saw a freighter riding low in the water, nearly stalled by the weight of her cargo and the worry of a headwind. She had to be hauling taconite from Lake Superior, now bound for Toledo, then back to Buffalo, then further East to the Erie Canal, and south for the Hudson River and beyond to ports all over the world. I would have given anything to be on board making passage to somewhere beyond the blood on my hands. To be out there in the flicker and blink of water knifed by the bow, the day and night alive with ports yet unseen. What more could a person ask for but more time away from the poisons of the land?

"I'll go to hell and back if that's what it takes," I said, enjoying the swell of my proclamation.

"You give new meaning to stubborn," Ruby said.

"Have to know the worst before I can let him go," I fired back.

"He may have failed you more ways than a banker."

"I need your help," I said, softening my tone, sick at the thought of sailing to Detroit alone. Sick at the thought of turning back. Sick at the thought of how little I knew about what to do next.

"You need a lot more than help, girl. You need luck. Money and food. And a gun from that burning farmhouse wouldn't hurt none either."

We gathered up to leave our cabin. Ruby foraged in a patch of wild raspberries on the south side, reaching deep into the thorns with no ouch in her. I found walnuts lying in the deep grass and offered one of them to Ruby.

"You like walnuts?"

"Love them," Ruby said.

"There's a slew of them on the ground."

"Leave them be," she urged.

"Can't be that bad," I said, peeling one of the green balls with my pocket knife to find the stone within.

"You'll regret that."

"Always wanted to taste a walnut off the ground."

I peeled away the outer rind of the walnut and proudly held up the wet, shining nut.

"Look at your hands."

"What?"

A mahogany stain ran the length of my fingers and into my palm.

"That's nothing but a stain."

"You won't be able to cut it with turpentine or gasoline." Ruby laughed.

"Why didn't you tell me?"

"I tried."

"Not very hard."

"You seem like the type that only learns hard and not often."

"How long does it take to bleed off the stain?"

"Some are marked for life."

"I hate you."

Ruby laughed. "No, you don't. You now hate walnuts."

I threw the walnut on the ground and tried not to look at my hands.

"Pretty place with a view of a lake," she said, changing the subject. "Might not get better than this," she added, looking out at North Bass Island across the sparkling water.

"That was my thought until I started peeling the walnut."

"Maybe your luck will hold and you won't be marked for life or maybe not."

We walked east on a corduroy-dirt road arrowed through stands of sapling ash and maple and bordered by cattail marsh littered with smart-walking, red-striped pheasant. Inside this open sweep, I heard bells bright as gunshot, and saw a lime-stone church with an adjacent rectory set back off the road. This little square oasis looked too sweet to walk on by.

"I want to stop."

"Think that's a good idea considering everything?"

"Just take a minute."

"I'll be outside."

"How do I know you'll be here when I come out?"

"You don't?"

I gathered myself to enter the church just as the bells quit. I climbed the tidy stone steps. My own footfall kept time with my heart. I told myself if anyone sized me up, I'd just turn around, walk away. A handful of elders were seated close to the altar, mostly women, bonnets and scarves showing bright color in that dim stone sanctuary. I closed my eyes, then I startled when an organ cascaded into a rumble, followed by a trumpet blast. No one cast a glance my way. I held still in the last empty pew like a rabbit at the edge of a garden, gazed up at two images of Christ, one a stained-glass baby cradled by Mary, the other a bronze man sequestered to a splinter of dark wood. I looked at the old ones in the sanctuary to see if I could tell which Christ their eyes were drawn to. Momma said Christ is the most interesting man in the world. He doesn't care if you're blind, lame, deaf, dumb, or dead. If he says you can get up out of your graveclothes, you walk on. No matter what storm seeks to dash you, he can quiet it with one wave. He comes in peace with no fear of the sword. I am the light of the world, he said. I figured I could use some of his interesting if I was headed for the brass of Detroit.

The limestone church felt cold to the touch like a secret breeze was seeping out of its foundation plate and pouring across my feet. I needed some warmth, the touch of a hand, reassurance. I closed my eyes again and prayed I could find my father before the slack-jawed pickerel marked out the measure of his vault. I stepped backward from the pew, hoping to pull away as silently as I had arrived. I could sense the pull of the door behind me when I felt a hand on my back. An old man, his face splotched from booze and sun, got down to cases. Next to him was a young boy who looked like an usher.

"Is your faith strong?" the man asked.

"What would I do without it?" I said, with no hesitation, hoping to throw him down.

"Would you like to meet some churchgoing ladies?"

"Just passing through."

"So I can tell," the old man said, tracking me like a hunter drawing a bead.

"Can I help?" the blond usher boy asked.

He motioned me to step outside.

"Not seen you before on Pelee," the boy said.

"First time here," I said.

"Not staying on for the summer?"

Ruby sat on the limestone steps, smoking, listening in.

"Not a summer tourist," I said.

"What are you then?"

Ruby smiled at me, curious as to what I was going to say next to this boy darkly clad in black slacks and pressed navy blazer.

"I'm a traveler," I said, looking into his clear blue eyes stoked with confidence.

"Never heard a girl say that before."

"I'm sailing on to Detroit."

"Sailing?"

"I'm a sailor," I said, putting a little spin on *sailor*.

"So am I," the boy said, all white teeth showing.

Ruby snuffed her cigarette on the steps.

"Her name's Norah Bow. She's wanted for murder in Ohio."

"What?"

"You're funny," the boy said to Ruby.

"Poor girl wanders in and out of churches all over the islands in Lake Erie asking for forgiveness wherever she goes, but it never comes. Look at her hands and you'll see a stain that won't go away no matter how much she prays to the baby Jesus."

I tried to hide my hands, but before I could stick them behind my back, he saw the ugly splotches left by the peeled black walnut.

"Bloodstains never go away," Ruby announced.

"Stop, Ruby," I shouted at her.

"What happened?" the boy asked, confusion wrinkling his face.

"Killed her mother and father with a filet knife. Made quite a mess of things."

When the boy backed up, Ruby started to laugh, more like a cackle thrown down by a crow.

"I have to be going," the boy said.

He turned away, looking as if he wanted to wave, but didn't, then he scurried inside the church.

I tried to kick Ruby but she swung her legs off to one side.

"Doing you a favor," she scoffed. "Getting sweet on goldilocks is not going to get you back on your boat."

"For five minutes I wanted to pretend today was just another summer day."

"He's not your type. You've gone too far to sit down with a choir boy."

"I was just starting to like you again," I said.

"Comes and goes for me too."

We left the church behind and walked for an hour on the east-west road in silence. We passed fields of soybeans, corn, beans, and felt the heat they held in their growing skins. Ruby didn't stop to steal much more than a bunch of radishes which she ate with dirt stains still clinging to the skin. I wanted to call her names and tell her how many ways she had failed this life. I wanted to hurt that tough hide of hers, but I needed her more than she needed me. Damn and alas, I had already lost track of her twice and I couldn't afford to lose her again. The wind was hot as steam off an iron and it blew Ruby's dress up and sideways. When the Lord set for the sea its limit, maybe he didn't imagine Ruby walking the road beside him, her dress uplifted and showing off her treasures. Maybe Christ would not have said, *Get up and walk* if he had known she would never bother to slap her dress back down. I couldn't wait to get back out on the water where good things came to me in blustery bunches. Ruby and I said nothing until we saw a familiar figure on the road mincing toward us. It was Blind Danny, fish peddler, impersonator of the blind, oracle of the island.

"Hello, ladies," he said, blinking hot light. "Did you find all you came for?"

"Not quite," I said.

"Detroit calls to you, then?"

"There's more I'm looking for."

"Sure there is," Blind Danny said. "By the way, I left you a package of fish at the smokehouse."

"How much do we owe you?"

"On the house."

"How did you know we'd be coming?"

"My job is to know who comes and goes."

Ruby threw me a big eye roll.

"Maybe you'll find your daddy on the whiskey river," Blind Danny said, pointing to the north.

"That's my only wish and prayer," I said.

"There are some sweet little islands on the river where a sour man can hide."

"I'll remember that," I said.

When Danny twirled his cane, Ruby reached out, grabbed it, took it away from him, then knocked him off his feet with a swift kick.

"I could use one of these," Ruby said.

"Give that back," I shouted.

"Trust me," Ruby said.

"This is so unworthy of you," Blind Danny said.

"I'm sorry," I pleaded. "She's not well."

We left Blind Danny sputtering on the road. I felt ashamed for what Ruby had done. The silence lay between us like a black Bible neither of us would crack open.

"Why do you like that babbling half pint?" Ruby asked, as I looked back at Blind Danny, already a slender, limping shadow on the east-west road.

"He offered us food."

Ruby swung the cane over her head. Got the feel of its heft in her hands.

"How do you live with yourself?" I asked, my annoyance with her breaking up my voice.

"I bet he could beat us both in a foot race," Ruby said, jabbing the road and the air with Danny's hickory cane.

Years later, I read about the ancient Greek belief in fate, the one ferocious fact from which you can't escape, the one storm that even the gods are helpless to prevent. Daddy said my fate was like his. To live within reach of the demon switch. For Ruby, fate gathered under the next flap of her wings. Me, I didn't know how to go back. Didn't know how to go forward. I was the toy of fate, maybe everyone is, a thing caught by some unseen cage and that's why any progress in the human dimension is painfully slow. On the other hand, I was now ready to seize my fate. In the name of the father, I had already squared up with beauty and death. Already, I knew about guilty. Already, I carried the stain of it on my hands. Maybe Ruby was right. I would have to learn how to feed on carrion before I would ever fly again.

13

After stealing Danny's cane, it took some guts to make a beeline for a gift he'd left us, but guilt didn't lay a claim on Ruby the same way as me. Truth be told, she didn't have much use for any of the raw feelings that dragged my anchor. She made her zigzag through an ordinary day seem straight and had a smile to prove it or, as Proverbs puts it, a cheerful heart is a continual feast. And so, when we stopped at Danny's fish house to pick up the bundle of smoked pickerel wrapped in cloth, she seemed unfazed by the threat that welcomed us inside. Jack Little, Danny's brother, waited for us with a pistol propped on his lap. Ruby looked at him like he was no more dangerous than a cartoon bleeding off a page.

"You two broke up the Rose pretty good," Jack said calmly from his milk crate perch. "I'll be needing some compensation."

"Fresh out," Ruby said, eyeing him closely.

"Not what I hear. You might as well be a bank."

"That so," Ruby said.

I saw Ruby tightening her grip on the cane she held behind her back.

"Do you know who this woman is?" Jack said to me.

"Sorry for what happened at the Rose," I said. "Had no idea there would be so much trouble."

"Everywhere this woman goes, a body turns up," Jack said, aiming the gun at Ruby.

"Let's talk this out," I said, pretending to be well-versed in the ways of mediation.

"Have another idea," Jack said to Ruby. "You give me all the money you have."

"All I have is a few dollars," I said.

"This woman is a professional."

I'd like to believe divine intervention comes at us in packages as small as pinpricks which is how I regarded the blue-tailed swallow that flew into the one window of the smokehouse. Jack glanced at the clunk against the glass and Ruby used that one moment to swing the cane and bring the full snap of it alongside Jack's head. He crumpled and fell off the milk crate as fast as the swallow fell to the ground. I rushed over and pressed my ear to his chest and heard a dull rasp. Made me sick to think of one more man dying on Pelee because Ruby and I had come to visit.

"I thought we might need this," Ruby said, spinning the weapon in her hands. "Damn, it's hard to argue with a solid walking cane. Smack somebody with a cane and they stay smacked down." I could tell she wanted to wax poetic at even greater length about the crack of a hickory against a man's head, but I thought it best if we take our leave.

"What now?" I blurted.

"Make better use of that lanyard around your waist and tie this little man to the next world."

I broke loose the lanyard cinched at my waist and tied off Jack's hands. I used another piece of rope from the smokehouse to lash his feet to a center pole. My stomach turned over when I saw a trickle of blood seep from Jack Little's head. There was nothing I could do for him. Nothing I could say. While Jack groaned and tried to rouse himself, Ruby grabbed the revolver off the floor. Ruby then tore into the bundle of fish like it held freshly printed bank notes. She sunk her teeth into a greasy filet and offered me one. I waved her off.

"We have to get out of here."

"I suppose we do," Ruby said, throwing down the remains of a filet.

I opened the smokehouse door, looked out to see if Blind Danny had gathered forces to help him retrieve his cane, but I saw nothing, so we stepped out into harsh afternoon light, then ran through marsh grass, our shoes swishing muck.

"What did Jack mean about you being a bank?"

"Beats me."

We got back to Mill Point by early afternoon with the wind brisk out of the southwest at ten to fifteen knots. The day was just right for a broad reach into Detroit, the one city Daddy said he hoped I would never see. When I asked him to explain the basis of his hope, he said Prohibition had turned men and women into fools with no greater ambition than to blot out their time there with stories they couldn't tell anyone. Remembering this made me wonder which kind of stories Daddy would tell, if he were still alive.

"My good boat is still here," I said, relieved to see *Odyssey* where we left her nosed under a sweep of willows and pleased she was unharmed after all that had gone wrong. Ruby threw Blind Danny's cane into bramble, then peered into the doghouse cabin.

"What are you looking for?"

"Nothing," Ruby said, with some catch in her voice.

"I'm sure your bag's still there."

"Everything I own is in that bag."

"So you said."

Ruby crosshatched her brow, some old anger smoldering her face.

"Can we get the hell off this island?"

"What do you think we're doing," I snipped.

Ruby saw me glancing at the walnut stain on my hands.

"Won't come off," she said.

"In time it will."

"Your hands are so dirty, you don't know whether to sit, run, or curl up into a ball. Welcome to the club."

If Daddy had been there, he would have called Ruby a counterpuncher. He once fancied himself an amateur boxer though I can't recall if he ever entered a ring. One of my earliest memories was sneaking into the garage and watching Daddy work over a punching bag hung from a beam. If he and Momma got backed up in a quarrel or something had turned south on a big sales call, he would rush out to the garage like some men rush to a bar and I'd hear him trying to peel the skin off that leather bag. Being a bookworm and not much wider and heavier than a pencil, Daddy nursed another life in the garage, jabbing and stabbing at a bag until he was a drenched man, his face glowing like he'd been staring into a roaring bed of coals, aiming with each punch to become the fire itself. I could tell Ruby wanted to spar but I didn't give her the satisfaction. What was the point when I knew she would win?

"This is going to be your second night sail," I said.

"I love holding on for dear life," she said, refusing to help me clean off the branches that camouflaged the *Odyssey*.

"Should come natural to you," I said.

I'd forgotten about Jack's gun until Ruby pulled it from the firewood satchel she'd found back at the farmhouse.

"It's a .38 Long Colt with a six-inch barrel and a sweet wood grip," she said, holding the gun in her right hand and taking aim over water. She opened the chamber, spun it, then tossed the weapon to me.

"Nice to have six bullets," Ruby said. "Don't you think?"

I caught the gun by the barrel.

"Please, don't do that again," I barked and quickly stowed the gun on a ledge in the stern lazerette along with the burlap food sack.

We pushed *Odyssey* from the bow and watched her reenter the drink. Once afloat, I felt my arm and leg strength returning. I knew my boat could stand up to whatever weather tested her keel bolts.

"You look like a girl version of Samson getting her hair back." Ruby laughed.

"Thought you had no interest in the Bible."

"I like a tall tale as much as the next person."

We hoisted sail, let out the main and jib, and ran downwind along the eastern shore of Pelee. I flicked tears off my face with the back of my hand.

"What's wrong now?" Ruby asked, already looking cramped and uneasy after just an hour on a dead run.

"Just happy to have the wind at my back."

The water rushed against the hull. The wind bellied the sail. We flew north, all swish and straight arrow. There were reefs ahead, swift currents, ore freighters, and channel markers we had to pick out of the Lake Erie haze, but none of these watery designations unnerved me half as much as the thought of looking for one man in a big city known for its cutthroats and machine guns. I looked at my chart and took some comfort from knowing we could hug the length of Pelee even though the water dropped from hundred feet to eight in places. Made no difference to me because *Odyssey* drew only three feet with the centerboard down.

"What's it like? In Detroit?"

"More pepper than salt," Ruby said, shifting her haunches.

"Some like it hot," I said, thinking it sounded tough.

"Everything starts and ends there."

I closed my eyes and the darkness took me in. I heard a dog barking for someone to come back or go away and caught a whiff of a wood fire near Middle Point, the fat spilling into flame. I imagined a family waiting to be fed, the smells and sounds of a life lived with simple pleasures protecting them from what they had done or failed to do. I could have broke down just then wanting what they had, but I was the skipper and I wasn't yet half way to anywhere. Tears, what were they anyway? A weakness I couldn't afford. Once you start, you just want more and soon enough you dredge up every old scratch as proof of your sinking situation and meanwhile the family gathered around the fire is telling stories, laughing, their forks and spoons clicking in their mouths.

"You know how to get us to Detroit?"

"We'll be there by dawn," I said, already fighting to stay awake.

"Then what?"

"Get some sleep. I'll need you eagle-eyed soon enough."

"Why is that?"

"Once we get into the shipping lane, we'll both have to keep watch."

"How do you know about all that?"

"Daddy made me study the charts."

"But you've never been there before?"

"After tonight, we'll both know plenty."

We rounded Lighthouse Point on the Northeast tip of Pelee and I set a course of 290 degrees to angle us into the Detroit River channel some thirty miles away, west of north. If the wind held, we'd be there for breakfast. If not, I'd have to take up the Lake Erie pastime of *wishing and fishing*. I reached down into the firewood satchel and grabbed the last apple that once belonged to the three dead men. I took only the smallest bites until the juice was full and round in my mouth and I was back home helping Momma make two peach-apple pies, me cutting slices, mixing them in a blue daisy-chain bowl with cinnamon, nutmeg, brown sugar, a dash of salt, and a splash of maple syrup. She said using an ice cube to make the water stand up and shout with cold was the trick to making a flaky crust. The rest was practice and patience. Hers tasted like heaven come-on-down to earth. Mine tasted like wet cardboard.

I saw nothing now but the moon walking on water and I was thankful for the light to steer by. Over my right shoulder I saw a freighter plying the skinny dogleg of Pelee Passage for Detroit. If the captain drifted just a hundred yards out of the channel, he'd be in low water hell. That's all the distraction it took for a ship to ride up onto a shoal, lose steerage, and go down lonesome into the drink. A few yards this way or that and bingo, Lake Erie will grab your bones.

"Where are we?" Ruby asked the dark wind as much as she did me.

"Can't sleep?" I asked her.

"The slosh of water makes me think we're taking on water."

"If that ever happens, there'll be no mistaking it for water slipping by."

"How deep is this lake?"

"Deep enough to bury a freighter."

Ruby looked out at the night dressed in a blue-steel ripple

of waves and freighters in the distance, their reds and greens scratching the greater darkness with some sign of life on the move.

"I can't stop thinking about what happened."

"They were going to kill us," Ruby said, "after they had their way with us." She shook her head, disappointed that the death of the three men still held me captive. Hard times in thin places had not chased Ruby into a sleepless corner. I couldn't help but admire her uncanny ability to leap back from doom, unfazed by the arrival of new troubles, unmarked by the memory of old ones.

"I could eat the rubber off a tire," Ruby announced.

"Have some peanut butter," I said.

"Can't do it."

"Better than smoked pickerel."

"Watch it now."

"Don't know how you can eat that stuff."

"Grew up with it," Ruby said.

"What else do you like to eat?"

"Doughboys."

"What's that?"

"Soup dumplings."

"Little wads of dough. That's what you like? There must be something else."

"Pork pâté made with onions, garlic, cinnamon, cloves."

"Set me a table."

Ruby told me how she loved to make poor man's pudding, an upside-down cake with caramel base, butter tarts made with eggs, raisins, vanilla, and maple syrup as well as sausage pies, strawberry crepes, pea soup simmered with bacon. It's funny how you can make your belly growl just by thinking about food.

"Miss your mother?"

"Her cooking," I said.

"You're coming into a time when your mother could help you plenty."

This talk about Momma made my heart sink. I was already

scared I'd come too far with nothing to show for it. Scared I'd find no answers in Detroit. Scared that Ruby would find a dozen good reasons to bail on me once we got there. I looked over my left shoulder at the Bass Islands to my south, tucked just under the U.S. border with Canada. For the first time, I missed my country, my mother, my dog, maybe even my baby brothers. I didn't want to die in another country where no one knew the name Norah Bow.

We sailed just outside the shipping lane, far enough north to avoid any drunk freighter skippers cutting corners on the hard shallows of Pelee Passage. The wind held steady out of the southwest at fifteen, brisk and orderly, the whitecaps visible in the moonlight like daubs of face cream on Momma's cheeks. I could see her trying to sleep but failing to find the hour when the good sleep comes, swinging her legs over the bed frame to stare holes into the darkness, raising her stuck bedroom sash, rubbing her temples in rhythm with Erie lapping the beach, every part of her wondering where I was or if her husband still numbered his days or had left all numbering to someone else. And I wondered where she kept her strength when I was not there to order about. Momma said you get wistful with age. When I asked her what she meant, she said wistful was like a pebble in your shoe. Old hurts could still make you limp. Think twice about doing something new. I had so many questions I wanted to ask her about what went on between men and women. I wondered if I would ever get the chance, and I wondered if she would tell me truth or only some version of it that glossed over the complications between her and Daddy.

"Where are we now?" Ruby grumbled.

"You ask that question a lot."

"All looks the same out here."

"See that flashing green to port?"

Ruby squinted at the fleck of green light hollowing the blackness.

"That's North Harbor Island Reef."

"How much farther?"

"Too bad sleeping doesn't come easily to you."

"Why?"

"It's your turn," I said, pointing to the helm.

"What are you saying?"

"I need to sleep. You need to steer."

Ruby and I switched positions. I longed for my sagging bed on the screen porch. I wanted to lie there listening to Lake Erie raking the shore. I closed my eyes to better picture myself back home. I couldn't see my bed and Bob draped on it. Instead, I saw Daddy and Momma through the open porch window, their voices snarled, teeth showing.

Sandusky is no bigger than a crackerjack box.

Your point is...?

You've been seen with other—

Rumors and gossip.

You have no idea how this makes me feel.

You can't believe what—

Stop lying.

I had no idea how long I slept. I sat up with a gasp and nearly caught the boom in the head. When my focus returned, I saw Ruby holding the tiller with one hand, but her eyes were closed, her body slumped in the cockpit. I glanced at the compass and saw we'd drifted off our heading. I faced aft with every intention of grabbing the tiller away from her when I heard an enormous wave breaking over us. I somersaulted toward Ruby, landed on top of her and felt the port side lifting to flip us. I leapt to the high side and hoped my hundred and ten pounds of girl flesh would hold my boat down. Ruby was upside down, clinging to the doghouse. I saw the mast flex like a toothpick and every inch of my boat shivered. The mainsail snapped, the mainsheet broke loose from its jam, the boom swung over our heads. We swerved sideways after being thumped and spit upon, but we didn't flip end for end. I peered under the sail and saw the wave's origin.

"What happened?" Ruby moaned.

"A freighter nearly ran us down," I said, grabbing the tiller. "We got lucky."

"You call that lucky?"

"We were pushed aside by the bow wake."

In moments, the freighter had pulled away, its white stern light dipping in the trough of its own push to reach Buffalo by morning.

"I thought we were going down," Ruby said, running her hands through her hair. "I must have fallen asleep," she added, making it sound like someone beside herself was responsible for nodding off at the helm.

"Must have," I said.

"Guess I'm not much for crew."

"Don't go fishing."

"Just making an observation," Ruby said.

"I would just as soon stay alive long enough to check out Detroit."

"That makes two of us," Ruby offered by way of apology.

"Then don't go to sleep. Any woman that can..."

"Go on," Ruby said.

"Never mind."

"I want to hear what you have to say."

"I need you to wake me if there's something out here you're uncertain about."

"Aye-aye, captain."

It hurt to keep my eyes open and it hurt to close them knowing Ruby couldn't be counted on to stay awake while I slept, so I slapped myself until it hurt.

"Take the tiller," I snapped.

"Again?"

The slapping didn't take. I leaned over the gunwale and dunked my head.

"That flashing green off to port at nine o'clock is Middle Sister Island."

"Meaning what?"

"Next stop is the outer channel of the Detroit River. Every-thing starts and ends there. Isn't that what you said?"

"I could sell tickets to all the heartache coming your way."

"Have a little faith in tomorrow."

"What about the gun?" Ruby asked.

"The gun?"

Ruby flipped open the stern lazerette.

"It's gone," she said.

"Never shot one anyway," I said, uncertain whether I was saddened or relieved to know the gun flipped overboard when the freighter caused our knockdown.

"So much for faith," Ruby said, with more sarcasm than pain caught in her voice.

Odyssey settled into a broad reach, her jib and mainsail pulling us forward through gentle swells. We made good time over water considering we sailed among freighters angling for Detroit from all over the world, our speed just a fraction of the longboats loaded with taconite, coal, limestone, sand and slag. Caught in a moonlight veil, the stern enders looked as long as the devil's arm. Ruby looked at me looking at the distance we'd come from Pelee and took aim with her own brand of troubled wisdom.

"Too bad," she said, stroking the tangles from her red hair with a brush, "this damn Prohibition gets so many killed. The little guy is just trying to put away some extra. Never seen a law I liked, and this one is all jinxed. Any time the government tells you to put a bottle down, you know that just gives men greater need to pick it up. No good has come from this law and a few are making more money than God."

"Prohibition didn't kill those three men back on Pelee," I said. "We did."

14

The first splashes of pink kerfed into a cloud bank behind us. The ore boats made strong for the outer channel of the Detroit River to unload their containers. No matter their size, *Odyssey* stayed true to her heading and let them slip by like so much dark water lit with oil. My sloop at my command was every bit the equal of those longboats until the wind petered out in the last hour of the graveyard watch and we stopped making headway. Erie heaved in slabs and fell sideways like something cleaved from a storm. Our sails snapped and rattled against the side stays. The dawn was not fully unwrapped and I could see Ruby greening up from the slosh. The rasp in her voice bottled up with a little more smoke.

"What's your father do for money?"

"Life insurance."

"I'd rather work with the dead," Ruby said.

"Honest work," I said in defense, knowing that Daddy didn't much like peddling insurance even though he was better at selling ten dollar policies than almost anyone in Sandusky.

"Being born is a gamble," Ruby mused. "Dying is the same. You can't pay down the risk with installments."

"You're living proof of that," I jabbed.

"Nobody promises us today, let alone tomorrow."

As usual, I gave her the last word because she needed it more than I did and I knew from the pale cast of the day, we were going to flounder and I didn't need more rock toss.

"There's more air blowing out a gnat's asshole," she muttered. She waved at a trio of men on a Detroit-bound powerboat that sizzled past us. "Can't we hail them for a tow?"

"Against my principles."

"Sweet Mary and Joseph, we could die out here before your principles would mean anything to anyone but you."

"You take what Erie serves up or you stay home," I said, firmly gripping the tiller.

"Felt sick for hours."

"Stick your finger down your throat and be done with it."

Ruby did what I said. She retched for almost an hour and I said nothing to her the whole time. Actually, I enjoyed her being helpless to help herself. It was about damn time she suffered some. For once, she didn't have any bluff. For once, she was hung out over the rail the way I had been since I left Rye Beach. For once, she had no pretty on parade. We each nodded off waiting for the wind to lift, but no trickle of sweet stuff found us. We saw nothing but ore boats entering their northbound turn toward Detroit. Heard nothing but the rumble of engines. Tasted nothing but black exhaust swirling down on us. The sun rose high, then slipped by inches, the slop haggling: *I'll give you this if you give me that.* It's been said sailing is either about boredom or terror. Too little wind or too damn much. Which is why I mostly sail alone. Either extreme doesn't set well with most people, and I've got no patience with most people and their need for sunny perfection, smooth sailing, whatever you want to call it.

"We're going nowhere fast, Norah."

The mainsail hung slack, whipped against the shrouds. They spoke for me. More hours in a back shuffle against the Detroit River current. Then a change came. Not the one I wanted, but then I was beginning to grasp the old saw Daddy preached, *Change is pain.* I dug two paddles out from down below.

"What the hell is coming at us?"

"Have no idea," I said, sizing up the shadow swirling inside the dusk.

"Looks like a waterspout," Ruby said, her mouth wide open.

I looked into a dull grayish-brown swarm hovering over the water and saw pieces of a maelstrom skittering. The muscles in Ruby's face tightened. Her tongue rolled over her bottom teeth like she was trying to clean away taffy.

"That's no waterspout," I said, still not knowing the shape

of what had come to claim us from our doldrums. More scattering in the air until the pieces smacked against the mainsail and I looked up into blackened sailcloth and saw the blur of mayflies, Canadian soldiers Daddy called them. The fury of wings triggered the snapping of jaws. The water whipped itself into breaking waves from the fish spinning and colliding in mid-air. It was hard to tell what was louder: the crazed fish or the mayflies they lusted after. The Canadian soldiers swept in like a squall, thicker than rain, more fierce, the main and jib scooping them up and dumping them on our heads.

"They're going to bury us alive," Ruby choked.

Before I could cover up my mouth with a kerchief, the soldiers descended, tangled in a cloud as smelly as fish bait until there was no seeing out but into their swollen eyes and withered mouthparts sucking air. I'd heard fishermen say Canadian soldiers could molt, mate, and die in one minute, then sink a boat with the weight of their dead bodies. Old wives tale, I thought then, but I was not so sure now.

"Paddle," I muttered. "We've got to paddle."

Ruby reached for the paddle, coughing, sputtering, and spitting out wings and legs while I sculled in hopes of moving us out of the mayfly swarm. We inched forward but my kerchief fell and my mouth filled with insects. I gagged and when I turned to spit overboard, I opened my eyes into a billowing mass. When I tried to open my eyes again, I fell back into the cockpit.

"What's wrong, Norah?"

"Can't see."

"What do you mean?"

"They got into my eyes."

I heard Ruby scrambling. She propped my head up on a duffel and grabbed a flashlight. "They're leaving," she said. "The cloud is moving off."

I wanted to believe her. I couldn't look for myself, but I did feel the increment of a breeze.

"Let me see your eye," she ordered.

One hand cradled my neck, the other stretched the corner of my right eye.

"Easy does it easy," Ruby said. "Going to dab a bit of cloth in your eye and get this devil out. You with me?"

I nodded and Ruby swiped at what was caught in my eye and grabbed it with her cloth. I blinked back tears and could see again through a murky squint. She lifted the lid of my left eye and stretched the skin until it hurt. She stopped, pulled back, sighed. I couldn't see anything out of my left eye. I gagged on the mayflies, then hung my head over the gunwale, lost what little food rose in my craw.

"Not good," she said. "Your left eye's a bloodshot mess. You need a doctor."

"You see any out here? You'll have to do."

"I can't."

"That's just peachy," I said.

"We'll have to find you an eye doctor in Detroit."

I looked into the sky with my good eye and sensed the winged army had turned south with a new wind pushing them on. My good true boat was painted with the skeletons of Canadian soldiers still heaving their wings and legs. The wind returned with a gasp. I nursed the tiller with both hands. We paralleled the Detroit River channel to the east. The wind jumped up a knot. The throb of my left eye made me hold my breath, then gasp, then hold. Sometime after midnight, we left the outer Detroit River channel and headed south of Hickory Island. We pointed toward Grosse Ile and Trenton Channel which tracked the shape of the city. Everywhere I looked with my one good eye, I could still see the remains of dead soldiers.

"Hand me the flashlight," I said to Ruby.

I lit up the folded chart and saw shoals no deeper than three feet. As I fought the itch and burn of my eye, I thought there were good reasons why most people never went anywhere in a small boat, especially to a dark island in a river beset with drown-

ing currents and all manner of jagged, foul-smelling debris.
Ruby looked into the inky foam swirling around us and held
her nose.

"Welcome to Detroit," she said.

I didn't reply because I figured Ruby would use any sliver
to help make a case I had no business in Detroit even though
now I did need an eye doctor, even more than I needed sleep
or food. Being mayfly blind was not going to help me spot one
thin man on the whiskey river. Just north of Celeron Island,
the wind died again, so we paddled toward the red and green
flashing cans that led us around the tip of Gibraltar Island.
Headlights drilled holes in the distance. The city hum was cut
with train whistles and the *ka-thunk* of steel wheels. The smell
of gasoline, smoke, tar, and sewage made me gag. Either Detroit was booming or tearing itself apart or both scenarios were
possible.

We paddled into a cove, my arms heavy as mud. Ruby
scanned like a cat crouched before a bird, lifted her nose, and
took in the stink as if guided by an unfailing instinct for how to
proceed. Abandoned dinghies and skiffs were upside down on
their gunnels like coffins without handles. No one appeared to
have come to this cove in years. We angled *Odyssey* into shore,
climbed out. I pulled out the rudder pins, and hid the rudder
and tiller in the crook of a nearby tree in hopes no one would
want a sailboat they couldn't sail. Ruby fished out her duffel
from down below and winked. "Come on, girl. The blind will
see again."

"I need to sleep."

"That's not what your eye needs."

"Where are we going to find an eye doctor at this hour?"

"Won't know until we try."

"I can't."

"If you don't find a doctor now, you might do some harm
you can't reverse."

I wanted to dig in and tell Ruby I knew better, but I didn't.

We walked away from the cove, each of us grabbing some far-off city light to guide us. I looked over my shoulder to get my bearings, but I couldn't snag a single landmark to show me how to find my way back.

Detroit, in 1926, the number one funnel for whiskey swirling into America from Canada. Detroit, the world's number one pleasure dome for spanking new Henry Ford cars. Detroit, boiling with cash and not enough ways to spend it down. Detroit, where a woman in a short skirt might ride alone on a streetcar, on a bicycle or drive her own car, then stay out all night with a stiff drink and the quiver of a saxophone. Detroit, the French word for strait, crooked as any city on earth in 1926. But what did I care for its plunder and fame? What did I care about the number of bottles it sent out into the world? About who bought and sold what and at what price? All of that was for some other sailor to deny or endorse. I was looking for a thin man from Ohio with big ears. Such a father as that couldn't be that hard to find, if only I could see.

15

Ruby and I walked through river marsh and scrub trees with the chatty complaint of ducks following us into a scrawny stand of poplar trees. The sound of dogs and sirens scratched a hole in my listening. No more than a few steps into Detroit and I walked like a marionette, stiff-jointed and bent over from being crouched in a cockpit. My vision was so blurry I wanted to grab Ruby's arm, and didn't. We spilled onto a dirt road with an up-flickering of grackles. I didn't see the wide-brimmed stone big as a cantaloupe. I caught it with my right foot, tripped forward, fell down, already feeling out-flanked and Detroit-stupid.

"We'll get you fixed up," Ruby said, holding her duffel close to her body.

"I'm not broke," I said.

Ruby chuckled. "That rock you tripped on was practically up to your knees."

No stone in the road slowed Ruby down. She walked easily, the prospect of the city opening its arms and giving her swagger. The distance between the quiet backwater cove and the approaching city shrank. I heard a truck braking hard, the squeal of rubber, the blare of a horn, the scrape of metal against concrete.

"Have any idea where you're going?"

"I remember a hospital down along the river somewhere."

"Won't it be closed?"

"Emergency rooms don't close."

We walked on and with each step I felt more uncertain about my strength to go on, one-eyed into the dice roll of Detroit. I felt more like half way to forty than fourteen. We passed fruit stands collapsed in on themselves and a row of storefronts, some boarded up, others burnt beyond repair. Little tornadoes swirled at our feet. The river hugged slabs of shadow and light. The dead-fish whiff followed us. In the distance, I saw a lit-up sign for Occident Flour stacked over one for Benedictine Cordial, a man in a tuxedo holding a long-stemmed sniffer to his nose. I stopped and turned to my right and saw a girl not much older than myself, her face carrying a wedge of lipstick and a hard splash of rouge, a cigarette notched in her teeth. When she waved to another girl propped in a doorway across the street, I saw sweat stains beneath her arms.

"Hey, ladies, you game for something not pictured in any book?"

Ruby reached into her pocket and flipped the girl two bits.

"Looking for an eye doctor," Ruby said to the girl.

"And I'm looking for candy in heaven," the girl fired back as she charged up to us like a dog pulling a chain. Seeing double came easy to me, so I leaned away. The girl said to me, "For a little more coin, I can take you to a different kind of doc."

The girl's eyes cindered the corner she stood on. Daddy called street people ruffians and she fit the bill, all rough and raw, the cigarette smoke spilling off her mouth. Something in the face still pretty and alive. She knew I saw that in her and she looked to hate me for looking too long. Ruby took a breath, pinched off a smile, all tenderness in her voice now cut with something like steel.

"One more time, I'm asking do you know where the hospital is. My skipper needs someone to look after her eye."

My heart leapt when I heard Ruby say, "my skipper." The girl pointed up the street.

"There's a hospital at Elizabeth Park. Half a dozen blocks up on the right."

"Many thanks," I said.

"Your eye looks like shit," the girl said to me. "What happened? Your old man smack you down?"

"You might say that."

The girl looked me up, down, and sideways, then she spit in the street.

"You can't turn pepper back into salt," the girl said.

"I don't follow your meaning," I said.

"Your future is long gone," she said, "and the past never happened."

"Don't know that song," I said.

"Maybe you helped write it," she said.

I couldn't tell if she described herself or if she could see where I too had fallen. Either way, her words made my skin bump down a ladder. Ruby pulled me away, but I stopped not twenty feet away when a black car with wire wheels and white sidewalls pulled up. A man in a long coat got out. He looked at the girl, told her to unbutton her blouse, turn around slowly. Even from a distance, I could see his thick lips, chubby fingers, pomaded hair. His face, one long lump of indifference. Ruby whispered, "You've no problems, Norah Bow."

The girl spun around slowly like she was a candle burning down a wedding cake. He stepped closer, ran his hand up her skirt, and I heard the tearing away of her undergarment. The girl winced, shrank back. He scanned the street while picking at his face with a thumbnail. He leered with his teeth glowing in his jaw. I hated his long coat, his baritone gobble and cluck.

"Get in the car," he said to the girl. She flipped her cigarette at me, but never looked me in the eyes. When the car door slammed and the car drove off, my knees went weak. How did she find herself so far from home? I sat down on the curb, my head swimming with the spark of that girl who was less to the man in the car than a cigarette flicked to the curb.

Ruby said, flatly, "Always a buyer. Always a seller."

"That's all you can say?"

"Her choice," Ruby said.

We started walking again. The silence between us like something that settles after a slap. She hung back from her normal stride so she and I could walk side by side.

"What happened back there was nothing," Ruby scoffed.

"Nothing?"

"You've already seen worse."

My bum eye had made me forget the dead men at the farm, and now that night came back, but I told myself to keep walking, one foot in front of the other. I couldn't afford to go back anywhere. The hospital looked like it needed more help than I did. Most of its lights flickering or blown out. This place must not be the hospital Henry Ford built for his executives. Men bivouacked on the sidewalk like they were waiting for a soup kitchen to fire up and still find them, this side of the angels. Ruby and I walked through broken glass, milk cartons, wilted flowers, cigarette butts, empty bottles, bloodstains, and the wind whistling between buildings. Last chance, slim chance, no chance, those were the sad mules who ghosted there with their heads down, breathing heavy.

"Sure this isn't the morgue?"

Ruby pointed to the Elizabeth Park Hospital sign. No part of me wanted to enter this building with or without Ruby. She could sense my holding back and reached out and touched my shoulder. We walked on through glass doors held together with cardboard and tape. A guard slumped in a chair pointed us to another set of doors. We passed through those and came to a heavyset woman at a check-in desk. Without looking up, she asked, "You been cut up with a knife or shot?"

"Neither," I replied. "I need someone to look after my eye."

"What's wrong with it?"

"We ran into a cloud of Canadian Soldiers and—"

"Whatever you say. Take a seat over there."

Two hours later, a stout nurse with a bandaged thumb walked up with a clipboard and said, "You the girl with the eye?" I nodded. "Come with me."

Ruby got up to join us. "Who are you?" the nurse asked.

"A friend," Ruby replied.

"Stay here."

"What happened to your thumb?" I asked the nurse as we walked through a dimly lit hallway jammed with bloodstained gurneys.

"You don't want to know."

"I do."

"A man tried to bite me as I cut his trousers off. The scissors slipped and well…"

"What happened?"

"A shooting down by the river. Happens twice a week. Purple Gang hijacks another gang's shipment, bullets fly, bodies follow. Some are shot up so bad, they hardly look like men anymore."

My gut tightened, then slow heaved but nothing came out of my mouth. I wanted to run back down the splattered hall, past the corner where the girl stood gamely before she melted into the car, and back to my boat where I understood the wind shifts and the points on the compass rose. The nurse led me into a room with a desk, a table, two chairs. She sat me down, put on her glasses, shone a light into my left eye, brought a hand of quiet into my own unsettling.

"Name's Sally. And yours?"

"Norah."

"Pleased," Sally said, while holding her pencil beam steady.

"Like I told the other woman, this cloud of Canadian soldiers fell on our boat."

"You're talking about some kind of flying insect?"

"Exactly."

"The doctor's going to have to rotate your eyeball and flush out the body parts."

The nurse pushed back in her chair, wrote a few notes on a clipboard chart, then sized me up over the rim of her glasses.

"It's none of my business, but what are you doing out this time of night with that other woman. Is she—"

"It's not what you think. I'm looking for my daddy."

"You traveled here from a ways off?"

"Ohio."

"Trouble at home?"

"You can call it that."

"This is no city for a girl your age," Sally said. "Bad country, front door to back."

"I can take care of myself."

"And that's why you're here seeing me?"

"How bad is it?"

"Your eye?"

"Detroit?"

"Running booze across the river from Windsor is gravy for half the city long as they can keep alive. The other half wants to stay out of the graveyard, so they keep their nose to the grindstone, then they sneak off to a blind pig for a pint."

"Blind pig?"

Sally canted her head, then spread the fingers of her right hand with her thumb pointed down her throat, then shook her hand like it was a bottle. The gesture made her look like a skeleton guzzling the bones of her hand. I wanted her to stop and I couldn't stop looking. She made it clear enough a blind pig is where you went if you wanted to get blind.

"Prohibition has never made so many bankers happy," she said. "Whiskey pays well except when it don't."

"I know all about graveyards."

"Sorry to hear that," the nurse said, taking my hand in hers. "When did your father run off?"

"That's not what happened."

"You sure about that?"

I nodded.

"See if Lonesome Bill will give you the time of day. He knows everybody who runs hooch across that river."

"Where do I find this Lonesome—"

The doctor walked in. He was a thin, bald man who grabbed the chart from the nurse, didn't bother to look at it, then sat on a stool in front of me and switched on a pen light. His white coat stained with every color of human weakness and breakdown.

"Look to the right," he said, brusquely. "To the left."

"We'll need to hold her head over the sink," he said to Sally.

"What are you going to do?" I said, as she guided me to the corner sink.

"You've got wing and thorax behind the eyeball. Your cornea is scratched pretty good. Your entire eye is red, but the good news is this. Our eyes are like tongues."

I pushed my tongue against my front teeth, more anxious than ever, thinking maybe I should bolt from that room and risk finding some other doctor. He saw the panic painted on my face.

"Eyes and tongues both heal fast."

"Okay," I said.

"Going to flush your eye, grab what's left of the critter, put a dab of ointment in there, give you a patch so you look even tougher than you already think you are. Then I'll send you on your way. How's that sound?"

I had misread this doctor. His brevity was not coldness. I just wasn't his most pressing case. If Sally was right, he had gunshot victims to sew up or send to the morgue.

"Fair enough."

"There's one catch. You've got to hold very still."

The doctor filled a syringe bulb with a solution from a blue bottle. I never liked rooms with no windows. This room was no exception. I couldn't see out and I couldn't be seen and the sweat broke on my forehead to prove my aversion to such airless places.

"Eyes glued to the ceiling," the doctor said.

Sally tied some kind of bib on me, then patted my back.

When the doctor shot the contents of the syringe into my left eye, everything went blank there as if my eye spun around in my head.

"You're fighting me," Sally said.

"That's what I do."

"Not if you want to see again," the doctor said.

He got my attention. I took a half dozen deep breaths. Sally refilled the bulb. On the second flushing, I saw her nodding at him like she wanted him to rush in and snatch some critter before a gate closed.

"Okay, we're making progress," the doctor said. "Now, there's one more piece to this, but I need you to sit in a chair."

Sally guided me to a chair. She pulled down my cheek while he pulled up just below my eyebrow. He held a long cotton swab. Before I could squirm off, he mopped up whatever wing debris was left, then reached for another swab. With my eye still leaking tears, he dabbed the scratch with an ointment. Sally reached into a drawer for a black eye patch with an elastic string and handed it to me.

"Keep that patch on for five days. Your eye took a beating. It can't heal if you take it off," the doctor said, his tone both cautionary and reassuring. Before leaving the room he added, "Your folks know where you are?"

I didn't know whether to lie, fudge, tell the truth, shrug. I was grateful for what he had done. I didn't think he had the time to find out more about me. I took a chance and said, "No."

"Take good care," he said, before leaving the room.

Sally squeezed my hand. "You'll be fine."

"About Lonesome Bill?"

"He works the docks for Hiram Walker, Detroit side."

"Where exactly?"

"You go past Fighting Island, past the River Rouge, just shy of Customs. It's a poke up there, but it might be worth making his acquaintance."

"How do you know this man?"

"Every woman has a soft spot for Lonesome Bill."

"Thanks for the patch," I said, with a quick hug, then pulling back just as fast.

Ruby and I retraced our steps to the waiting room by following the thin animal wheezes of the men and women tucked in there. With my one good eye, I saw teenage girls, mothers, fathers—all of them whacked by something they never saw coming. They were slumped in chairs and in no hurry to leave as if what brought them on foot was only waiting for them to return. There was plenty of broke to go around. I didn't need two eyes to see that.

Outside, a breeze found us, lifted my spirits, calmed me some.

"There's some pirate in all of us," Ruby said, admiring my patch.

"From what I know, pirates steal most anything," I said.

"It may come to that," she said, never one to offer comfort when a shot of distress would do. Everything about our first night in Detroit made me more tired than spit. With only one eye working the angles, my balance was none too keen.

"Ruby, we have to stop somewhere."

"That makes two of us."

"Really? You look light on your feet."

"That's only because you can't walk."

"I've got twenty-five bucks."

"That should get us a roof and a breakfast and then some."

Ruby found a policeman stationed at the hospital door while I went outside, sat down on the curb.

"Is there a cheap hotel nearby?" she asked him.

"Lady, I got news for you. The night's almost over." The policeman's gut hung over his belt like Sunday ham. His face cascaded in a series of loose, drooping folds. His teeth stained black from tobacco chew. The brightest thing about his body was his badge perched high on his chest.

"We need to catch up," Ruby said.

"Hard being a working girl?" He looked at Ruby's floral dress splotched almost as bad as the one I found her in.

"You have no idea," she said. The policeman cracked a smile, almost a smirk.

"Check out the Rusty Nail," he said, "up on your left, two blocks. There's speakeasy booze up front. Rooms in back. They'll take in anybody, even you."

"Much obliged," Ruby said to the cop, then she helped me to my feet.

We walked on, my thirst unrelenting. My voice cracked when I told Ruby about Lonesome Bill. She said nothing about her willingness to seek him out. I hoped this night would end soon, and I'd have no memory of it except for the good doctor and nurse Sally who was kind enough to tell me about Lonesome Bill. My mind was a swamp of cogitation with no purchase. I saw again the hard-bitten girl entering that long-finned black car and I wondered what rough beast had thrashed her about, never pausing to remember she was someone's daughter or sister or friend with a name once spoken in tenderness and now maybe unspoken forever.

Ruby led on to the Rusty Nail. The stools were turned upside down on tables. The few stragglers leaning over the bar looked at us plain as butter on toast. Maybe they were retired cops friendly with the badge who sent us there or maybe they were just river men with no boat to catch. Each of them looked like they were born with a broken tooth, their faces lit with sweat and grease and something like the smear of disappointment.

One of the drinking men piped up to the bartender, "Hey, bottleneck."

"I told you, last call's over and done with."

"Got some late-night jelly roll coming in."

Ruby walked up to the barkeep, his hands clouded with suds.

"Bar's closed. Take it elsewhere."

"Need a room with a private bath and linens," Ruby said.

"You need some fries to go along with that shake," one drinker said, his jaw square as a liquor box.

The other men at the bar threw their heads back.

"A room with a lock and key will do," Ruby insisted.

"What tricks do you carry?" the barkeep asked, looking at her bag, then wiping his hands on his apron and taking more than a nickel glance at Ruby's shape. "Maybe you should give us a dance before you retire."

"Let's go," I said to Ruby. She waved me back.

She said to the barkeep, "We have money."

"Eight bucks for the two of you. Out by noon. I don't reckon you'll need that much time for what you've come for." I dug into a pocket and gave Ruby a twenty dollar bill. She handed it over to the bartender who made change, but held two dollars back.

"What's that for?" Ruby protested.

"Damage deposit." The three stragglers slapped each other on the backs. The barkeep dipped his hands into a tub and dunked a pair of beer mugs, pulled them out, rinsed them in another tub and set them on a shelf behind the bar.

"No crying out, either. I room down the hall from #11 and I need my shut eye."

"You won't hear a peep out of us," Ruby promised. The men laughed again, but I was so tired I didn't care what they thought. The barkeep pointed down a hall, his wet hand stroking the air. One of the men called out after me, "Sweet dreams, peach tree," and I thought how sweet could anything be in a place called the Rusty Nail. I turned back to say something to the man who spoke, but Ruby steered me away by the shoulder.

"Tomorrow's another day," she said.

"What that nurse said was right, Detroit is bad country."

"Plenty of bad here, some good," Ruby said, fitting the barrel key into the door lock. "The trick is knowing the difference between the two." She wiggled the key, pulled on the door, pushed, and we shuffled in. I snapped on a light switch and heard the sizzle of a bulb without much life left. The small square room had a musty smell which reminded me why I planned to live my life on boats with my head in the wind. The floor was rough-hewn white pine and perfect for snagging a splinter. There were drapes on the streaked windows and the sagging bed came with a yellow fringed coverlet.

In the bathroom, I tilted an oval mirror, saw an eye-patch girl caught in the smudge. I sat down on the toilet and felt my eye twitching beneath the patch, heard pipes knocking, the short squeak of faucets, the hard turning of keys, the bar and hotel winding down into its worn steps and hollows. I put my ear to the bathroom wall and heard a man and a woman fighting. First, a slap, a moan, a "please no," then bed springs squeaking, the man grunting, the woman pounding his back, the dull roar of skin against skin, then a flare and a charge, "Get the hell out of here." Whimper and slam, then nothing more. Ruby took

the room's one wooden chair and slanted it beneath the door
knob, then wedged the feet into a groove on the floor. After
she secured our door, she slid her duffel under the bed. I laid
myself down, thankful the bed was big enough for two and
thankful that Ruby knew all there was to know about hotels
with thin walls and jackals down the hall.

"Your clothes?" Ruby asked. "You're not going to sleep in
them, right?"

I dragged myself out of bed, dropped my shorts, peeled off
my T-shirt and slid beneath the sheets. Just before I fell asleep,
I heard Ruby singing some French song in the bath, the lilt of it
easy on the ear, a love song or lullaby or a mix of the two. After
Pelee, how could she gentle such melody?

I woke in the night, all jittery and singed by the heat of the
room. I saw Ruby's floral dress on the floor. I gathered it in my
arms and took it to the bathroom. I bunched up the dress and
pulled it down over my head. With no breasts and hips to speak
of, the dress hung on me like a potato sack until I retrieved the
blue sash from beside the bed and cinched it at my waist the
way Ruby did. I stood before the mirror, then reached up to
pull the light bulb chain. With a black eye patch and my brown
hair sticking out in three directions, I was a fetching sight. Still,
I stood there admiring the design, the brightness of the flowers,
the drape of blue ribbon. I tried to imagine the woman Ruby
was when she wore it. Fearless or ruled by fear? I could never
tell the frill from the marrow. We are all cursed with some piece
of fear, but she blended the curse with a blessing and wove it
into her sashay. I pulled the dress back over my head, pulled the
bulb chain again, and returned to bed. I'd just played dress up
for the first time and in a Detroit hotel with a woman who had
killed three men on a boat, then helped to dispense with three
more on land.

I heard nothing else until first light brought a garbage truck
into the alley and sparked a yowl. Ruby kicked away the draped
sheet and I saw her backside. I imagined how a painter might
warm to such a slope. Never once had I looked upon Momma

given to waking without a nightshirt on. Such a bed behind a bar would have been more than I could have weathered on my own, but here with Ruby, this dim hotel room doubled as a safe harbor. The cat in the alley would not quit, but the chair, canted at the door handle, had not moved since Ruby had lodged it into place.

Memory: What is it? Something quivering like the first snake in the garden or the only life raft that God allows? Guilt or freedom? After so many years, I can't say with certainty how much of what I recall really happened or whether I invented some of it for consolation. I can't tell you whether I am remembering Detroit or whether Detroit remembers me and I am only a last-minute boat for any number of small agonies with no place to make landfall. I can't tell you I understand how time can swerve out of its blind progress and funnel you back to a place as if you never left a certain cul-de-sac of confusion and revelation. And given the inevitable perils of aging blood, I may soon be able to remember only those things I would rather forget or I may become that dreaded thing bobbing in a corner, a blank slate, where nothing more can be written or recalled.

16

When I stepped out of the bath, I figured Ruby would be still asleep, but she sat on the edge of the bed brushing her long red hair, the tangles slowing her strokes. I still felt funny about getting dressed in front of her so I pretended to have left something in the bathroom and stepped back away from her.

"Modesty's the better part of a sandwich," Ruby said, glancing up. "Your mother tell you that?"

"Thought you were asleep," I said, dodging her question.

"You sleep with one eye open in a place called the Rusty Nail."

"Better than the Irish Rose," I said from the bathroom. "I had raccoons and mice in my room there."

"Bravo, brave skipper, you've now slept in two bars before you could drink in either one of them." I looked again at the stain on my hands. I had already scrubbed long and hard, but the dark splotches remained.

"Last night was just a tease," Ruby said.

"I'm so close," I said, trembling so hard I dropped my towel. I picked it up and wrapped it tightly around my body.

"Those men last night in the bar," Ruby said, her brush skating effortlessly through her hair. "Those were the nice ones. Hell, they might even pay taxes, take vespers, leave a coin in the Sunday basket, kiss their wives and children goodnight."

"I've got no problem going on alone."

"Why do I bother trying to talk sense?"

I had no idea if I had what it took to go on alone, but I couldn't turn back without knowing what happened to Daddy. That pledge wasn't fed by some fierce obligation to tell Momma what happened to her husband. Like I said earlier in the night, my forward was born of my own fire, no bigger than a match head, stoking me, warming me, calling me, telling me I owed it to the man who helped bring me into this world. Who taught me how to sail, read the wind, walk again after that killing influenza swept through without mercy. And, yes, I almost forgot. I did still carry some guilt that maybe I was responsible for him being stolen away at gunpoint. What I had seen on the beach, I could not unsee, but I could keep looking even if it made no sense. Ruby offered me her recipe for living: a blend of smile and sneer. Her tough could be tender. Her steady could be shaky. Her rasp could be smooth. This morning was no different.

"Okay, then, Lonesome Bill here we come."

"I didn't think you heard me tell of him."

"It doesn't pay to miss anything."

I expected to see Ruby digging into her duffel for a change of clothes, but she never opened it. She grabbed the duffel from under the bed, and we left our room behind, the bed unmade. Ruby and I walked down the hall toward the bar, the wide pine flooring creaking with our footfall. The barkeep was where we left him putting beer mugs back on a shelf. He glanced up, the hazel glow in his eyes no more friendly than pig iron. Ruby laid the room key on the counter.

"I've come for the deposit," Ruby said.

"Haven't seen the room." The barkeep laughed. He opened the register, smacked a roll of quarters on a tray and handed over eight coins.

"I prefer bills," Ruby said.

"Fresh out of those."

The barkeep placed the stack of eight wet quarters in her right hand.

"Where you from, darling?"

"Everywhere and nowhere," Ruby said.

"You look like yesterday."

"You don't look like anybody."

"Can't place the horse you rode in on."

Ruby closed her fingers around the quarters and flicked the suds off one rim. We turned our backs on the barkeep and walked across the floor toward the exit. I held my breath. Those few feet turned cold as river bottom against my ankles.

"I know you're a working girl," he shouted. "Maybe I've seen you at the Seadog or the Flagpole, I don't know where, maybe some gambling room. Gonna ask around about you. Find the fat and the skinny."

Ruby stopped. Without turning around, she spoke her mind. "Damn sure no one is gonna ask around about you."

"Shine up a penny any way you want, darling, but you still won't make a dollar."

Ruby didn't answer him. I had to quicken my step to match her stride. Her speed told me she was rattled, her mind at odds with a threat not easy to uncoil, a sweat bead gaining weight over her lips, her fingers pressing against one another, her nails digging against skin.

"What's the Seadog and the Flagpole?"

"Another couple names for death," she said.

"Have you ever seen that man before?" I asked.

"Hell no," she said, staring at me with pity and wonder split even in her eyes.

We stopped on the sidewalk and Ruby took a breath, then another, gathering herself. I looked out on the street and saw a horse-drawn milk wagon making an early morning run. A car honked as it flew by the wagon, then another car accelerated inside a puff of exhaust. Cars and wagons, one eating up the other. The milkman checked the street address on his clipboard. He clamped his hand strap onto four glass bottles and jerked them into the air. He glanced at us as he carried the milk toward a house next to the bar, the bottles swinging under his arm, heavy and fragile and firmly gripped. I looked after the man in a jaunty white cap, smiling to myself like maybe milk delivery was Detroit's most revered profession and not the running of whiskey. The milkman's blinkered draft horse looked better to me than a church. The horse was tall and true and patient for its task that had started early and would end late and pay nothing more than a pail of oats.

"I could eat the scales off a fish," Ruby said.

"I could eat the eyeballs."

"I could eat the tail," Ruby said.

"I could eat the stink hole." I laughed.

We stopped at a sidewalk diner serving off a counter. Ruby ordered black coffee, blueberry muffin, scrambled eggs. I wanted to order donuts, muffins, toast, eggs, oatmeal, bacon, link sausages, bananas, everything. Momma said oatmeal sticks to you longer than eggs, but I passed on the porridge and ordered four fried eggs over easy, bacon, two muffins, milk, orange juice, coffee. The Black man behind the counter cocked his head.

"You've got two hollow legs, little sister."

"Breakfast is my favorite," I told the man, who was a one-man order taker, griddle cook, cashier, bottle washer.

"You don't say."

We sat at his counter lit up with steam from a hot cloth. Feeling protective of my haul, I used one arm to wrap around my plate. Ruby glanced every so often over her shoulder. We settled up and moved along, my full belly making up for more than a few lost meals. Funny how a little food can make you believe in something other than dark clouds on your transom. We walked down the street just as the storefronts opened for their morning trade, the stir of a new day a steady mix of laughter and groans, trucks braking, then backing up, someone yelling to stop or come on back, men rolling up their sleeves to load up dollies, the engine of the day already plied with muscle and destination.

An older man in a faded suit coat and tails guarded the corner of Tyler and James where we needed to cross. He wore a block-lettered placard, *The saloon must be closed.* His eyes were blood-rimmed dimes long since spent on the Lord's work. He staggered in a tight circle like a dog leashed to a stake. I stopped to hear him out because on that day Detroit was new to me, not yet gripped by the many dark intentions Daddy and Ruby had spoken of.

"Praise the Lord in hard times," he said, his voice one long scrape through a drain pipe. "Praise for any one of you who have resisted the call to imbibe, guzzle, and otherwise indulge. Praise for any who has spent what precious money you have on food for your family, or for your church, or on those far less fortunate. Praise for any who wants to join me right now to close the claw of the devil that has sprung up all over our fair city. I'm talking about the luckless, sweet-talking saloons found on every street corner, more common than churches. I'm talking about the blind pigs everywhere fouling our city with the promise of free lunches, but nothing, my friends, in this blink of a life is free except God's love and his mighty wrath, and I urge you now to resist the zigzag to hell and hold out for a much greater reward, a much greater satisfaction, a much greater hope of the good everlasting. Praise for heaven and for hell and for your knowledge of which one is looking out for you. Praise in good time, your time, any time, this time, won't you please join me in God's time and make your displeasure heard as a clarion call. And the crooked shall be made straight and rough ways made smooth as Luke tells of it, so the Lord's work can take hold without fail and the new day without poison can find us again in the light of praise."

"Hard way to make a buck," Ruby said.

I looked at the preacher's hat and saw inside more than a few bills and a scattering of coin and thought a man could travel handsomely on the road of praise if that road starts with damnation.

"Never trust a preacher who swings a hammer," Ruby said, summing up my feelings.

We found no free lunch at the Rusty Nail, no free newspapers, no free peanuts, no welcoming conversation. Still, we found some sleep there and no one died because we had entered and caught a few winks. No matter the sidewalk warning from the preacher whose wallet was swelling, I would return to such a speakeasy if I thought for one minute such a place could help me find Daddy.

"Got a couple of nickels?" Ruby asked.

"You're not thinking of giving them to him?"

"Not a chance."

Ruby hailed a trolley and hopped on board while I fished for nickels. She turned back to grab a coin and dropped it in a fare box. The conductor was hunched over the wheel pouring over the funny papers, his pillbox skewed on his head. He didn't look up until he heard coin skitter the trough, then he levered the car forward, the street slipping away from us as we plunged toward the river on crackling sparks of electricity. On Biddle Avenue, we clipped through Riverview and into the village of Wyandotte facing Fighting Island. Each brick bungalow came with a pink flowering crab, a bucket of red begonias, and a black Ford. The downriver hooch business delivered its own rewards to this postcard neighborhood. The trolley turned right and dropped back down toward the Detroit River. Mind reader that she was, Ruby spoke to the crook of the moment.

"Now or never."

We jumped off the trolley and doubled our pace toward the river. I saw a sailboat headed south back to Lake Erie and felt a slow ache burning into me at the stray thought that I could be on that boat with Daddy leaving this city.

"Wake up, girl," Ruby said, as I nearly stepped into the path of an oncoming truck. I jerked back, but then got caught up again looking at the Detroit River lit up like a rare blue pickerel running fast from a trolling hook. How could such a thing of beauty be bogged down with so many whiskey bottles and bodies? Before we crossed the avenue to drop down to the river, I saw another man working a sidewalk corner, a hat flung down by his side. This man was as thin as a railroad spike and black as engine oil and he was playing a guitar hung around his neck with a piece of tri-colored fish twine. He held his guitar to his chest like a baby. His voice was raw with more hurt than help coming anytime soon. He sang about the devil whiskey, but I couldn't tell from his words whether he thought whiskey was a good or a bad thing or something forever lost in between the notes...

My woman took my good drink.
Said I could die tomorrow.
Tonight I let her love me,
No matter what the river thinks.

I stood there with the man, mesmerized by the drag splinter of his voice. Like he had found a way to take me with him to the beginning of all rattle. His playing brought me to some feelings strangled in my own throat. How I could hardly speak of them, so they were speaking through me. I watched his fingers bend the strings, and when he did this, his voice climbed up out of my tangle and into the clang of the street. I can still hear a few of his words: *pork chop, gravestone, red dress, turpentine.* I reached into my pocket and put two bits into his hat. He nodded. I nodded back. Our coming and going, real and gone, like that, a bent note that hangs in the air like an invisible spill of gasoline. His guitar never turning back from pain, no matter what the river thinks.

"Some singer," I said to Ruby.

"He's seen the moon's dark side," she said.

"Where is he now?"

"Just one step ahead of something," Ruby said, both of us taking a last look at the man with his eyes closed like he'd been singing to himself all his life. We dropped again toward the river and hugged a planked wall held together with rusted spikes. Creosote piling ran out into the water like stubs of crumbling teeth. You could almost walk on the backwash of glass bottles, beer cans, the broken legs of tables, fishnet, corn cobs, garbage, snarled fish line, shoes, pillows, underwear. Perched over the slosh, I looked out at the river flashing south and took some pleasure knowing that this current washed upon my shore in Rye Beach. Ruby and I both saw the Hiram Walker distillery sign at the same time.

"I wonder how this works?" I asked Ruby. "Thought we couldn't bring whiskey into the U.S."

"Looks like boats come to the Detroit side to re-fuel before they load up on the Windsor side, then they set out from there."

"One hand feeding the other?"

"Something like that."

Men in stained T-shirts scrambled across the decks of the tied-off boats. Two of the boats were steel tugs with bulkheads running aft. Hard to imagine these rigs would get loaded in broad daylight, then set out for ports lettered on their transoms. One man in red suspenders directed the other men and I figured he must be Lonesome Bill. He was bald, barrel-chested, and had white eyebrows so bushy it looked like he was wearing a visor over his eyes. His sun-kissed head with no neck looked like pictures I'd seen of overripe mangos. Ruby and I looked at one another, knowing one of us had to sidle up. The dock workers pretended to be busy when he was near and they backed off to talk and smoke when he stepped inside the dock house. I walked toward him.

"Looking for Lonesome Bill."

The man glanced up from his clipboard. I could see neat squares and columns of numbers.

"What's your pleasure?"

"Have reason to believe my daddy's running whiskey here."

"What business of that is mine?" He still didn't look at me straight on.

"I was told on a good authority by a nurse named Sally that you might be able to help me." Lonesome Bill turned toward me and some hard gleam in his eye softened.

"Three quarters of all the whiskey in the world is flowing across the Detroit River right now. I imagine there are a lot of daddys caught up in that."

"Which is why I need help."

"Don't we all need some of that." He squeezed his left hand into a fist and the muscles in his arm snaked up his chest under a sheath of grease stains. His eyes drew themselves back to his clipboard.

"I've come a long way," I said.

"I can see that."

"Please."

"You have any idea what sort of party you're trying to break into?"

"A private one?"

"Just the opposite."

"How so?"

"Everybody and his brother is chasing whiskey money."

"That's not what I'm after."

Watching our push and pull from a safe distance, Ruby threw down the hint of a sashay into her stride. When she was near a man, Ruby angled her body so more of her could be seen and fussed over. Her legs, her arms, her hands scissoring the air. Lonesome Bill sized her up the way a rider might look at the rump of a horse. He lingered on her hips, wet his lips, swallowed. Lonesome Bill had the same goofy look Zane did. Like he'd just won a new roadster at a raffle. Wonderment, I guess you'd call it. Death and revival under the same tent. Ship come in at last. Horse headed for the barn. The coin toss, yours to call.

"Where you from, darling?"

"Montreal, all day, all night."

"You two together?"

Ruby nodded.

"Where you staying?"

"No fixed address," Ruby said.

"Just a couple of dolls off the trolley, that it?"

I slipped between Lonesome Bill and Ruby and made myself known once again.

Lonesome Bill gazed at the Windsor side of the river like it was the Promised Land. He too was looking for something as yet unclaimed. He turned back toward Ruby with a grin and it was clear from the burst of light skidding off his front teeth he had the means to help us, but wanted something in return.

"May I have the pleasure of knowing your name?" He held out his right hand to Ruby. She looked at him straight on like she knew full well the terms of this exchange and offered her hand.

"Ruby Francoeur."

"Charmed."

"Gets me where I want to go."

"Like I was saying." I interrupted by stepping between them. "I'm looking for my father. He's skinny as a pencil. Got big elephant ears. And he knows everything there is to know about engines." Lonesome swept his arm from the north to the south of the visible river, then he launched into an unexpected sermon intended to impress Ruby who let her eyes graze on him, each look like a little finger tug.

"What you see out there is thirty-two miles of gold. Nothing less than the busiest strait in the world. Just with the flat-bottom scooters, there's a thousand bottles of hooch coming into Detroit every damn day. Hiram Walker says they know nothing about whiskey shipments because they don't own the docks. Coast Guard can't stop it. Police can't stop it. Whiskey makers in Windsor are feeling no pain and neither are we."

"I'm not trying to blow some whistle," I said.

Lonesome Bill fetched his eyes on the swell of Ruby's breasts peeking out of her dress. Like he suddenly got struck by some sickness. She had no problem with his looking and his brushing one hand along her backside. If she stood any closer to him, she'd be a mile deep in his arms.

"I'm not going away," I said, "so you might as well tell me everything I need to know."

He turned his back to me and faced Ruby.

"Can I buy you a drink this evening?"

"Don't see the harm in that," Ruby said.

"This day's looking up."

"Where?"

"The Blackbird on the Windsor side. Around eight." Lonesome Bill cocked his head like a lost dog hankering after a biscuit. He waved to a patrolman on the next dock, then he turned to me.

"I've seen a man like the one you described, but I can't say whether he's still here or scattered to the four winds."

"Where was he?"

"On the Windsor side. He popped his head out of an engine room with grease stains on his face and shirt. Not every day you see a man with ears like that."

"Name of the boat?"

"*Martina.*"

"Where is she?"

"Not my turn to watch where she goes."

"What is she, then?"

"She's a whoopee ride and cash cow rolled into one. Custom-built forty-footer with steel plating over wood and twin two-hundred horse engines. Coast Guard can't catch her even when she's fully loaded. Boat like that can make a man twenty thousand clams in a single night."

"That a fact?"

"You don't want to get in the crosshairs of money like that."

"I'll do whatever it takes."

"Attagirl." He laughed, then Bill ogled his eyeballs back on Ruby. I wasn't about to stand there and pretend nothing was going on between them, so I hailed a boy in a flat-bottom scooter patrolling the dock's underbelly. He grimaced and kept coming on. I figured the smaller the craft, the bigger the view we'd get of the river.

"Can I pay you to take us over to Windsor?"

"There's a ferry boat leaves on the hour," the boy said, miffed for my asking.

I dug into my pockets and pulled out two dollars.

"Forget it. You can't afford me."

I looked into his skiff and saw a dozen jute bags cinched off with twine.

"You can't afford not to take me if I tell the blue uniform over there about the giggle water you use for ballast."

"Well, aren't you a one-eyed bearcat."

"Been called worse."

"Reckon so."

"I ain't got all day."

I called out to Ruby. She put away her lipstick and kicked one leg back to give a flare to her leave-taking. Lonesome Bill finger waved and she waved back with her whole hand. I decided at that moment men were ridiculously weak and silly creatures against a succubus like Ruby. Clutching her duffel, she broke into a run which made Bill look after her. I could almost see his heart thumping. She waved again. He wiped the sweat off his forehead with the back of his hand. Made me a little sick and envious how Ruby turned every man she met into a hay burner.

17

I climbed down a slimy ladder into the flat-bottom scooter boat. Ruby handed me her duffel, then followed me down. The boy yanked the starter cord and the engine turned over, coughed, died. He had rough hands with engine oil smudged into the knuckles. Every part of him was tense and nimble like a creature born to the task of bringing life back into a dead mechanical thing. He had a scraggly thatch of sand-colored hair, a skinny, sun-baked face, and narrow blue eyes that skipped easily across water. And he had something else: the rare crackle of readiness and gamesmanship that such a river demanded. I liked him right away.

"Having some trouble with my horse," he apologized, wiping his hands on the blue bandana loosely clasped at his throat. "That's why I paddled in here. Otherwise I'd be to hell and back and never would have met up with the likes of you two." He yanked again and again and I saw the wavy play of muscles beneath his T-shirt. The engine sputtered, spit black smoke, then a prop kick.

"I'd say you need a new set of plugs," I offered.

"That's what my last teacher said," the boy said.

"You don't go to school?"

"What's that?"

"Your folks good with that?"

"Don't have any of those."

His line about not having parents broke my line of thought and I didn't know how to commence another line of parley. The boy coaxed his outboard. "Come on, baby, talk to me." The engine sputter turned smooth enough under the quick of his hands and the prop turned over and spit water.

"You ladies don't mind if I unload some cargo before I take you across?"

"We have a choice?" Ruby asked.

"Suppose not," he said.

"If we get caught—"

"No worries. I'm in the export business."

"What did you say?"

"I'm in exports. That's what we call it."

I remembered a name from the night I caught Daddy on the beach unloading crates of whiskey.

"Ever come across the Mexican Export Company?"

"There are dozens of export companies in Windsor. Too many to count. You can take any name you want for a company. Nobody looks twice or everybody looks the other way or everybody is blind to the power of the wallet."

The boy smiled at me like he meant it, then flipped the outboard around to back us away from the dock. Once we pulled away, he whipped around the engine head, and off we went on a rooster tail, away from the jellied scum, the floating boots, the tangled rope, and the whiskey boats Lonesome Bill made ready for distant ports. From what I could tell, the whole whiskey business was done with a wink and a nod. Hiram Walker made all the whiskey they wanted and they sold it through an army of anonymous distributors at whatever price the market would bear. I didn't care who made millions under the table. I didn't care if the line between legal and illegal was no wider than a river. What I did care about was progress. It was not yet noon and already I had a solid meal, got a new bead on Daddy, and now I was skipping along the shallows of the Detroit River in a rumrunner's craft, faster than a monkey's paw in a snake bag.

"We have far to go?" I asked.

"That depends on what you mean," he said and left it at that.

The day was a blue sparkle secret spilling in all directions. There was a stiff breeze from the south setting up river chop, but that clash of elements only bristled my spirit. Like maybe I belonged there, nose up in the Detroit River. For the first time since I'd left Rye Beach, I was not looking over my shoulder to get back home. Right then, I didn't hear the hinge of some dark memory. No suckers on the tobacco leaves. No bullet holes, no flames, no broken teeth, no crooked smiles leering from the sidewalk. No fear that Daddy was already face down in the slime. Only this ride with a boy on a river, my heart bouncing like it now knew life had more in store for me than dying.

"Why do you carry hooch in those burlap bags?"

The boy muffled a laugh.

"You won't make a lot of friends in Windsor like that."

"Don't need a lot of friends."

"If I have to dump them fast, I can dive down in the shallows and pick them up later. That's why the bags are tied off with grabbing ears."

"Sounds dangerous."

"Most occupations are."

The boy ran upriver no more than a mile to a broke-down marina patched together with two-by-fours and truck tires. A man greasing a marine railway glanced at us through a hank of blond hair smeared black. He wore gray overalls and yellow gumboots. He nodded to the boy who tipped his brim. Oddly enough, the man at the rails looked very much like my preacher back in Rye Beach, the Reverend Raymond Francis, who said a man without creed makes a daily covenant with chance and confusion, and I wondered what the dear reverend would have said if he'd seen me resting my dogs on a mess of jute bags packed with hundred-proof longnecks. In heaven's name, he would have nosed me toward Solomon and the *little foxes that ruin the vineyards.* I would have told him sometimes you've got to run with the foxes if you're looking for a father taken at gunpoint.

"Stay low," the boy said, "as we coast in. Don't want either of you making a fuss." We drifted the last ten feet into a dock where a pile-driving rig was tied off at a rusted bollard. The boy pointed to the jute bags cinched at the top with pointy ears wrapped in shipper's twine.

"Come on," the boy instructed. "Earn your keep."

Each jute bag weighed a good twenty pounds. I dragged

each of the twelve jute bags out from under the thwarts. I made sure my feet were planted before I handed off to another boy who stood on a floating pile driver.

"Beans for breakfast," he said, after I unloaded the last bag. "I could use someone like you," he said as he laughed into the freshening breeze.

"How much are those twelve jutes worth to you?"

"One dollar a bottle. Ninety-six bottles in all. You do the math."

"What's your name?" I called out to him while he loaded the bags into a wheelbarrow squirreled behind a dock shed.

"Fat chance."

I saw a shiny black Willy Overland waiting in the lot, engine running, bonnet open. The boy loaded the bags into the car, grabbed a handful of cash which he didn't bother to count and returned to the dock. He smiled at me for the second time like maybe now I'd treat him with more respect.

"Norah Bow," I said to the boy. "This here is Ruby."

Ruby winked at the boy which made him look twice. I half-blocked his view. I didn't need her flapper girl routine getting in the way of my learning something from this river rat. I figured this boy knew more about the Detroit River than any chart could tell me. Momma said if you want to make an impression, make someone feel smart, so I took her counsel from afar and put it to good use.

"Hey, why does the river have so much current?"

The boy wiped his palm over his mouth. He yanked the outboard starter and we puttered out of the fire-trap marina, leaving only a thin line of wake as if we'd never been there.

"River's got to kick in the difference," he said, "between Lake St. Clair and Lake Erie. About three feet I figure."

"How fast?"

"Fast enough to drown a good swimmer. Where you headed?" the boy asked.

"Looking for somebody on the Hiram Walker docks."

"Start at the top and work down."

"Only thing I know to do unless you say different," I said.

"You ain't never watched a catfish get fat smart."

"How so?"

"Lives off the bottom for a reason."

"Camouflage? That's your secret to a long life?"

The boy smirked in triumph. If he ran out of gas, he could always draw on his spare tank of cockiness and mud-soaked reserve.

"Ever been to Cedar Point?"

"What's that have to do with Hiram Walker?"

"One thing doesn't have to follow another," I said.

"That's just like a girl," he scoffed.

I loved how his eyes twinkled just then. Like two dings on the hood of the river.

"They've got a roller coaster over there that's faster than a bullet. Some grown men are afraid to ride it, but I bet you could ride it blindfolded and no hands."

The boy showed a few jagged teeth and had a scar on one cheek the size of my pinkie nail. From the looks of it, he'd been knocked around some and dished out a few knocks of his own. He pulled a wide-brimmed fedora low on his forehead, the crown of it stained red like maybe the boy plucked the smart hat off a man shot full of holes.

"My daddy runs Cedar Point," I added.

"Eye patch and all, don't you hit on all sixes," the boy said, spitting downriver.

"It's true. Daddy was taken by rumrunners out of our home. I've come here to fetch him back home." Ruby cocked her head, curious at the change in my story.

"Why would someone make a grab for your old man?"

"He's rich," I said. "Filthy rich."

The boy's flat-bottom scooter boat flew over the river like a piece of black slate. The snarl of foam and current was no match for the boat's speed. I had to hurry if I was going to turn the boy my way.

"If you help us find my daddy, I'll get you a weekend pass to every ride in the park. And find you a place to stay. Everything paid for."

"I've got money to get me there and back," he said, patting his shirt pocket.

"I'll show you around myself. Could even be more fun than running hooch."

"How do I know you're fishing with live bait?"

The boy looked at the traffic on the river, shielding his eyes from the brightness built into the river's kick and churn. He struck me as wild and kind and wounded in almost everything he said, and I sensed a kinship with him that scared me and turned my breath shallow.

"Ruby, tell him what I'm saying is the god's honest."

"This girl saved my life," Ruby said to the boy. "Pulled me out of the drink in the middle of the night after the boat I was on shot up in flames. Far as I can tell, whatever she says is straight and true."

The boy squinted at Ruby over the whine of the engine.

"What's this free trip gonna set me back?"

Ruby swiped at her own smile. She too liked this boy who wouldn't give us his name and who slapped a price tag on free.

"We need a ride back across the river tonight."

"You're not moving no rotgut? I only carry top quality. Nothing but the best. That's the kind of business I run."

"I told you, I'm here to collect my daddy. If he's not here, then I want to clear out sooner than later. Can you run us back?"

"Tell me where and when and I'll be there."

He reached out his hand and I extended mine, wondering how in the world I was going to snag free tickets to Cedar Point if he should come to Sandusky. The boy's peek-a-boo smile told me trickery had its place in this world.

"We'll be at the Blackbird. Midnight, I figure, before we get out of there."

"Midnight?"

"Too late for you?"

"Ain't nothing too late for me. It's just—"

"What?"

"Where you needing to go at that hour?"

"Way downriver."

"Where?"

"Gibraltar Island where my boat is dragged up on the bank."

"That's halfway to hell."

"An all-day pass at Cedar Point is not cheap."

"You'll show me around there?"

"And all the food you can eat."

"Midnight it is. At the Blackbird."

"Thanks," I said, as we approached Windsor, just south of the Hiram Walker docks. Everywhere I looked up and down the river I saw that the mumble and slur trade was already engaged in a brisk business. Boats of all sizes were rafted up and jostling like so many horses at the starting gate. I saw steamers, tugs, speedboats, rowboats, and flat-bottom scooters. Men with dollies loaded crates down companionway ladders and into flush-mounted hatches with the threads of their songs and whistles reaching out across the water. The boy saw me trying to read the compass of this commotion.

"Customs like to clear early," the boy said. "So they can go drink down their hush money."

"You mean all the whiskey gets loaded into boats with a green light?"

"All bound for Cuba, St. Thomas, Argentina, or some such made-up place with a little detour into the Detroit Gold Coast. Yours truly has been cleared for Peru and Panama twice in the same day."

"How much whiskey gets through?"

"Between Lake St. Clair and Amherstburg, there must be fifty export companies loading up whiskey boats, plus decoys to greet the Coast Guard, then another fifty right in the belly of Windsor, so I guess you'd have to say the pipeline is wide open, all day, every day."

"Hope you don't mind her asking you so many questions," Ruby said to the boy.

"I don't get to talk much."

The boy recognized another flat-bottom scooter making a Detroit run and waved at the boy fast at the throttle.

"Who's that?"

"I trained him as a spotter. Then he got his own boat."

The boy read my baffled face and explained over the whoosh of the wake about decoy boats, signal lights, and spotters who watched for Customs Border Patrol, Coast Guard, police and the Prohibition Border Patrol. To cool myself off, I reached out to catch the spray. I put my other hand on his knee. "Why doesn't anyone come after you?" He saw my hands. How each fingernail was rimmed in black stain. I kept my hand on him where he could see it.

"The only boats the Coast Guard runs down are the ones they want to drive. Me, I'm a mosquito, not worth the bother."

"You're safe out here?" I asked, letting my hand slide off slow but not my gaze.

"No one's safe on the whiskey river."

I wanted the one-mile ride across the whiskey river to last longer than a bottle. I was hungry for the silver flash between me and this river boy. I liked everything about him, his long-distance squint and his cracked hands on the throttle, his patched denim shirt stained with sweat and engine oil, the blue bandana at his throat, the broad-brimmed hat, how he blended his flat-bottom boat with the islands and coves like he'd been anointed in the river mud itself and whatever might manifest on land and shout out his name could never be as delicious as the bump and glide over this river of legend. In Windsor, I climbed out first and Ruby handed me her duffel. She nearly lost her footing on a ladder slicked with seaweed which chuckled me. She looked pale green from the skipping ride where I felt singled out by the new day. The boy swiveled the engine and backed up his scooter. Before he left the dock, he called out.

"Friends call me Catfish."

"I like that," I said and waved him off.

Ruby plumped her hair, then smoothed it, then pulled out

a compact mirror and lipstick. In a flick, she changed from a wind-blown, green-at-the-gills passenger to a fetching place to roam. How did she do this? Pull, brush, swish, smooth, *voila*.

"Quite the vixen," Ruby said, slipping her compact into a hidden pocket.

"What?"

"With your daddy's gift for lying, you've got Catfish dangling from a stringer. That boy would ride the roller coaster on his own dime if you just put your hand back on his knee."

"I never said he was a liar."

"You hardly need to defend his honor. It's not like he's running for sainthood."

"What's a vixen, anyway?"

"Men spend much of their lives in a fox hunt."

Ruby ran her hands over her dress as if to iron out the wrinkles or maybe she just wanted men in a dash to pause and imagine what it might be like for their own hands to wander there.

"Lose the eye patch. You don't need anybody looking twice unless of course those eyes belong to Catfish."

"Stop it," I said, muzzling a laugh, "or I won't hand it over."

I swung the bag at my side wondering what it would be like to travel so light and fast and never know how the day would start or end and if the drowsy middle would be pleasing, full of shame, or given over to another dead run.

"Just having fun," Ruby said, reaching out for her worldly belongings.

I'd be lying if I didn't tell you how confusing it was to travel with a woman like Ruby who viewed her body like a knife in the pocket, wild card in the deck, guest book at the long kiss hotel, the next ticket for the train. Momma was all hush and hurry about bare skin. Ruby was all shiny curve and wink in the morning. Between those two, I didn't stand a chance of knowing how to read the flicker in my chest for a whiskey boy named Catfish. I just had to give my unknowing more time to unsettle me. I had so much time back then and now I have so precious little, or do I have the clock all wrong and I have just enough time to tell my story, all hands on deck, and still get home?

18

I need to say more about Catfish and the undertow of the whiskey river and how I came to taste the flutter secrets in my own blood, but first I hear Ruby again and the thump of pettiness in my chest like the gavel of a tribunal.

"Need a new dress," Ruby said, running her hands again over her hips.

When she used the words *new dress*, I knew what she really meant was she needed a new life, a new game to play, a new man, or a Canadian blend of all three.

"How you fixing to do that?" I asked, not wanting to look at Ruby's hourglass figure that could make any dress sing. Even as we stood there, two men walked by craning their necks. Her generous bust combined with a tapered waist and wavy hips were enough to draw attention, but then her flame-red hair was the bonfire topper. It was comical to watch men stare and stumble after her, but then I wasn't much better. I looked back at the Detroit River blinking south knowing everything in me felt envious of her curves, daunted by her bravado, jealous of her power, hungry for her crossing of any threshold, and not wanting any of it if I couldn't have it all.

"Back on home soil," she said. "Something good is bound to come my way."

I glanced at my cut-off jean shorts and my shabby, stained T-shirt and wondered what a new dress would do for my broad shoulders and straight, no-curves-anywhere frame.

"I could use your help," I said, walking toward a flurry of cars, trolleys, and people on Riverside Drive. Not yet nine in the morning and the city already jangled with promise. Laughter and doubt sprung at me through gossip, lecture, and worry. Knots of people drew down to the river, some clearly light-footed, set upon a goal of catching the Detroit ferry. Others held back, blaming, scolding, hands outstretched as if saying, *Come back, get away from me, time to go, why did you leave me so little money?* Canadians they may have been, but they seemed not unlike the folks in Detroit: some happy, some not, some ready to go back to sleep, some clocked in, tumbling toward the demands of another ordinary day, others already in a party mood with no glance toward burden and obligation.

"You've graduated to the next level," Ruby said. "After what I just saw with that boy, you can make your own way in Windsor."

"That mean you're calling it quits?"

"Nobody said anything about that."

"You've got your traveling bag. What more do you need?"

"Can't trust my worldly possessions to a river rat."

"His name is Catfish."

"I only said I need some new threads if I'm going out tonight. I mean, really, look at me." Ruby did a twirl. Wanting me to think her innocence was her strongest suit. All smiles, just then with a little hide-and-seek thrown in. "I've never looked this dusted over."

"You looked a lot worse the night I picked you up," I said, envious that Ruby was going to spend the day shopping while I had to trade my safety for a mouthful of perilous questions.

"Don't even go near a Customs Office along the river," Ruby advised. "We didn't exactly get you into Canada on the up-and-up. No telling what they'll make of you."

"The Blackbird, then. Should we meet earlier?"

Ruby revealed a flush at the base of her throat.

"Come late."

"How much later?"

"How about eleven?"

"That's better than twelve hours from now."

"I figure you'll need a full day to learn anything."

I stepped back from Ruby thinking this was the moment when she sprung loose from her pledge to see me through. This was the moment she crossed over to her old life, when she happily returned to doing what she did best. This was our time to part company without saying it because that was her breezy, ruffian style. Some long hurt part of me was surprised she hadn't slipped away the moment we arrived in Detroit. She was starved for a brand new dress and there was no way on God's green she cared more about me than herself. How brainless was I to ever consider some other conclusion?

"You're right," I said. "I'll find my way."

"No doubt you will," Ruby said.

"Good luck finding a dress," I said weakly.

"Good hunting," she said, striding north up Riverside like she knew exactly where to find more dazzle for a little money. I fought with myself not to think about her as I walked toward the docks of the Detroit-Windsor Ferry Company, but I didn't fight long. The noisy cheerfulness of the ferry dock stood in bright contrast to my forlorn. The ferry had just arrived and I couldn't help but ache after what the women had: the expectation of meeting someone or going somewhere fun inside a summer day and a ticket to prove they knew how to get back home. Hard not to stare at them just off the ferry. Like seeing a whole cotillion of Aunt Coras with their bobbed hair, rolled stockings, eyeshadow, and scarlet lips. Everything about them eager to enter the hotels, shops, bars, and restaurants clustered at the river's edge. This throng of sleeveless dresses could have sprung out of a *Vogue* magazine I sometimes saw Momma stealing away to read. It took me only five minutes of staring to realize that Ruby and Aunt Cora didn't have the corner on flirt and fast. When I didn't see anyone who looked anything like me, I walked out to the last piling where the ferry was cinched to its bollards and looked back across the river toward Detroit. I wanted to grab a seat on that Detroit-bound ferry and have it swing south and take me all the way back to Rye Beach.

If you spend any time around boats, you know this much: there is no ride as comforting as the one a ferry offers. All that freeboard and beam irons out any waves your mind bumps up against. The leather seats are forgiving and if the ferry is crowded, there's always still enough room to get away to sort yourself out in your own time. On a ferry, the light offers a grazing of gold, pink, and mauve. Like it has no qualms lofting you or wetting your eyes. On a ferry, the wind is always brisk and you can imagine it will have your back. On a ferry, the monsters of your own making are no longer mean enough to swallow you whole. On a ferry, everything that is long way off is still a wonder and not a worry. On a ferry, you might as well stay a while longer in the generous, big-fendered swell of the womb.

I saw a man in uniform at the far end of the ferry dock with a nightstick bumping his thigh. One look at him and a sudden debate banged my head. If I asked him anything, he could send me back across the river or he could help me make short work out of an impossible task. Worth the risk? Everything, Daddy said, is a risk including not taking one. *Yes, no, yes, no, maybe.* I saw a vendor on the same dock as the policeman selling bags of hot sugar donuts. I made my way over to the stand.

"How much will two dollars buy?"

"U.S. or Canadian?"

"U.S."

"Three dozen."

I handed over the cash and the man handed me a steaming bag of sugar donuts.

"Have a serving tray?"

"What?"

"Making a delivery."

The donut vendor flipped open a cardboard carton, cut it open with a flick of his knife, folded up the sides, and handed the makeshift tray to me and said, "That'll be two bits more." I gave the vendor a dollar and told him to keep the change. I gathered myself and walked toward the policeman who had stopped to talk to an elderly woman planting a box with geraniums. I waited for the policeman to glance my way.

"Sorry to interrupt," I said to him. "I've lost my way."

"Girls," the woman said to the policeman, "are always getting lost. Go ahead and help the poor thing."

"Yes?" the officer asked. His face was story book bright. Just by looking up into it, I felt confident selling my next lie.

"I need to make a donut delivery to the Mexican Export Company. I know it's right around here, but I can't remember where."

The policeman took a whiff of the hot sugar donuts.

"Please, sir, try one," I said.

The policemen dipped his hand into my tray. I offered the woman one too.

"Thank you," she said, the powdered sugar from her donut flaking off onto her gloved hand.

"Not always safe down there," he said.

"My boss told me just to leave the donuts at the door."

"Smart idea," the policeman said.

"Safety is my number one," I said.

"I believe the Mexican Export Company is just two buildings over," the policeman said, pointing downriver.

"Silly me," I said. "I walked right past the building. Care for another?" The policeman and woman both nodded. He took one more and the woman took three, shaking each one. I tried to leave the ferry dock quickly, but couldn't make good headway. Another ferry boat from Detroit had arrived and a drove of brightly lit couples poured off the ramp like hot taffy. I dipped my hand into the bag of donuts and ate one in two bites, then another. I ate six more powdered sugar donuts before I spotted the Belle Isle restaurant next to the ferry ticket booth and a familiar face there.

"What are you doing here?" I asked, surprised and pleased to see Catfish leaning against a lamppost like he had been there for some time watching my donut routine.

"Thought you might be hungry for real food?" he said in a mocking tone.

He grabbed my arm and we sidled up to the back door of the Belle Isle. He held open the back door and we crept past the kitchen help who were scrubbing pots and talking French or some other language I couldn't make plain.

"Need to use the ladies," I told him.

As if he were a regular customer, Catfish pointed the way. I entered the lavatory thinking I needed to be quick, but once inside I stopped my rush. The white floor tile had been buffed to a shine. There were three white pedestal sinks and a cushioned bench in a calico chintz. Wainscoting, floral wallpaper, oval mirrors, and a sailboat mural made the room feel more like a gallery than a restroom. I stood in front of the mirror looking like something fished out of the river. My sunburnt face smudged with grease. My eye patch askew. My mouth dusted with powdered sugar.

I opened a built-in linen cabinet and saw a stack of freshly laundered hand towels. Then, I saw a pair of sunglasses left on the bench. I looked around to see if another woman was in a stall. I was alone. I picked up the glasses, dangled them in one hand, hoping no one would return to reclaim them. I'd never seen sunglasses like these with green sea glass and tortoise-shell frames. I removed my eye patch, slipped on the glasses and voila, I looked more like someone else. The girl I now saw had just stepped off the Detroit ferry. With somewhere fun to go and some hint of a burning riddle in her distant past. I left off the eye patch, tucked the sunglasses in my pocket. I used the toilet, wiped off the powdered sugar, wet my hands to push back my hair. I took one more look in the mirror and smiled this time the way I wanted to smile at Catfish when he looked at me.

Once back in the hallway, I wanted to sit down in this swanky restaurant and order a meal, but Catfish had another idea. We crept back toward the kitchen. I saw two plates of food ready for a waitress to serve them, but before that happened Catfish snatched the order off the counter. We wasted no time returning the way we came. Just before we left the restaurant, Catfish handed me a turkey sandwich smothered in cranberry sauce. Might have been the single best thing between two slices of bread I'd ever tasted.

"This is how you live?" I asked, wiping my chin with my hand.

"Catch as catch can," Catfish said with a lilt.

"I've got to find the Mexican Export Company," I said, glancing downriver.

"That can wait," Catfish said. "It's not going anywhere."

"I've waited long enough," I pushed back.

"Let me show you *my river*."

I guess it was the way Catfish took possession of the words, my river, that made me think the Mexican Export Company could wait. Standing there in front of me waiting for my reply, Catfish was springy on his feet, loose-jointed like a marionette, all risk and reward in one package. He made me smile just to look at him. All his ropey, sunburnt muscles showing. I couldn't tell if he was lonely or if he liked me. I was glad I wasn't wearing the movie-star glasses. In that moment, I didn't want to hide from this boy behind big round anything. Catfish grabbed me by the hand and we ran from the restaurant, laughing with each step, and I thought a stolen moment like this must be worth stealing again.

"Why are we running?" I asked him, out of breath.

"Someday we won't be able to," he said, giving me the impression he was not just talking about the stoop of old age. We stopped near the ferry and he bought me an ice cream, two scoops of strawberry. He had three scoops, more chocolate than anything else.

"You have no family?" I asked, biting into my first scoop like I'd never had one before.

"That's right," he said, licking his ice cream smoothly. "Just me and the river."

"How does that feel?" I asked, thinking I was risking almost everything to find my daddy and he didn't even have one or seem to need one for that matter.

"Never knew who bore me. Got dropped off with a neighbor, I guess. Was told my father left first on a westbound train. Mother cleared out not long after with another fella. Been standing on the river's doorstep my whole life, fishing, trapping, delivering this and that. I like it and the river seems to like me."

"Don't stop now," I said, entranced by his every word and by a gap between his front teeth wide enough to whistle through.

"Some things you don't want to know. Others might suit you."

Catfish was not all clown. His face radiated a lost shining and a lucky streak. Like he knew all about both in spades. He was easy to talk like he had already lived once and knew lots of things I would never grasp. There was definitely some broke in him, but those forfeit parts didn't keep his head down. He did like to tilt his head off-center when he looked at me. Like he was puzzled, amused, ready to leap out of the way or not let a camera grab his soul in a single shot. That's what I remember most. Lost and found at the same time. Like most of us feel if only we would come clean with the hard ground we stand on.

"I should go," I said. I didn't want to leave him, but I was afraid to stay, and lose the link to Daddy calling to me from the most slender of threads.

"You need to see my playground."

He grabbed my hand again and I liked it just as much the second time.

We found his scooter boat tied off at a floating dock. I looked downriver wondering if I was having second thoughts about even bothering with the Mexican Export Company or if the only thoughts in my head were how much I liked being with this reckless one from the river mud. "Come on," Catfish urged. He climbed down a slicked wooden ladder and I followed. I sat on the center thwart facing Catfish while he fired up his Evinrude.

"Where we going?" I asked over the throaty engine.

"You'll see," he said. Catfish cranked the throttle and the flat-bottom scooter rose up, smacked the bigger waves, skimmed over smaller ones. With just two of us, the scooter was a fast, smooth kiss. I had no business giving up a day, but I couldn't stop how good it felt to be out on that river with Catfish. I let my eyes leave behind the Windsor shoreline. Hard at first to let go of why I came this far, then it got easier when I took in the rush of the clouds. No matter where I looked, there was only a big sky as blue as a gas flame, the river swirling beneath, and this boy letting his eyes grab at any good chance. In that moment, on a river only a mile wide, it felt like I could be a million miles away from the blood and ash that had brought me there.

Catfish raced out to the sharp southern point of Belle Isle and nuzzled his boat into a crack in the shoreline no bigger than a doorway. We idled into a leafy lagoon. He cut the engine and we drifted toward a pair of canvasbacks who dove before we got too close.

"This is one of my homes," he said. Catfish pointed to an osprey nest stuck in the fork of a lightning-sheered oak.

"Fish hawks will show you where the big fish gather," he said.

I looked at the heap of driftwood sticks and seaweed and wondered how something so fragile could be strong enough to hold up such a big bird.

"No one goes hungry around here," Catfish said.

"What are we doing here?" I asked, a little jittery once we had stopped.

"I thought we'd play a round of golf." He beamed.

"Golf?"

"Nine holes."

He nosed the bow into a hidden cove, stepped by me, took a line up on the shoreline and tied off his boat to the osprey oak.

"Come on," he said, reaching for my hand. "Welcome to Belle Isle. It's not Cedar Point, but I promise, you'll like it."

No more than two minutes walking north and I could tell the island was really one big park with roads, bridges, flower gardens, man-made lagoons, picnic shelters, fountains, and signs pointing to a petting zoo, canoe rental, bath house, aquarium, riding stable, dance pavilion, casino. I had come to Detroit expecting to find thieves as hard as iron. Like the girl Ruby and I met near the hospital. Like the men at the Rusty Nail with narrow eyes undressing you. On Belle Isle, the mood was playful, expectant, and hopeful with young families, couples

strolling under parasols, musicians practicing scales. And there
was Catfish, like a pickle balanced on my nose, who made me
laugh by doing almost nothing. We walked to the west side of
the island past the boat club and bath house. The beach was
crowded with bodies lying on striped towels. I saw a mother
with two toddlers. She had long chestnut hair like Momma's
and her skin was satiny white. I wanted to ask her something,
just hear her voice and watch her take her boys into the water.

"You hungry again?" Catfish asked.

"Always," I said.

We stopped at a concession stand. Catfish ordered hot dogs
with relish and potato chips, two chocolate shakes. I had never
met a hot dog I liked, but this one, smothered in catsup, mustard, and sauerkraut, was something to hold out for a postcard.
Or maybe I felt a ripple because Catfish tucked a napkin under
the paper tray that held the hot dog. Or maybe my new flutter
was Belle Isle itself set in the middle of the whiskey river like
some kind of jewel clenched in the hand of a drowning man.
What I mean to say is, I felt safe with him at that concession
stand and there was no place else I wanted to be. The Black
woman at the stand made friendly with Catfish.

"What are you good for today?"

"A round of golf," Catfish said.

"Who's your friend, Cat?"

"Norah Bow," I said. "And yours?"

"Destiny," the woman said, smiling fondly at Catfish like he
was forty going north as Daddy used to say, although I never
really knew what he meant by that.

"Hey, Cat," she said, "you know the course is closed today."

"Never stopped me before," he said.

"Take care, you old river."

From a narrow rise, I could see the golf course set between
a yacht club and a stand of hardwoods, a southwest wind flap-
ping the underbelly of leaves. I had never played golf. Didn't
know the first thing about the game, but when I looked at this
course set beside the Detroit River I thought I'd never seen a

more inviting stretch of secluded green. It looked to be an oasis at the fringe of a city given to the crime of revelry. A sign read, *Belle Isle Golf Course Closed for Repairs.*

"What gets broke on a golf course?" I asked him.

"The greens," he said. "They're doctoring the greens, but that won't stop us."

"Why doesn't that put me at ease?"

"Come on," he said, winking me on.

We walked behind a Greens Keeper's shed. Catfish lifted a tarp draped over a barrel and pulled out a set of golf clubs in a snappy two-toned khaki bag.

"Finders keepers," he said.

He pulled out a club from the bag.

"This is a driver," Catfish said. "It's the biggest club in the bag. And that green stretch in front of us is called a fairway."

And that was how my first and only golf lesson started. Catfish showed me how to tee up the ball, how to stand about two feet from the ball and bend my knees, how to make a full hip turn with my swing. At the first hole, he teed up, took a breath, exhaled, bent his knees, lifted the driver past his shoulder and swung it through to the ball in one loose but controlled motion. The golf ball flew high and straight down the fairway and for a moment I lost sight of it, and then the ball dropped to the grass, rolled forward. There was no one else around. It seemed as if the rest of the world had retreated to some raw and stormy place and we were left behind in a pocket where nothing could touch us. A sweet, grassy smell hung in the air.

"Your turn," he said.

I teed up the ball. Took my stance. Bent my knees and swung. The ball dribbled off the tee. Catfish smiled some.

"You're all tied up in knots," he coaxed. "Take a deep breath. Don't try to bomb away at the ball. Just make one complete motion. Like you're dancing alone and no one can see how happy you are."

I tried again. Same result. Same clumsy dancer.

"Don't look," I told him.

He turned his back to me and said, "You can do anything, Norah Bow."

I moved a little closer to the tee, thinking maybe I was reaching for the ball. I pictured Catfish and I at the dance pavilion. I let the tension go in my elbows and shoulders and the ball launched itself off the ground, higher than the trees and down the middle of the fairway.

"You're a natural." Catfish beamed.

We played all nine holes, unfazed by the sign that said the course was closed. As if clocks had not yet been invented. As if there was no trouble behind or ahead of either one of us. All the while, I was uncertain whether we were tramps or kings, but for those few hours the whiskey river and its underworld my father had been dragged into was held at bay. I couldn't remember feeling the nameless dread of my past decisions. I didn't think once about Daddy. I loved playing, but I loved being there with Catfish more. He made me laugh from my belly. If he flubbed a putt, he'd turn his putter into Chaplin's defiant cane, sometimes spinning his body around it or pointing it toward a ball as if to call the ball back to the cup. Catfish was a natural ham. He didn't take the game seriously and he didn't bother to keep score, but someone else did. We saw three men running toward us waving rakes and shovels. Why, I wondered, did ominous men always travel in threes? I wasn't about to stick around and find out.

"Guess our game is over," Catfish said.

"Sure was fun," I said, searching his face for what to do next.

"Look," Catfish said, watching the three men draw closer. "I'll head toward the woods. You make your way back to my boat. If I'm not there in an hour, take the ferry from the south end, back to Windsor."

He read my puzzled look.

"I'm the one they want. Not you."

"You sure?"

"I'll find you there."

The three men were only a hundred yards away.

"Get going," he said.

I ran south while Catfish ran east toward the woods. The men paused to consider our splitting up, then they forgot about me and ran after Catfish. He was slowed down by the bag of clubs over his shoulder, but still he looked fast enough to give them the dodge. Just before I lost sight of him, he waved and my heart leapt in my throat. I found his boat with no problem. I wanted to take a nap on the bank, but I didn't want to risk having someone else stumble upon me. I waited for over an hour, but Catfish was a no show. I walked slowly to the ferry dock hoping he would pop up and light my path, but he never came. I bought my ferry ticket back to Windsor half wondering if I had only dreamt our time together or if it really happened. Even while I stood on the upper deck in my movie-star glasses, I thought maybe I'd see Catfish following the ferry back to Windsor, but there was no sign of his boat to unfreeze the moment of my going on alone. I stood at the rail of the *Belle Isle Queen* watching the wake, wanting to be like Ruby in search of a dress and a party at a roadhouse bar, and not a fourteen-year-old girl looking for her daddy who might be hidden, dead, or undiscoverable by his own lights.

No, that's not even close to the whole story about that day. I wanted to be with Catfish who didn't care whether I wore sunglasses or not. Didn't care if I knew a driver from an iron or if I even had a father. Didn't care if I had a shape that favored a dress. How many years since the tilted mischief of his smile on that golf course? Eighty or is it more? After so much time, aren't we entitled to invent what we said and did and even imagine a different outcome? So much in us tangles and collapses and even a bright, crisp memory like this one seems not to be mine alone, but to belong to the place itself set down in a river with fierce current. This memory has waited all this time to return out of hiding and now when I can hardly carry a teacup, some unsorted awakening takes hold of me like a virus or a stray enzyme in the blood, not yet finished with me, not yet started, and the long night of my sleeping is coming on fast.

19

I walked off the ferry thinking it was best that Catfish wasn't there. He made me want to play and laugh and forget what I had already seen and done and what more I had to do. I had no business asking him to take risks on my behalf with the hope that getting away would be as easy as outrunning three men with rakes. Whatever I had to do there in Windsor, I had to do alone. I walked two buildings down, entered the parking lot of the Mexican Export Company and saw three Reo Speeds. One was parked so its windshield faced the river, one was backed up to a dock, and another waited to unload. There was a man in a tweed cap fielding a line for a boat. The river chopped hard against the piling. The waves were confused as if by the light cut with gray clouds. Nothing about this dock said to me, *So glad you could stop by.*

I took off my sunglasses, spun around to look behind me, then slipped inside a white dockside building. I walked down a hallway patched with squares of angled window light. I found an office on my right with the air squeezed out of it. The walls were bare. The few shelves held leather-bound ledger books. On a desk, I saw Mexican Export Custom Forms marked Peru, Argentina, Trinidad, Cuba. I turned on the desk light and the room took on the tinge of green glass shade. I walked around the desk to open a metal file cabinet. I tried the drawer handle, but it was locked. Daddy kept his keys close to the places he kept locked. I felt underneath the desk, on the carpet corner, and found the key in a magnet box on the backside of the cabinet. I didn't come this far not to snoop. I let out my air, then quickly held it again.

I looked through a window and saw the first Reo Speed pull away. The second car, waiting to unload, backed up. I turned back to the cabinet, turned the key, and started flipping through marked folders. I saw the names of Hiram agents, engine part suppliers, dock workers, pile drivers, boat builders, carpenters, Customs agents, gas and oil purveyors, handy men but what I wanted was the names of mechanics who worked for the Mexican Export Company. Sweat trickled off my face and wet the back of my hands. I told my hands to work faster. My throat turned to sandpaper. I didn't dare try to swallow. I saw a file marked *Bermuda Exporters* and read a letter from a Jimmy Longman to a Cecil Thomas talking about raising the price of beer by a dollar a case. I saw files on setting prices, guaranteed delivery schedules, the leveraging of credit, billing cycles, damage and inventory adjustments, taxes, debt collection. At the end of Longman's letter: *all business on the Detroit side will be cash-and-carry. Nobody gets a free ride.*

Another file: *10 Commandments of the Mexican Export Company.*

1. Thou shalt not use wood alcohol to cut good whiskey.

2. Thou shalt mind thine own damn business.

3. Thou shalt not talk to the police about anything.

4. Thou shalt not talk to newspaper reporters.

5. Thou shalt know nothing about river crimes.

6. Thou shalt not steal from other rumrunners.

7. Thou shalt not welch on debts.

8. Thou shalt not use counterfeit cash to pay for whiskey or beer.

9. Thou shalt not undercut another rumrunner.

10. Thou shalt not work the river on one's own time.

Whoever violates these 10 rules will be sent to the <u>coroner</u>.

The underlining of the word coroner made my lip quiver like maybe the investigator of violent deaths had already laid me out on a table for examination. I saw photos of boats with notation of their loaded and unloaded estimated speed. I flipped through a file marked *Women.* Inside, photos of naked women with phone numbers on the back. Then, tucked inside that folder, between a photo of a woman lying in a four-poster bed with her legs wrapped around a man and a photo of another woman bent over a horsehair loveseat, I found another file with the words *Engine Repair* scribbled on top. My fingers flew through this file, but mostly I saw only the names of shops: *Jake's Marine Engines, The Hull Truth, River Fuel, C & S Marine, Detroit Engines, Charlie Hood.* Then, I found a piece of paper labeled *Mechanics* at the top and below, a short list of names: Clarence More, Johnny Carpenter, Charlie Benoit, Stanley LaSalle, Vital Bow. I read the last name about ten times, then I told myself I had not seen it.

There was no mistaking that name, nor the memory that grabbed me right then out of nowhere of Daddy cornering Aunt Cora on our porch. I had just come from the can and neither one of them knew I was listening in. It was dark enough to cloak me where the porch doglegged. I heard him boasting to her how his first name meant *indispensable to the continuance of life* and his last name meant *a knot tied with two lovely loops.* Prancing like a pony, Daddy thumbed his belt and put a slight hitch in his pants so she couldn't overlook his most vital sign, then he backed her against the wall and kissed her hard on the mouth. I froze there, repulsed and drawn forward when she raised one leg and wrapped it around his thighs. "Is a bow anything like this?" Aunt Cora cooed. They kissed for some time, neither one able to escape the other's grasp until I went back to the outdoor head and slammed the door. When I returned to the porch, they were gone, and I wondered if I had only imagined their locked legs or had I really seen them twined there, not twenty feet from Momma's kitchen. Reading his name again, I wanted to tear out of me the sounds, colors, and smells of Rye Beach.

I thumbed the folder faster looking for which docks these mechanics favored. I saw the bookkeeper's file with a cartoon clipped to the outside. The picture showed a bottle of whiskey with a bent neck kissing a man with glasses holding a pencil. The caption read: *If I didn't love my bookkeeper so much, I'd have to drown him.* I found nothing on *Martina,* the speedboat that Lonesome Bill spoke of, in connection with Daddy. But I did see something in the file that caught my breath. It was a photograph of Vital Bow stuck inside a file and he had his arm around a woman, and that woman was Ruby. I clenched the photo and felt my blood trickle scarlet up my neck. My eyes burned. At first I thought the floor was shaking, but it was only me. Like I'd been running hard, but I was standing still. I told myself there had to be some good explanation. And there were only two people who could give me that. I grabbed the photo out of the file. I had it half way stuck in my pocket as a man's voice boomed.

"Who the hell are you?"

I turned around to see a man in a droopy, tent-like overcoat. Like other men I'd seen in Detroit, his gut hung over his belt so far it looked like he was hauling stone. He had a whiskered double-chin, dark circles below his eyes, tobacco-stained teeth, just enough hair on top not to be a snooker ball. His skin mottled orange and red like the scales of fish gone belly up. Honestly, I thought he was so fat and slow, I could dart past him, but then as if reading the flex in my legs, he pulled out a revolver.

Swagbelly said: "I used to stand on the dock every morning and throw out a soup can. At first, I just made a lot of holes in the water. After a hundred mornings, I started to get good with this long-barreled .38."

"You don't scare me," I lied.

"Give me time."

His words jabbed like hot wire.

"Looking for my daddy," I said.

Swagbelly jammed his two fingers into his mouth and let out a piercing whistle. Two men from outside came running.

"Look what I found, boys. Says she's looking for Daddy. Ever hear that one before?"

I recognized one of the men who'd been tending a dock line. He too wore a long coat with a nightstick dangling from his belt like he was an off-duty cop making an extra buck.

"Tell us what you're looking for and maybe we can help you find it," the man said with a smirk and a dare.

"I told you, looking for my father. His name is Vital Bow."

Swagbelly set his gun down on the desk, tipped his hat back, and rubbed his eyes. Then, he pressed his palms flat against his eyes like he was hoping to shut out what little light held me in his office.

"Who are you?"

"I'm Norah Bow. I'm not trying to steal anything."

"That paper in your pocket?"

"I forgot to put it back."

"Shit, girl. That's not real smart."

Sweat found the back of my neck. My gut tightened. Everything in me breaking and burning. I looked at the other two and wondered what Ruby would do if she were there. They looked bored like they couldn't read the profit in conversation. They too were on the heavy side and short, and looked none too nimble in a tight space cast with poor light.

"This photo means nothing to me," I said to Swagbelly, flicking the picture of Ruby and my father on his desk.

"Don't believe you," the big man snorted before he sat down and put his feet on his desk and lit a cigarette.

"You don't look like you believe much of anything."

"Smart mouth on you."

My arms prickled like they'd been dipped in hot sauce.

"Just tell me where I can find Vital Bow and I'll be on my way."

"If I tell you, then my boys here will take you on a one-way ride. If I don't tell you, I might let you go. Then again, I might not. In this business every decision you make gives rise to the need of another decision and that's what troubles me. I don't like surprises because they require an unwanted decision and that action prompts the threat of a miscalculation. Can you see how your turning up here has made me feel agitated? Like maybe I should have seen someone like you coming from a long way off. A speck of something that blinds me to some bigger trouble that will require me to make another decision I don't want to make."

"I'm afraid I don't follow all the turns of your thinking."

"Then, let me speak plainly."

"Please, sir."

"I'm a hammer and you're a fucking nail."

No matter the ten commandments these men swore by, I figured Swagbelly was bluffing. My mind threw sparks in all directions, looking for some crack to slip through. I couldn't hurt him. Swagbelly ran an export business. I didn't run anything and I didn't know anybody. Nobody in Windsor or Detroit would believe anything I might say about him. I didn't even know Swagbelly's real name.

"I'll take my chances with knowing my father's whereabouts," I said through parched lips.

"You got moxie, girl, but you've got mush for brains for coming in here."

"My father worked on a boat called *Martina.*"

Swagbelly picked up the photo, glanced at it, threw it down on the floor.

"Don't know anything about the *Martina.*"

"Vital Bow. What do you know about my father?"

Swagbelly scratched his left ear, then his nose. Like he was trying to remember something through the skid of a fingernail.

"Last I heard, Vital Bow was on Middle Island. He services the fancy speedboats from Detroit, Cleveland, Toledo, all over."

"Middle Island? There's nothing there."

"Nothing but a high-class casino and plenty of girls and booze."

"I sailed right by him?"

"The photo you lifted should tell you he's feeling no pain."

"Let me walk out of here," I said, fiercely. "I've done you no harm."

"You cut yourself a low card."

"I'm meeting somebody tonight. If I'm not there, they'll know I'm missing. They will come looking for me and for you."

"Somebody's always looking for me," Swagbelly said, his eyes shrunk to pinpricks.

"Everybody knows what business you're in. It's not like there's some big secret. There's no way I can hurt you."

"Can't take any chances," Swagbelly said, "on what you saw or didn't see. Nothing personal. I'm a father myself. And God knows, I like girls, young ones at that. Just taking care of business. We live and die by certain rules on the river."

"My name is Norah Bow," I announced again as if the men in the room should know who they planned to kill. The quaver in me was like a branch starting to break way up the trunk.

"Sweet name," Swagbelly said.

He nodded to one of the men who sidled in my direction. The third man stood in the corner digging at the fur of his front teeth with a toothpick.

"I'm fourteen years old," I said to Swagbelly. "I live in Rye Beach. My dog's name is Bob. I came here in a sailboat I built with my father."

Swagbelly's eyes rolled back in his head, two icebergs adrift in black current. The one man came at me fast, his body crouched and ready to tackle.

I swung with my arms and kicked at empty air. The man grabbed me by the legs while Swagbelly dug his thumb into my throat and lifted me off the floor. With both hands, Swagbelly squeezed harder until the burn of air in my throat gagged me. I felt my eyes bulging and I fought to breathe through my nose, the tears flooding my eyes. I squirmed and swung my elbow and caught Swagbelly in the cheek and he lost his grip long enough for me to fall backward. I pushed away from him like a crab scuttling the floor. He backed away from me, pulled on the lapels of his overcoat, straightened himself, and ran his hands through the few knotted strands of hair on his head. He looked away from me quivering on the floor. Like maybe strangling me was beneath his station and he didn't exactly know what had come over him.

"Tie her up, boys," Swagbelly said. "Get her ready for deposit."

I curled up, rasping shallow air, but I knew I had something left. I kicked at the man who held me down by my arms. When he eased his grip, I leapt up and kicked a desk chair on rollers toward Swagbelly. It caught him in the shin and he doubled over and I felt some fire returning until the third man whacked me in the head with his nightstick. The last thing I remembered was this: I fell a long way and saw again all the water I had crossed and I even got one glimpse of Middle Island, damn near in my own backyard, where Daddy was once photographed with a woman named Ruby Francoeur who had been draped around his shoulders.

20

Something sharp dragged across the roof of my mouth. I swished my tongue until I found a tooth sheared off. The blood was warm and sticky and tasted like fork. The side of my head throbbed and it was near impossible to swallow after Swagbelly had gripped my throat and thrashed me in the air.

I found myself in a warehouse packed floor to ceiling with whiskey crates stamped with the Mexican Export Company label. I was snug-tied at the ankles and behind my back and lashed to a chair. Swagbelly said something about a deposit which I didn't read as dropping me off at a bank. The thought of drowning with my feet and hands tied made me work up a sweat so I squirmed good and hard, and dug my nails into the rope. I inched backward in the chair looking for something to rub my tied wrists against. I'd seen Keaton and Chaplin free themselves this way, why not me?

I saw a whiskey crate with a splintered edge. I had one thought only: If whiskey brought me there, maybe whiskey could get me out. I pressed up against the crate and wiggled my wrists up and down against the jagged edge. My hands tired quickly and I stopped, started again, stopped, no way of telling whether I was cutting a strand or just heating up rope. I kept at it. I heard voices. The same men.

"Please, let me go," I said as forcefully as I could muster.

"Shut up," one man said. The man who hit me with a nightstick had a baby face and a soft rubbery chin that made him look young old at the same time. The second man wore thick brown glasses and combed his shag to the left to cover a receding hairline.

"There will be hell to pay," I added.

"Heard that one before."

"What have I done to you?"

"You broke into our office."

"Just looking for my father. Give me a chance."

"What kind of chance?"

"Take anything you've got."

"How old did you say you are?"

"Fourteen."

The two men looked at each other and shook their heads at the same time like they had rehearsed it.

"Maybe we could take her for a joy ride before we make a deposit," Nightstick said.

"You know the boss doesn't like our detours."

Nightstick held a large burlap bag. Hairline cut the ties at my hands and feet.

"Get in there," Nightstick said.

"What?"

"You said you wanted a chance, get into the bag," Nightstick said. "If you know how to swim, you might make it out, might not."

"That's my chance?" I said.

"Better than nothing," Nightstick said.

Not wanting to risk another conk, I shimmied into the bag, relieved for one moment to have my hands and feet free. What I didn't bargain on was having Nightstick cinch the top and knot it off.

"Hey, I thought you said—"

"We have to make it look real for the boss."

The two men carried me out. One grabbed my feet. The other my head. I couldn't see much more than a crosshatched blur of dock lights through the opening. Swagbelly offered his final instruction.

"Throw a little cement in the bag and she won't pop up at all."

Once Swagbelly said this, I fought to catch my breath, my body its own cold river. The two men swung me onto a stack of whiskey crates. I wanted to cry out at the sting of the landing, but instead I bit down on my knuckles, thinking maybe they would give me a chance. The engine started with a growling idle. One man cast off. The other took the wheel. No need between them to talk over something they had done before. I couldn't hear myself think over the rumble of the engine, now running, I figured, at twenty-two hundred RPMs. Not too fast, not too slow. The waves lifted the bow. The speedboat entered a pulse and rhythm I recognized. My heart wanted to stop when the boat idled back down. The men said something. They had to be checking for other boat traffic, scanning all directions, waiting for some moment when they'd let me take my chance in strong current and they could slip away unseen.

"Untie the bag," I shouted.

I repeated it. The two men said nothing, then one taunted, "Sucker born every river minute."

"Please," I said, but their silence told me they had no intention of cutting away the knot, so I might try to swim.

"You said you would—"

One man grabbed my feet. The other my head. They held me above the water like they were getting ready to release a fish.

"Stop. Please. Stop. I didn't do anything."

I sensed some hesitation as they swayed me out over the water. Made me think they had a change of heart but they were only being cautious, and then a cry leapt out of me as the river cold smacked my face. The shock of it was so great it was like some Muskie had risen out of the depths to take a bite out of me. I sucked up as much air as I could, my fingers making no sense of what was happening, the cold clawing at me as I lashed out at the bag's opening, the darkness of that wet chute dragging me to bottom. I cocked one eye through the slit of the bag to where the boat used to be, but the dark of the river sewed up the gash of my descent. There was nothing I could do but tear at the knot above my head until something gave way or the thick river mud settled into me, and I had no more light of my own to shine back into the world. A great gong clanged in my head. I thought at least if I was going to die, I wanted to look at the dark swirl and call it my own and tell the river it was all right if it had to take me. I didn't hold a grudge against the current because I sailed away from my home and I had to take all that was not home and still call it mine and death shall hold no dominion, and the valley was a green pasture after all and my cup runneth over during my time on earth, and then as I was about to burst, the clanging shuddered and stopped, my sinking into a gorge took on the quality of a rising, someone had my hand, I swear it was the hand of God or some river angel that feathered the dark into light and she didn't want me to die just then and so I looked up into the face of Catfish who had severed the knot and was willing me to rise on something other than air because I can't tell how such a rising could happen after I'd sunk so far into the Detroit River not known for releasing its citizens short on air. Weeping may endure for a night, but joy cometh in the morning, and sometimes joy reaches down for you and you can't explain it or even speak to it but you trust this joy because there is a buoyancy that comes with it even though I had slipped into a temporary blindness from the river cold knifing into me.

We broke the surface, his arm wrapped around my chest, so he could side stroke with me to his scooter while I was gasping and flailing and making his job that much harder, but damn if he wasn't a Catfish accustomed to river hardship for he made short work out of my blinkered madness. He tied me to the gunwale before he climbed into the scooter, then he hauled me in and I vomited and then I told him he must really be a Catfish because how could he find me in such a drag of current at the entrance to the soul and he said he'd tell me everything but right then I needed to flop around and be sick because the river had siphoned off the best of me. I was as cold as death but not dead and he was glad to be of service and I tried to tell him through the chatter of teeth that his words were so formal but welcome for such a moment stolen from the river that wanted to claim me.

I did what Catfish said, coughing, sputtering, retching, what little food in me was pitched out and he just looked at me like he'd seen it all before, like he'd seen everything that could happen on this river because he was a bottom fish looking up at the world's stream of mischief that never ends but only keeps circling back for more of us like a shark that has tasted a geyser of blood and thinks to taste more. That look of his, of almost blank wonder that couldn't afford to sit in judgment, was unlike anything any I'd ever known before or since. He lit a cigarette as if leaping in after girls sewn up in burlap bags was all in a night's work, and maybe it was for him, but for me his kicking the long way down was a river gift I never have fully understood. After what might have been an hour of drifting out on the Detroit River in his flat-bottom scooter, he helped me sit up and take stock of a world I'd almost lost.

"You were down in the river for some long-ass time, maybe four or five minutes, maybe longer. Don't know how you stayed alive that long. I thought maybe I was the only one who could pull off a stunt like that."

"Wasn't part of my plan," I whispered.

I dug my hands into my stomach thinking I might be sick again.

"You found out where your father is."

"Something like that."

"He's here in Windsor?"

"He's on a fly-speck island in my own backyard."

"That must have some sting to it."

"A lot," I said, my voice not yet my own. I took as many deep breaths as I could and while I gulped air, I caught the whiff of some river vagrant pan-frying a mess of corn-breaded walleye and onions and my stomach growled. Then, I heaved again.

"What now?" Catfish wanted to know.

"Got a few questions for Ruby at the Blackbird."

Catfish wrinkled his brow like that was a silly question. He yanked on his starter cord and his scooter boat jumped forward.

"How did you find me?"

"How did I ever lose you?"

His reply was just about the sweetest thing I'd ever heard anyone say to me.

"How?"

"Gave the man at the ferry office a fiver and he told me he saw you go over to the Mexican Export Company. I figured there was a better than even chance you'd get jammed up, so I waited till I saw a boat leave. If they had you, I knew they wouldn't be traveling fast to draw attention and I would be able to keep up. Even without their running lights on, I knew where they were by the drone of their engines. They never saw me holding back. When they heaved a bag into the water, I thought something was all wrong."

"Everything slowed down when I was in the river."

"Lucky they dropped you in shallow water. Another hundred yards out and I never would have caught you in time."

"I owe you."

"Maybe so," he said, both acknowledging my gratitude and undercutting it with his Catfish brand of modesty.

"It's a miracle you were there," I said, looking at the stars and thankful it was dark enough to see them doing what they could to lift me back up into the human element.

"No one in the great beyond will ever mistake me for an angel."

"You were tonight."

"Who did this to you?"

"Swagbelly."

"Who?"

"That was my name for the man at the Mexican Export Company. He tried to strangle me first."

"Before he dumped you in the river?"

"He took pleasure from it all."

Catfish studied my neck.

"Looks like you're sporting a purple scarf."

I touched my own throat and felt the swollen muscles there.

"Who else was there?"

"Two other men. They put me in a sack and dumped me in the river."

"Same thing happened to another friend," Catfish said. "The fat man you described said my friend made a delivery on his own. He was a mosquito like me in a scooter. A week later he washed up on the beach south of Fighting Island. His neck looked like yours and his head was stove in like they'd beat him with a claw hammer."

"Damn, that's awful, Catfish."

Catfish looked out at his home, the current quick as the slash of a knife and as pretty as the moon in a mirror.

"I like you," he said, flicking his cigarette in the drink. "You're different from other girls. Hell, you might be different from anyone I've ever met." I liked the way he said this because that was exactly how I wanted to be, different from other girls.

If not for needing answers from Ruby, I might have said to Catfish, I've had enough of the whiskey river, but we flew back to Windsor, the lights of the floating docks twinkling the river bank, saying the day had nothing on the night. The export business was open twenty-four hours, every day of the week, the dockworkers like unseen ants loading longneck bottles into tight bulkheads. No matter the hour, business on the whiskey river was brisk, but now I had business that was even more urgent.

"Ever get scared?" I asked. Inside the shrill whine of the engine, it seemed safe enough to ask just about anything of a boy I could hardly see, but who saw me when I needed him most.

"I've learned how to get some miles out of being scared."

"Miles?"

"You sure ask a lot of questions," Catfish said from his stern perch.

"I want to know you better."

"Sure about that?"

I paused, then I heard again Daddy's voice describing the final tuning of a piston for how certain he was that he and I were connected by the same demon switch.

"Top dead center," I said to Catfish.

He nodded again, smiled to one side of his mouth like he too had been snagged off the river bottom by a trolling hook.

"Talking to myself gets me through most everything."

"I do a lot of that and I talk with my dog," I said, watching the shoreline draw closer and thinking about what I was going to say to Ruby when I found her. I figured if Daddy had been on Middle Island all that time, maybe she had been there too and not in Toledo like she said when I pulled her off her dinghy. Maybe she had known all along he was there. Maybe she used me to get back to Windsor. Maybe everything about my going after Daddy had been just a thread torn off her party dress. The only thing that was not a maybe was Catfish. If I knew anything right then, it was this: Catfish was born with the same demon switch as me. How else could I explain how he fished me out of the river when I was nothing but a stone?

"Will you come with me?" I asked Catfish.

"What do you mean?"

"Don't want to go on alone."

Catfish looked at me with some fidget like I was aiming to set a hook in his jaw and he didn't know whether to spit it out or start running out the line. He cocked his head, fiddled his broad-rimmed hat, cracked his knuckles. Even in the best river sparkle, he was not exactly the most handsome boy I'd ever seen, but he had green eyes, a slow, blooming grin, a little jagged everything working in his favor and that scooter boat that seemed part of his ligature.

"Sure, I suppose, I mean, what the hell else have I got to do?"

Catfish went mud-flat quiet while he scouted out a marshy inlet where he could hide his flat-bottom boat. I wanted to ask him more questions about his river life, how he fought off loneliness, the threat of something going wrong, but his pursed mouth told me he was not used to spending this much time with anyone. He ran at trolling speed looking for a sliver in the marsh weed. He stood up to crane his neck and shook his head. The boat was like a watery limb of his own body, the bow nudging quietly along the edge of cattails, lily pads, shoreline muck, as he found what he was looking for. We motored through a cattail gleam no bigger than a doorjamb. Catfish cut the Evinrude and we slipped in sleek and easy. He handed me a paddle for the bow. He took the stern. We worked well together, the rhythm of our strokes easily matched along with our breathing. Dip, pull, glide, the motion easing into me. We ran the boat up into gravel shallows. The night around us unlit by the city. No Reo Speeds there waiting shipment, just the squeaking of bats and one long croak of a great blue heron stirred from its pocket. I stepped out and he followed, taking a line from me so he could tie off the scooter boat to a tree.

"Your boat have a name?"

"*Sweet Ride,*" he said. "She's all I own. With the money I got today, I'm planning on buying a new engine, keeping this one as back-up."

What happened next surprised me, but not Catfish. He was more comfortable than not in most every circumstance as long as he was near his river. Maybe from exhaustion or fright or just because I have clunky feet, I stumbled on the bank and sprawled forward like someone conked me from behind, again. Catfish caught me like I'd seen in the movies and pulled me up and I didn't hesitate to throw my arms around his lanky frame which felt as hard and smooth as stone. I kissed him on the mouth. He didn't pull back. I didn't let go. Just like that I tasted his mouth and I liked everything about it. I did it again and I didn't want to stop. I came up for air for the second time that night and said, "Your life here on the river is how I feel."

"What are you saying?"

"I'm tired of chasing a man who doesn't want to come home. Nearly got myself killed just for trying. I want to stay here with you."

"What?"

"Back in Detroit after we finished unloading the jute bags

you said maybe I should come work with you and I'm propos-
ing we do exactly that."

"Did I say all that?"

"I know more than you think. I've done things."

In the wet, marshy dark, I could see Catfish drawing his
right hand over his mouth like he couldn't swallow or maybe he
didn't want a single word to escape or he was guarding against
another kiss. He leaned back against the cottonwood that held
his *Sweet Ride* as if he needed help standing up. As I remember
it, there was even a catch in his voice like a click from a fishing
reel. I leaned toward him to hear his words and I could taste
again his mouth.

"Never heard a girl say she wants to work the river."

"Figured as much," I said, some strength returning to my
voice.

"Always worked alone."

"I'm not saying I need anything from you."

"What more are you...not saying?"

Catfish pulled back into the dark like the bottom feeder of
his namesake seeking a soft shoulder of mud.

"You and me, we should be...together."

"Together?"

"You know power boats. I know sail. We can teach each
other."

"All that stuff about Cedar Point?"

"Wanted you to think I was worth taking a risk."

"I knew you were lying. Liked you anyway. You were like
another kind of fish from an ocean I've never been to." When
Catfish said all that, he could have been reciting *Romeo and Juliet*
from a balcony for how it sounded to me. Another kind of fish
from an ocean he'd never been to. I have never forgotten the
furious pause of his words and how they held me steady before
the unholy reckoning of the next unraveling.

"Never had a girl," Catfish said, his voice a cross between a
croak and whisper.

"Me neither," I said. "I mean, I've never been with a boy, but now's as good a time as any to find out what the fuss is all about."

"Okay," Catfish said. "Guess it won't hurt to see how it goes."

"Kiss me," I said. "Like you want me on your river." He pushed himself off the tree and leaned into me and I have to say he was a quick learner because he gently put one hand behind my head like he was cradling a baby and he kissed me on the mouth with a tender forcefulness that made me tremble hot, then cold, then hot again. I didn't want the kiss to stop even if the kiss was from a Catfish, and some ancient shiver flared in us and our legs locked and his hands moved downward from my head to the scoop of my spine. My hands crawled underneath his shirt and the fumble of us nudged closer to fire when he heard the backfire of a car that could have been the distant plink of gun shots, and he pulled his lips away from mine and said, *What about Ruby?* My throat choked up when I heard her name. Our river kiss evaporated so fast, I couldn't even remember what brought it on, and the only piece that was left of that rushed, grabbing urgency was a sudden hollow in my gut that felt like a long way down.

"What time is it?" I asked Catfish, who looked like he'd been parked somewhere between lost, hurt, and eager for more.

"Do I look like someone who wears a watch?"

"Let's go find the Blackbird," I said. "I doubt she'll be there, but—"

"Why do you say that?"

"Ruby's a moving target. Someone's always after her and now that someone is me." I took Catfish by the hand and started walking toward the city hum.

"I thought you two were—"

"Close? Is that what you thought?"

"Ruby's not close to anyone except the next man."

"That's got some bite," Catfish said.

"Any man who gets close gets sucked into her web. He may

watch her wiggle out of a dress and think he's died and gone to heaven, but really he's just up and died with his pants down."

"What the hell are you talking about?"

"It's a long story, but she's in the middle of the whole thing. This morning, she told me she needed to find a new dress, but now I know why she left me this morning. She didn't want me to find out anything about her."

"You're just thinking the worse."

"You haven't seen her in action."

"In action?"

"Lonesome Bill got lost in her eyes. He went crazy looking at her back in Detroit where we met you. Hell, I've gone dreamy looking at her. She's not like other women."

"I thought you liked…different?"

"Don't tell me what I like," I said, mad at myself that I had not suspected that Ruby was tangled up in Daddy's disappearance.

"Let me give you something," Catfish said, trying to vent my steam.

"What?"

He put into my hand a pearl-handled pocket knife.

"What's this?"

"The knife I used to cut open that burlap bag those men stuffed you in. You might need it tonight."

That knife belonging once to Catfish, the one he used to cut me loose from the river depths, I still have it somewhere. Most little things you lose over time. Too many boxes. Too many changes of address. One street name crossed out and another one added. The nature of all things, to find us, then lose us, then return again from the drawer of lost causes. Safe to say, memory is more valuable to me than a hammer, wrench, or screwdriver. On some bare-assed long night when there is no exorcism or psalm I can summon up, and all I can do is wander in a closet, memory helps me locate a time and a place no one else on

Earth remembers. Memory, my anchor to windward. Memory, the invention of things forgotten. Memory, the old stone in the shoe. No matter the violence that comes to the whiskey river, memory is with me a little longer. Memory, all that holds me to the earth and takes me by surprise and prompts me to make a decision that I never wanted to make. Here we go into the hour of the long-ago knife.

21

Laughter thrown from a doorway, the squeal of trucks, a sidewalk harmonica, the bark of a dog, the cry of a woman backed up against a car. We walked up to a road with the city notes clicking like scissors. Catfish and I didn't say anything for the longest time. He reached out for my hand. I pulled it back. A soft touch wasn't going to help me find the hard edge I needed, but I did touch the pearl-handled knife and took comfort knowing where it had been, what it could do. No matter the poise of the blade, I felt like such a patsy for not knowing Ruby had no intention of helping me find Daddy. The photo I found at the Mexican Export Company told me this much: *Ruby knew more about my father than I did.* How else to explain her cozy smile in the photo? Her not wanting us to stop at Pelee just three miles north of Middle Island? Her prickly answers when I asked her anything about her past?

I wanted to kick and thrash about, the anger in me caught in a froth that had nowhere to go. When the silence banged more noise in my head than what I heard on the river road, I reached out for his hand and he took mine. His big hand felt strong. All that hauling, trapping, diving, cutting things loose, right there for my touch. Everyone knew cats had nine lives, but I wondered then, with our hands wrapped together, if the same number applied to catfish.

I stopped on the road with cars whizzing by. I heard words from a car radio spinning backward as if caught on the needle of a record player: *If ever you want me, you can have me the way I am.* I saw again the streetwalker slide into the back seat of a black-finned car, how everything was for sale between Windsor and Detroit, how deception was threaded into smiles, songs, cars, how the line between crime and comfort was no wider than the lip of a bottle. And I knew with certainty that just as Catfish had to use the knife to free me from the river, I would have to use the knife to get Daddy back home. As we walked, I tried to explain to him how many things had gone wrong. I told him how I found Ruby, about Zane, about the three men who died on Pelee. He offered no verdict over the clash and flap of my story. Maybe he thought I was keen on embellishment. Maybe he already knew so much of his own rumble, there was nothing I could say to scare him off. Or maybe he thought it was time to pop the champagne because he would never have to dress down any of his own troubles if he spoke of them to me. I talked fast of these things, but what I didn't tell Catfish was about the slow river of sadness that held me just then and wouldn't shake me loose. With each step closer to the Blackbird, I knew I would not be staying on the whiskey river with him. I had to get back home and make my own deposit.

"I get pieces of what happened to Daddy, then I lose them. Ruby's the only one who has the whole story."

"Then she needs to clear things up so we can be on our way."

When Catfish said this, I heard his words like they were part of a song, but not the one trailing from the car radio, but a song he chose for me. *So we can be on our way.* "Where's the Blackbird?"

"Next bend," he said. "Out on the point."

"I'm ready."

"If Ruby's not there?"

"Can't think that far ahead," I said, already sick of feeling trapped inside my own stewed brain playing back the last month, looking for clues for how Ruby played me like a long running fish.

"And this Lonesome Bill, do we need to worry about him?"

"He's all spit and muscle."

Catfish shrugged. "Leave him to me."

The parking lot at the Blackbird was jammed with Studebakers, Buicks, Hudson Super Sixes, Chandlers, Reo Speeds, even a Maxwell like Daddy used to polish. Catfish pointed out the spotter's shack in the parking lot. If the police dropped in, he said, the spotter would smack a buzzer alerting the bartenders inside to flush the sauce. Catfish said all of Canada had repealed a ban on booze except for Ontario. All the watchful eyes were for show. Still, it was good to know the score, he said. That someone might blow a whistle and come running. The authorities had to make a bust look real, but it seldom meant jail time for anyone. On the whiskey river, there was too much money in play to stop the speed of bottles.

The Blackbird was nothing fancy from the outside, just a big square white clapboard with dozens of windows facing east and a window to catch the sweep of the Detroit River pouring south into Erie. Men and women mingled on the wide verandah and leaned against the white picket rail to watch river traffic. One man sneered, his eyes rolling over when he saw how I was dressed in cut-off jean shorts and a denim shirt. Peacock proud with black hair slicked back, he wore suspenders and spats and he smelled like a vase of lilies set out in the sun too long. His female companion wore a black-beaded chiffon dress and a bored smile. She too looked unhappy that Catfish and I were there among the lovelies. I turned away from their eyeballs to read the sign over the entrance: *Fried Chicken, Perch, Frog Legs & Sturgeon Dinners. All you can eat for fifty cents.* Catfish saw my tongue wetting my lips.

"You like frog legs?"

"Never had any."

"The Blackbird has got the best legs on the whole river."

Suddenly, hunger grabbed hold and I got greedy thinking about big, steaming plates of food soaked in butter, lemon, cornmeal. "We'll get some of those legs. Maybe some perch and sturgeon while we're at it. Fries and slaw wouldn't be all bad."

"After your plunge, some legs might just be the thing," Catfish said.

We walked through an arched doorway to find a pair of bouncers in floppy tweed caps posted at a second interior door looking over every customer to see if they looked fit to dice and drink. Catfish stepped up without delay, safe in the knowledge of how things worked in such roadhouses.

"Here about kitchen work."   '

"Around back. Ask for Burt. Maybe he's got something."

We left the main entrance and walked around to the side. I saw men stationed at every other window—small eyes under broad rims. Catfish fiddled with a storage door off the kitchen and sprung it open with another knife he owned. Nothing rattled loose and fell when we broke in. Catfish went fluid through the door, struck a blue tip he pulled from behind his ear, and held the match steady until we saw a shelf with napkins, placemats, towels, aprons.

"Put this apron on," he said like he had done this before.

We entered the roadhouse wearing aprons and grabbed a wooden tub for busing dishes before we entered the main dining room where a few couples sat over large plates of steaming food.

"Where's everybody?"

Catfish pointed to the ceiling. The sound of happy feet thumped the floor like so many thrown dice. I glanced at one man's watch while he flaked off a section of perch filet with his fork. It was nearly eleven.

"Brother, that looks good," I whispered to Catfish.

"Eat on the way out."

We found the stairs, hugged the rail as one tipsy couple glided down, the woman spilling out of her dress. The man pinched her bottom on the stairwell. The woman squealed in protest. Any idiot could tell she was faking disapproval. Seemed exactly like Ruby's kind of place. Cut with slim odds, tight dresses, the thrill of money, the pinch of skin. I wanted to reach out for Catfish, but we both knew that gesture wouldn't buy us any friends, so we pulled apart, worked the margins of a large room, each to their own. The women nursed tall glasses of something. The men had beer mugs and shot glasses. Nearly everyone smoked. Made it hard to see. The room throbbed with itch and thirst. Everywhere I looked I saw someone grabbing, gloating, mouths gaped with laughter, and glasses clinked and gulped. The faces blurred into creeping fog, some distorted with lipstick, others drawn with fatigue, reproach, old-school flirt, tease and slap. I slipped through dice games, card games, roulette and stacked chips, worn smiles and eyes, men waving money clips like miniature fans, and women stealing glances at the gains and losses. All of it knit together with kisses along the neck and hands seeking a backside.

I saw Ruby from the back. There was no hiding all the curves she carried beneath her flaming hair. She had magically traded her tangles for a distinctive red helmet with bangs and a fringe at the ear. She wore honey-beige stockings with black seams and black-strapped Mary Janes with two-inch heels. In the crowded room, with the benefit of many people blocking her line of sight, I circled through the smoke to make sure. The straight hair threw me off and made me wonder if she'd picked up a wig when she slinked into a new dress. At her neck, a string of fake black pearls and an overblouse of kerchief linen with a long jabot. I'd never seen a woman look more cool in the midst of so much heat. I almost wanted to laugh at the staging of this new look. Ruby was somebody. Ruby was nobody. She was just passing through and she had never left. Here and gone, a tickle feather with oxblood lipstick. Lonesome Bill stood beside her, a man who had been wounded by that feather and had no more strength to lift it. He wobbled against a stand-up round table like he'd already knocked down a fifth. He looked old and harried compared to the light-footed, clear-eyed gamblers and their slim-waisted companions. His eyes were glass rivets pinned on Ruby's breasts.

Ravishing was the word Daddy used on more than one occasion to describe Aunt Cora. I hunted that word down in Webster because the way Daddy said it to Cora, the word sounded like something you did rather than what you are. Cora only smiled demurely and said, *Oh, thank you, Vital Bow. How sweet of you to notice my new dress.* While I watched Lonesome Bill tip his head to rattle ice cubes against his teeth, I wondered if I could make her talk. When Lonesome Bill left to find the Men's, I walked up behind her ravishing.

"Nice outfit," I said. "Did you think to leave anything to the imagination?"

"What's the point of wearing a dress unless it dares a man to take it off?"

"You're coming with me," I said with as much jolly command as I could muster.

"So glad you made it, Norah."

"Now," I said.

"What's your hurry?"

"Middle Island," I said. "That's my hurry."

"What?"

"You know that island with girls, gambling, and booze, not far from where I picked you up. That's what we need to talk about. Now." Ruby scanned the room for Lonesome Bill. She took a swig of gin, then reached for a cigarette, just as I had seen Louise Brooks do in the movies. Like the slow end of a waterfall.

"I can explain," Ruby said.

"Outside," I said.

"What about Bill?"

"Seems like you've already done pretty well by his lonesome, what with your new dress, shoes, stockings, and new bob."

"Don't get mean just because you're mad," Ruby said.

"I fished your hide out of the lake, now at least you owe me an explanation."

Ruby looked again for Bill. I showed her the knife that Catfish used to cut me loose from the pull of the river mud. She studied the room. I didn't need to study anything. With each second of her stalling, I was more determined than ever to get her outside. I stood behind her, nudging with the butt of the knife and in that new conjugation, we shuffled toward the stairs, each of us both nuzzling and sidestepping the crush, the merriment of the room standing in sharp relief to the grimace riding beneath Ruby's grin and the flash of my gritted teeth. I walked faster thinking there would be a tap on my shoulder or a hand wrapped around my wrist or even a whistle blown. Tracking Ruby's every step, I scanned the room for Catfish, but he was nowhere to be seen. Just before we entered the stairs, I saw Lonesome Bill and he saw me. Ruby and I both turned and watched him set two drinks on the table. He looked puzzled, maybe even lost like he'd been cast adrift with no name. She waved him over, her face wearing a wild shine.

"I know you can walk faster than that," I said.

We entered the stairwell while Lonesome pushed through the clot of drunk gamblers. At the bottom of the stairwell, I saw Catfish and gave him a nod. He climbed past us with a tray of empty beer bottles. As Bill entered the top of the stairs, Catfish collided with him and the two of them tumbled.

"What happened back there?" Ruby asked.

"Some drunk fell down the stairs," I replied.

I wanted to say drunk on lust, but I held my tongue. I stayed behind Ruby all the way to the arched entrance. Once in the parking lot, I told her to keep walking, hoping that Catfish wasn't hurt and he'd catch up. I wanted to get clear of the Blackbird, but part of me couldn't wait any longer to fix her with the one question burning a hole in my throat.

"You knew my father was on Middle Island?"

Ruby stopped near the valet shack. "I don't follow."

"You were with him. I saw you two in the photo."

"What photo?"

"Too late to play innocent."

"No one here is innocent, Norah Bow. Not even you."

"You're a liar, maybe a professional one."

Ruby staggered back as if I'd smacked her, her eyes widened, her Blackbird poise and self-assurance flown off.

"I was adrift in a dinghy," she sputtered. "I'd just been raped."

"You told me all that, but you left something out. My father was on Middle Island same as you and somehow you two ended up in the same photo."

"What you see is…not all you get."

"Okay, Ruby, then please turn on the damn lightbulb."

"Not here."

I looked back at the Blackbird and saw Catfish walking. As promised he carried a steaming platter of frog legs on his shoulder like he was a waiter delivering an entrée. I waved and he returned mine and something in that exchange made me think everything would turn out all right because at least Catfish and I had found each other, and his *Sweet Ride* was not far away. Even amid the glint of polished hoods and fenders, I could see the boats' red and green lights winking the river darkness, a skein of unexpected hope skittering through me, starting with the smile on that boy who must have shimmied out of river mud for how easy he was with the outer claw of unseen things.

"You're coming with us," I said to Ruby.

"Where?"

"Out to the whiskey river."

Catfish nodded his approval and I was glad he was there in case she tried to bolt on those long legs of hers. The three of us walked on with Catfish looking back to see if Lonesome Bill followed. He and I wolfed perch filets, frog legs, chicken wings, the juice and flakes of meat clinging to our chins. I used one hand to eat, the other I clamped to the pearl-handled knife.

"I have to get something," Ruby said.

"Get back here," Catfish said, shoving away the tray of food.

Ruby glared at me.

"All I own is…in my bag."

Catfish looked to me for what to do next.

"Give her one minute."

Ruby ran to the edge of the parking lot and fished her duffel out of the lower branches of a lilac. I kept watch on the precious seconds we lost and sure enough Lonesome Bill stumbled out of the Blackbird just as Ruby returned with her bag.

"Now is when we run," said Catfish.

"What's the point?" Ruby said. "Lonesome will never get his car out. He's blocked front and back. He's not going anywhere without his shiny new wheels."

"He's still got legs," I said.

"I'd wager he's too tuckered out to give chase," Ruby said.

I was never much of a runner, but it felt good that night to let my legs own the speed my heart had come to. To feel the air swooshing me with the knowledge I had won a sliver of the puzzle Ruby held back. It had to be well after midnight and you might imagine the river would be slowing down, but Windsor was lit up like a Ferris wheel on the skyline. Roadhouses, restaurants, and export docks flickering with late trade. Like Detroit, Windsor was a cash cow that couldn't afford to bed down, not with so much booze to pack up, float, and so many customers eager to swizzle and stockpile. No end to this city's thirst. No end to milk and honey. No end to the grab, the blur, the run, the wink. I told Catfish I wanted to head downriver as fast as we could. Like a house on fire, I think he said. He said he needed to make a stop.

"Where?" I asked

"One piece of unfinished business."

"Can't it wait?"

"'Fraid not."

"Sweet Jesus, doesn't anyone but me want to get the heck out of here?"

Ruby held her bag tight. Catfish wore a fleck of blood on his lower lip.

I was only moments away from the truth, but something was wrong. I could smell it like a wind shift bearing down from a great distance, but I didn't know how to stop it, so I went into it like every other storm, with my eyes wide open, one hand on the tiller and the other over my heart or was I still gripping the knife?

22

As we entered the marshland where *Sweet Ride* was beached and tied off, I figured Ruby would complain about how her fancy new dress would get wet, but she said nothing, her rouged face drawn down into something dark unreadable, gone. Catfish and I each grabbed a gunwale, nudged the stern out. He climbed in, then Ruby followed with her precious duffel under her arm, while I untied us from the tree. I climbed in last and this unlikely trio broken loose from the Blackbird was now eager to make wing. We threaded cattails and marsh grass until Catfish found a portal and we freed ourselves from the hot grip of Windsor. The wind from the south whipped up the south-flowing current. Catfish gunned the engine and we peeled south and close to the bank to avoid most of the chop. In the dark, I didn't recognize a single landmark until he cut sharply left and I caught a glimpse of the Mexican Export Company.

"What are you doing?"

"Paying my respects," he said.

"What do you mean?"

He slipped into another marshy bank, grabbed a gas can from inside a thwart, and leapt past Ruby and me. I wanted to stop him, go with him, be with him, kiss with him, feel his body pressing mine, root there in the dark with the body of that cottonwood holding us like we belonged there, a trunk of tangled limbs that no one could say where one of us started and the other ended. Old and new braided into one river giant and my tongue in his mouth.

He called out, "Back in ten minutes, tops. Promise."

"Go after him," Ruby urged. "Stop him."

The sweat ran off my nose like rain off a gutter. Ruby was right and she was wrong. I couldn't leave her, not for a second.

She would fly and I would be left with nothing for my troubles. What else found me just then? That old valley of the shadow. The burn of the shiver. My coffin of cloth. The current drawing me downward into the forever after, the air crackling out of me like the ash we all come to. After what happened out on that whiskey river, like I was nothing but a sack of bones to be buried in the mud, I was scared to twitch a leg in the direction of the Mexican Export Company. No, Catfish would have to pay his respects on his own.

"Middle Island," I said to Ruby. "Remember that sweet spot?"

For the first time since I found her adrift in a dinghy, Ruby looked like she had no more comfort to call forth out of her charms.

"I deal cards, mostly five-card stud. I met Vital one night at the casino."

I winced when she said Daddy's given name.

"He liked to drink and gamble," she went on with the glazed look of the defeated.

"Daddy?"

"Big spender. Always had a stack of chips."

"Go on," I said in disbelief.

"One night, maybe the second or third time he was there, he won big. When my shift ended, he asked me to join him at a table. Why not? If he wanted to spread cash around, I wasn't going to shut him up. We got friendly. Offered me fifty dollars to sleep with him."

As much as I was sickened by what she said, I was also frozen with fascination, starved to hear more, blood beating in my ears.

"What happened?"

"I brought him back to my room, but he passed out before we could," Ruby said.

"And?"

"Next time, he picked up where we left off. Said I was the most beautiful woman he'd ever seen. Said he would do anything. Buy me anything. Take me anywhere. He was like a schoolboy. Said he couldn't live without me. I told him to prove it."

"You did what?"

"I called his bluff. Never thought anything would happen. I'd seen his type before. Next thing I knew he was there all the time. Told me he was the house mechanic for the speedboats that pulled in there. I didn't know who he was, but he kept coming on like Christmas and Easter."

The thought of Ruby and my father stole my breath. I sat in the bow of *Sweet Ride* drenched in sweat. I glanced from Ruby into the river bank and grew fearful that Catfish was messed in something dire, worried sick and chafing to hear more from Ruby and terrified the whole story would never come out of her mouth. As quickly as he had spun off with a gas can, Catfish returned, out of air, his eyes wild in his head, sweat beads rolling off his face. He dove over me and Ruby for the stern, yanked the starter, and we backed out from the shoreline in a watery skid.

"What did you do?"

Catfish didn't answer me, but I saw my answer.

Flames shot out of the Mexican Export Company followed by the sound of voices barking instructions. The night was now a ball of fire that made Ruby's revelation pale. For one moment, the blaze struck me as a thing of beauty that couldn't be denied, and then I saw it as something else, a doubling of whatever trouble we had, something so big and bright that it would burn us down even as we flew from shore. The light from the crackling spiral allowed two men to catch sight of us and I saw them leap behind the wheel of a boat, cast off.

Catfish said, "I'll take us into the shallows where they can't follow."

I couldn't see the speedboat behind us, but I heard it like some flat black stone rolling down on us from the end of the world. The whine of the Evinrude turned into a scream. Catfish's green eyes were so full of flash they never blinked. When the spotlight found us, a bead of blood fell into my mouth.

"Get flat as pennies," he said.

We ducked below the thwarts.

"Don't you know what flat means?" he shouted.

We squeezed down lower into the boat. Catfish zigzagged out of the light and *Sweet Ride* leapt forward under his grip. The spotlight from the trailing boat crisscrossed the water and threw out so many threads it felt like a web looping and knotting around us. I peeked over our rooster tail, cupping my eyes with one hand to shield against the light aiming to bevel us there. With my other hand gripping a thwart, I felt the vibration of the engine and the river boiling the thin skin of the hull.

Sweet Ride slapped the water so hard, it felt like she would splinter apart. Catfish's face was drenched in spray and crouched so low our lips nearly touched again. He smiled at me like this was where he wanted to be, one swerve ahead of doom and just one moment removed from splendor, the wrongness of it made right by his smile. The bigger boat careened off our transom, its light slicing us in half, its speed so much greater, the sound of its hull flattening out the distance between us. Between the blinding spray off the bow and the glare of the spotlight off the stern, there was nothing left for me to see except Catfish's unflinching gaze fixed on the darkness ahead. My hands slipped off the gunwale and so I gripped his feet and felt the throb and burn of the engine through his ankle bones.

"One more minute and we're safe," Catfish said, but then bullets starting dropping all around us like hailstones.

"They've got a Tommy on us," Catfish said. "Imagine that. First time for everything." He guided *Sweet Ride* into the southern shallows off Belle Isle. The spotlight fell away as we sped into rocky shallows. Catfish opened his mouth to yell something, but I couldn't hear what he said.

"You did it, Catfish. You did it."

"Told you," he said, slumping forward. I reached around and felt a jumble of holes in his back the size of quarters. Blood gushed out of him and I wanted to scream; instead, I bit down on my lips until I tasted more blood, and by the time I laid him down in *Sweet Ride,* he was gone. Catfish was there one minute, greedy for mischief and escape, and the next minute, full of holes. With flames still leaping in the distance, I cried so long and loud my body was no longer my own but something more like his, limp and crooked and cold as bottom mud.

Ruby let me be and steered us south for what seemed like ten years of misery. I never let go of Catfish. Something about my clutching him made me picture again how he cut me loose from that burlap bag and drew me up out of the river, me clawing into him with a fierce hunger to live and him smiling all the while like every day is Saturday.

"Don't know where we are," Ruby said.

I didn't care where we were or where we went or how we got there. All I could think about was this boy at my feet and what might have been.

"Help me?" I asked of Catfish but he was now as long gone as the oil rag lying in the bottom of his flat-bottomed scooter. "Help me," I said again to the river darkness.

"He's gone, Norah. We have to do something."

Before Christ rolled away the stone of his undoing, there was no evidence of anything beyond this life. Right then, holding Catfish and then not holding him, it was hard to think of Christ as the master of any stone in this world or the next. He was just another dead man betrayed by a human spear. And maybe that's all he ever was, another man whose days were numbered and unregarded by the Romans who saw him coming into town on a donkey and started to salivate. Harder yet, from the hold of *Sweet Ride,* was to conjure a prayer that would reach one boy gone into God's river. With more blood on my hands, I asked God what to do and he told me to look up and I saw the north end of Fighting Island staring at me like the transom of a freighter. Catfish must have prowled Fighting Island. He would have trapped muskrat there and used its coves for hiding jute bags. The name of the place suited him given how his own life took shape, flew fast, and ended just as he figured he might be safe enough to kiss a girl one more time like he meant it.

"We'll stop and find some stones," I said, raising my head off Catfish's chest.

"Stones?"

"We'll put Catfish into the bag he found me in, weight it down, and lower him into the river."

"You don't suppose he has family?"

"He told me the river was family. On the bottom is the only place he'd want to be. I aim to make sure he don't get too lonesome."

Ruby steered us into the land and lifted the prop like she'd seen Catfish do. I climbed out and used the moonlight to find round, smooth stones free of seaweed, fish line, and river foam. Without saying anything, I pulled out the burlap bag stowed under a thwart and opened it up so we could slide Catfish in. First we had to carry him out of the boat. Me at his feet. Ruby holding his shoulders. The weight of him made us both clumsy and anxious in the dark and then we started laughing. Clutching our sides, almost falling down. Nothing said. Just the pain of this moment, the unbargained gravity of him in our hands, we couldn't hold it all. All we could do was let the laughter tears spill out on the ground and then I held myself up with tight arms, my ribs hurting.

"Careful," I whispered.

"He can't be hurt anymore," Ruby said.

The sting of bile rose in my throat like maybe it was bleeding up from the soles of my feet. I tried to heave, nothing came out, then something did.

"This is as close as he'll ever get to a church."

I couldn't look at his face now because if I did I wouldn't be able to finish what had to be done. Then, I did look at Catfish when I remembered the Bible saying somewhere, *Keep still, child. I will fight for you.* A boy his age shouldn't have crow's feet and raccoon eyes, but he had both. Maybe it was the angle of the moonlight, but I made out the token of a smile or I put one to his face because I needed to fix him that way. Catfish had come to Fighting Island, but his fighting days on the whiskey river were over and someone else would have to run scooter hooch from there.

"We should empty his pockets," Ruby said.

"What? And take his money?"

"Catfish would want you to have it."

I looked at her sideways like I couldn't believe we were even talking like this. "No two ways about it," Ruby said.

Ruby reached into Catfish's pockets, drew out a thick wad of wet bills and handed them to me. I took the cash and put it back into his shirt pocket. I wrapped his legs with rope, then his arms so it would be easier to scoot him into the bag, and after doing all that, I undid the rope. I couldn't stand the thought of him being bound even if he was dead. It took a long time to get a bullet-riddled Catfish into a burlap bag, then more time to load in the stones and then lift him back into the boat. Ruby backed us out. We motored due north to the red, four-second flasher, #104, right on the dotted line between America and Canada, at the north end of Fighting Island at the fork between the east and west channels, right where I knew Catfish would be anchored for as long as this river found its course.

"Going to say anything?" Ruby asked.

Even though we were out in the river in the middle of the night and there was oxygen pouring into us from every direction, I couldn't find air. All I could squawk was a cobbled version of the 23rd Psalm:

Thou preparest a table before me in the presence of mine enemies.
Thou anointest my head with oil.
My cup runneth over.
Surely goodness and mercy shall follow me all the days of my life
and... I shall swim... in the house of the Catfish forever.

We lowered Catfish into thirty feet of cold, clear water, then drifted downriver before Ruby started the engine. I told her to follow the red and green cans of the west channel hugging Detroit. I sat on a thwart, hunched over and struggling with the words *goodness and mercy*, and wondering if I believed either one of them anymore, every part of me seeing him in my arms with holes in his back. Whiskey and hard water with no cup runneth over. I couldn't stand thinking about all that had gone wrong and how little could be fixed and how my heart was so full it could no longer hide, and while we skimmed the west flank of Fighting Island I understood for the first time why men and women turned to drink. They wanted hard stuff to wear down hard memories. They wanted to forget. Maybe they even wanted to forgive, but all they could do was fall down and fail to grasp anything that does not last in this sorry world.

I didn't let myself think about the fire that Catfish set at the Mexican Export Company until we entered the long stretch of water running past Grosse Ile. With each river mile, I saw again the fireball behind our wake, the sparks spiraling and popping like firecrackers, and then the cruiser tailing us as if it had leapt out of the fire with all the speed of hell to draw from.

Why did Catfish do it?

He took pride in his river smarts. In being able to hide in the mud, wiggle there, eat anything, spit anything out, live another day. Did he really believe he alone could punish the men who threw me in the drink? Did he fear they might try it again if they saw me with him? Or did he do it to avenge his other friend who'd died at the hands of Swagbelly? The more I tried to grasp his misbegotten sense of setting things right, the more confused I became. Sure as sugar, I'd never know if the fire caught Swagbelly sleeping unaware, but one good dear life was now gone and there was no way to bring Catfish back from the netherworld of poor choices. All I knew for certain was I had failed to save him the same way he had saved me. No, that was not my only certainty.

I had to get more out of the whiskey than another riddle. I had to make good use of the sweet air Catfish gave back to me. Ruby was going nowhere until we both had plunged to the bottom of all this pain and surfaced with some answers. I was as mad as Cain. I carried my own gas can and I was looking for a match and if that failed to reveal all I needed to know, I still had the knife that Catfish gave me.

23

We motored back to the cove on Gibraltar Island and arrived at first light. *Odyssey* was there just where I left her. One trustworthy thing in my life had held fast, waited me out no matter how far afield I had skittered. Death had nearly claimed me as its own, and I had been the sole cause of death's harsh visitation in two countries. But then, seeing my sloop, a little outline of heaven came sharply into view and I thought there was still hope for the hands that had crafted such a sweet set of lines.

When I saw Ruby flick tears, I grew stronger, bold even. I needed to press my advantage. She might have used her size and strength even then to break away except for one hitch. What every other death couldn't touch in her, Catfish did find a portal. Her pluck was gone. The card dealer couldn't hold my eye. I needed to engage this lapse. I needed to break her. I needed the whole story, start to finish.

"What now?" Ruby asked.

"You're going home, the long way."

We pushed off from the southern tip of Gibraltar and the river current carried us south. I could see the wind rippling Lake Erie in the distance. Praise for Erie. I recognized her and she recognized me and we said without saying a word, *Hello, how are you?*

"Take the tiller," I said to Ruby.

"Why?"

"I want to show you what Catfish gave me," I said, crawling into the doghouse cabin. I pretended to look for the knife that was in my pocket.

Ruby called out, "Can you come back up here?"

"In a minute," I said like I was a harried mother snipping at a daughter. I heard a panic in Ruby's voice, but it was not from any river traffic springing up around us. I needed to take a peek in Ruby's duffel: the one possession she protected most, the bag that contained all her belongings, the only thing she cared about as if it were her child. She had buried the bag under lifejackets and fenders. I opened the bag, pushed aside a dress, a lace brassiere, underwear, and makeup, digging to the bottom until I felt the bricks of cash. I closed the zipper. I never knew so much money could weigh so little. I climbed back up with the knife Catfish gave me, but the blade was not tucked inside.

"What really happened the night those three men took you on the boat?"

"I told you."

"Not even close," I said, brandishing the blade.

Ruby blew the air out of her lungs. It reminded me of the gasp I released when I surfaced out of the Detroit River into the arms of Catfish.

"They caught me at the casino."

"Caught you doing what?"

"Skimming."

"What?"

"I know how to skim a table when there's a spender in the house."

"You stole money from the casino?"

"On the quick."

"Not quick enough."

"Stayed an hour too long."

"Tell me everything, right down to the minute."

"The owners sent three men to my room. They found me packing."

"And they found the money you'd stolen and put into your bag?"

"That's right."

"You got so close," I said, with knife in hand.

"They told me if I made them happy, they might let me live, but I knew they'd tie me to an anchor after they were done."

"Charming company you keep."

Ruby winced, her eye sockets growing darker like two bruises in a bloom. She gripped the tiller with both hands to hold steady.

"I know there's more," I said. "With you, there's always more."

"I slipped a Mickey into their bottle."

"I don't care about your dead. Let's get back to Vital Bow."

"Like I said, I called his bluff."

"You're going back with me to find him on Middle Island."

"They'll kill me," she said, with a flare to her nostrils. "You must know by now we're dealing with bad men."

"You're going to hold up your end of the bargain."

"You've got the truth now. Isn't that enough? I had a couple of chances to leave you stranded but I didn't because—"

"You knew from the start the man in the picture was my father."

"I was in shock when I saw the photograph."

"Shock? That's a joke, right?"

"I wanted you to find him, but I thought he was probably already dead by the time you fished me out of the drink. I couldn't break that news to you."

"Would have saved a lot of lives if you had told me something."

After I said this, Ruby sank down in the cockpit.

"Now that I know where he is, I'm going to get him out of there, and let Momma sort him out," I said, folding the knife and sticking it back in my pocket.

"How many bullet holes do you want?" Ruby asked. She was a doll crumpled in a corner.

"With you as my shield, I should be safe enough," I said.

"You don't mean that, Norah Bow. You haven't fallen that far. You're just hurt and mad. I'll give you that, but I won't give you my life."

Ruby looked wistfully at the last boil of the Detroit River and the shadow of mainland Ontario. Her bloodshot eyes matched the color of her hair.

"Why did you say Daddy was probably already dead?" I asked.

Ruby rocked herself like someone at a burial.

"Tell me."

"I figured the casino boys took him from Rye Beach because they wanted to find out what he knew about me."

"The casino boys wanted to know if you two were skimming together?"

"I suppose," Ruby said, the fake remorse sticking to her words.

I looked at Ruby, realizing I knew even less about her than I did when I first picked her up out of the drink. She was a riddle fog-bound inside a riddle. Red lantern floozy, card skimmer, bone cracker, roadhouse tease, confessed killer, escape artist, seeker of slim chances and fat paydays—who can say how many lives Ruby could lay claim to? Maybe she didn't even know. When you live your entire life out of one bag, there's no end to the number of costumes and disguises you can wear.

24

We left Gibraltar Island on a 140 degree heading which I hoped would take us into Lake Erie, but the wind knocked us down into shallows. I had my story, but I had no idea what to do with Ruby. I didn't want to take her back to Middle Island. If she had killed the three men from there, she would get anchored to the bottom of the lake. I couldn't stomach the thought of linking my short life to one more death. As she read my confusion, she dug out the binoculars from down below and watched two speedboats, one closing on the other.

"Who are they?"

"Two boats from Middle Island."

"We are a long way from there."

"I studied most of the boats there. There wasn't a one I didn't dream of stealing."

"Studied?"

"Show me a faster horse and I'll ride it."

"What?"

"I knew which boats were fast and which ones were faster."

I grabbed the binoculars from Ruby. The boats looked like two comets in search of another sky, each one leaping and skidding.

"The one out front is the *Martina*," Ruby muttered.

"How can you be sure?"

"Better than even chance."

"Why now?"

"All this time you were looking for him, maybe he was looking for you."

"More like he got word you were alive," I said, giving her nothing in return.

The lead boat didn't have running room to outpace the boat

that dogged it so the lead boat headed for the western shore of neighboring Celeron Island. My chart showed the island dotted with exposed rock like beads on a chain. Ruby clutched the binoculars like a pilgrim with a cross.

"I know it's the *Martina*," Ruby said.

"My father took you out for a ride in a speedboat used by the rumrunners?"

"Yes."

"Where?"

"I don't know."

"Yes, you do."

Ruby crossed her arms over her chest and cast down her eyes. "Cedar Point."

The air wheezed from my throat like she had just stabbed me with the knife Catfish gave me. She saw me struggling to say something and went on talking.

"I'd never been to the amusement park so he said he'd take me. We raced over there one Sunday morning when everyone at the casino was still sleeping off a drunk."

"Cedar Point?" I said, unable to grasp that Ruby had gone to my playground with Daddy.

"We never should have gone back to Middle Island," Ruby said.

"Why did you?"

"I don't know. He froze up inside when we were at Cedar Point. When I asked him what was wrong, he said your name. I thought it was his wife's name."

The lead boat entered the cut separating two chunks of the island and threaded the exposed rocks. The faster boat closed the distance. Both boats were running out of water.

There was no time left to know what I believed or disbelieved about anything Ruby had told me. The lead boat skipped between two exposed rocks, skidded sideways, flipped over. The second boat slammed into the same rocks, flipped end for end and exploded.

"Can you get over to those two boats?" Ruby asked.

"You could be wrong."

"What if I'm not?"

"It's too hard to tack upriver because of the current. We can't make it. I'm trying to leave the Detroit River. Not go back. We just buried Catfish, not far from there. God, I hate this place."

Ruby had lied so much it was hard to believe she could be right about these two boats. I looked for some trickery, but she couldn't hitch a ride on a speedboat that was now in flames. She and I had played so many different roles where I was the boss, then she was, where she was lost, then I was, where the land was her kingdom and the water was mine. Now she showed me yet another side: Ruby on her knees, pleading.

"Please," Ruby said.

"Why?"

"It's the only thing I have to offer."

"The truth?"

"I'm not proud of what I've done."

"That's a shocking confession."

"I'm trying here, Norah. I know these two boats. Your father is over there," she said, pointing to the wreckage.

"Okay," I said, tacking into the shallows in spite of my disbelief, fluky air, and miserable current. In four tacks and thirty minutes, we found the wreckage of the trailing boat still smoldering. You couldn't escape the smell of gasoline. I saw splinters the size of my arm, a navy-blue cushion, and a carton of cigarettes all floating together. The lead boat was farther away still and we had to paddle to reach it. I read the name *Martina* on the transom. A man in the drink held onto a strip of burnt planking, his arms draped over the half-submerged board. I leaned over the gunwale and peered into my father's face. His eyes rolled back in his head. His ears were filled with blood. Delirium and cold had taken him better than halfway into the next life. I tried to haul him on board, but his wrist bones were already too slick to grab, so Ruby helped me grab

Daddy by the belt and drag him over the gunwale. Without seeing us, he curled his hands over his chest and drew his knees up, teeth chattering, lips swollen blue-black like chicken fat in a cast-iron skillet.

My body shook thinking he might die even before I had a chance to say a word. I told my body it was no time to be heaving over the side. I didn't know much about reviving a burnt man who'd been stuck for thirty minutes in bone-cold water but I knew this much—Daddy would die on my boat if I couldn't heat him up like a slow-roasting bird. I had no stove, no heat source, just two blankets from home.

"He's going shiver himself to death, isn't he?"

"Maybe not."

"How do we bring him back?"

"Only one thing to do."

Ruby ducked into the cabin, grabbed everything strewn there and threw it out into the cockpit.

"Start peeling off his clothes," Ruby said.

His trousers were soaked into his skin. His bones white and brittle like something long buried, then dug up out of the worm-threaded dirt. He had ugly burn marks on his face and hands like a man who had already passed over and wasn't too keen on coming the long way back.

I repeated, "He's going to die, isn't he?"

She scrambled topsides and we laid Daddy out as best we could. She snapped off his shirt buttons in one jerk. She dug her thumbs into his skin at the waist to grab hold of his pants and we rolled them down to his knees. I lifted him up from behind and Ruby wiggled his pants and underwear down to his ankles. Ruby took him by the ankles. I held his shoulders, a move we had already rehearsed with one dead boy from the whiskey river.

"Back down into the cabin, easy like," she said.

We both crouched and lifted him into the cabin and laid him down on one of Momma's blankets. Daddy was as cold as an anchor wedged into muck, but he did offer a trickle of breath. When I bent over him, I could feel it against my mouth. "Put the other blanket on top of him and rub slowly," Ruby said.

I was too tired to cry so I just squeaked again some of the 23rd Psalm, the words like sparks in my lungs, a little heat rising through my mouth, the glimmer of something holding my head up, until I glimpsed Ruby doing a shimmy shake in the broad daylight of the cockpit. She slipped from her dress, brassiere and underclothes, and crawled below, all naked and shining, and nudged me aside.

"I'll take over from here," she said, pushing me out of the cabin and back into the cockpit. Her breasts swung against Daddy, her breath hot against his face, her hands around his torso.

"What the hell?" I asked, miffed she planned to steal my last with him.

"He'll be dead in twenty minutes."

Ruby laid down next to my blue-burnt daddy, pulled the blanket over her nude body and slid her arm beneath his head. His eyes were pinched shut as if to freeze out the cold by not looking at how completely it had consumed his body. Her eyes as big as apples swinging in the wind. I knew the book of Genesis as well as most preachers but I never figured I'd see such an Adam and Eve as this: Adam just a raw, shriveled man, trembling uncontrollably, moments from a watery grave, and Eve bursting with skill and cadence, each naked and unknown to the other in a Biblical sense, laid out in the smallest boat cabin in the world and sandwiched between scratchy wool from Momma's hope chest. This Adam sipping air through blackened teeth, and this Eve, all breasts and thighs, sucking down gulps of air and blowing it into him like some bellows from the earth's oldest fire. In the speed of this collision, the moment made me slow down and wonder how many hundreds of people gave birth to this chance coupling that was not a consummation, not a commingling of flesh and spirit sanctioned by holy contract, but something almost like it.

I could hardly look. I couldn't look away. Letting no small thing go unnoticed. Life and death dancing between the pendant of her breasts. Like having a bird's eye view of the first elemental scuffle between ice and fire. Ruby wrapped her legs round my father until she encircled and held him back from the purple cold that sets in after your teeth stop snapping air. He put a chatter into her own teeth, the ice of his bones seeping into her. She fought back with her body rocking him into hers until, like a chafing rope holding a surging boat to a dock, I couldn't tell where she started and he finished. Even though I knew this wasn't the sex thing, it looked like everything I'd heard or read but never been told about from Momma. It was confusing and terrifying, but if what Ruby did with Daddy returned him to the steady tick of this life, I wouldn't say a word, not now, not ever, and Momma would never hear from me how much good use her blankets had come to.

One hand on the tiller, I knelt in the cockpit while Ruby and Daddy wrestled in the doghouse cabin below. I prayed and pinched my eyes because there was no way I wanted to bring him home dead so we could have a funeral and say a bunch of platitudes everyone would forget two minutes after they bit down on a sliver of sweet bread. I asked God to pay Daddy no mind for thinking he didn't exist, but rather to see beyond his shortcomings to the long ride back to Rye Beach and two little boys who surely needed him, for as it is writ in gospel somewhere I was hungry and you gave me food, thirsty and you gave me drink and I was a stranger and you welcomed me. I got so lost in reverie, I didn't hear the moaning below. I thought the sputter must be tangled debris against the hull or some ancient wind sound caught in a pocket over the island we laid next to. Then, more groans and gentle pounding. I was afraid to look down below and I was afraid to ignore what I heard.

I thought, dear God, Ruby had slipped far beyond the bounds of human decency by trying to revive a dying man with some kind of sex ritual. I couldn't bear to look, but I did, and what I saw was something more beautiful than a hummingbird locked in front of a picture window although it was just as small. Daddy was pounding his fist against the hull like he was trying to claw loose the latch on a cage. My stranger had come back from the dead and he wanted to be heard and welcomed.

"He will vomit any minute," Ruby said, from under the blankets, her voice muffled, tired, and full of fire all at the same time.

"Getting this cold is like killer flu. He needs water. He needs more warmth. He needs everything all at once."

"Keep doing what you're doing."

"I saw him look at me once and blink."

"He got more than an eye-full."

"He's so close to gone, I don't figure he even knows I'm naked."

"Pity," I said, remembering what Ruby told me about how Daddy passed out after the two of them were alone in her room.

"We're going to need that fisherman's bucket," Ruby said.

Then the vomiting began. I had my daddy back, such as he was. He took one look at me, struggling for air as the sickness in him started with a shudder, a kick, and then a heaving fury like all the poison of his whole life was screaming to spill out. I went below to be with him.

"I'm here, Daddy. It's me, Norah." The tears ran off my face and then a laugh born of all the fear and misery we had come to.

"We're going home, Daddy."

His mouth didn't work and he couldn't say my name, but I saw something in his eyes, a recognition, a wonder, and this wild rolling panic like he was dreaming some piece of his life from the dead side of things and he was grateful for the bright thimble of what he saw shining into him.

"I'm here, Daddy. This is me, your Norah Bow."

He nodded, collapsed, rose up to heave, his eyes spinning in his head. He wrestled his angel in her naked glory and his life was spared. What more could a lost man want? Death followed by a revival and to hell with any kiss of betrayal. Looking into the burnt and swollen smudge of Daddy's face, I wondered if he would ever be able to tell me who he was and why he needed this kind of death by water before he could get himself home.

25

Moments after the thrill of seeing my father return from the waters of the dead, it occurred to me with a sickening taste like bile on the tongue, that he might not have been a man worth saving. Worst yet, his having come back meant that Ruby could leave. Her contract had been fulfilled. I never saw Ruby put her clothes back on, but when I looked at her, she bore some resemblance to the woman I remembered seeing with Zane and Lonesome Bill. The chill she had absorbed from Daddy had left and a fleshy glow had returned. The bloodshot web had lifted from her eyes. The humbling, the pleading, the sagging, baleful confusion, not to be found. While I was not looking, she had made her face ready for the next man, the next roadhouse, the next hand of cards.

"Everything Daddy did was about you," I said to her.

"Who can say for sure?"

"I can say it."

"We found your father, Norah," Ruby said, putting a hairbrush back into her duffel. "Take him home."

"He wanted you and you didn't want him."

"I told him as much."

"You stole his heart and his money."

After my father expelled all the sickness he could summon, he slept like the long dead sick and never again looked at Ruby Francoeur, naked or clothed, real or imagined. The rasp in his lungs was none too comforting, but he slept on with a rueful smile as if he saw without eyes open how foolish he had been to chase Ruby across Lake Erie. Ruby watched me watching him, then she too closed her eyes and spoke her next truth.

"Can you take me back to—Canada?"

The land to the north was only a stone's throw and a million miles away. As much as I wanted to hate Ruby Francoeur, I wasn't ready to part company. I had nothing in common with her, nothing of hers I wanted to claim, and yet now she seemed a part of me like the memory of an explosion or the first summer wind through a screen door. How could I spend one more minute with her and how could I let her go? How could I not love and hate her for what she had done? All that was unsayable in me wanted to say more and maybe only Ruby of the flamered hair would be able to hear me out or draw me in. Only many years later did I learn that the ruby, the blood-colored stone, is thought to preserve one from all perils. Only years later, did I hear someone tell how a ruby when placed in water could bring it to a boil. How only a ruby could shine through a shroud. How only the ruby could be used to torch-light a cave. Long before I heard such stories, I learned what a ruby could do and I wanted to keep one for myself just in case I could not throw off enough heat of my own.

"If the winds holds, I can be there in an hour," I said, pointing to Bar Point on the chart. Lucky Ruby. The wind did hold at fourteen knots so we could sail across the southern tip of the Detroit River channel back to Canada in one tack. There was no harbor, but the sandy shallows let me ride in and kick up the rudder. Ruby hopped out and helped drag *Odyssey* onto the beach.

"All stories reach an end," she said, fingering at her throat a string of colored beads she had pulled from her traveling bag.

"You can do better than that," I said, my tongue wagging from one side of my jaw to the other. Looking at her in that sandy light, I saw why it hurt to let her go. She was a bent note from a street guitar, an open door fronting the sea, a red dress unfastened and falling to the floor. She did have something I wanted. A willingness to trust whatever the wind broke apart and call it good eating. Daddy must have seen all this life in Ruby. He must have told himself it was worth any risk because she had the vital force he lacked. If I were him, maybe I would have suffered the same recklessness. Maybe I would have chased her to the ends of the earth to learn what fed her appetites, her strength of will, her choice to live and die by the flick of a card. At fourteen, I already knew I wouldn't have many friends. Didn't want many. But one or two like Catfish and Ruby could make all the difference in weather bearing down from the troubled west. I put my arms around her. She stroked my hair and said, "You and I are sisters now and that's never going to end."

Her tears wet the back of my neck.

"I'm never going to see you again, am I?"

"I wouldn't bet against us."

I pulled back and peered into Ruby's face. I painted in my mind her hawkish nose, her high cheekbones, tossed freckles, her fiery hair that wouldn't cooperate for any comb, her hazel eyes, the pretty mouth she gave easily to men. She did the same with me, holding me out, then pulling me in like we were trying to memorize the difficult grammar of our days together.

"Promise me, we'll see each other again," I said, my lips trembling, "then I can let you disappear into the Klondike or some such place. Promise me you and I will meet again someday."

"You are something else, Norah Bow. Sure as that Bible of yours says there will be more good things tomorrow, you and I are not done."

Our arms were extended like two bridges and our fingertips touched.

"Thanks for...the truth," I said.

"You pried it out of me."

Ruby looked down at her duffel.

"The money?" she asked.

"I don't want any of it," I said.

"This is real money, Norah. You could buy yourself a bigger boat."

"It's blood money. Somebody will be looking for you. Got no great need to keep looking over my shoulder."

"A good part of it I took from—"

"He deserved to lose it all."

Ruby turned away and walked up the beach, then gave a little wave back over her shoulder. I pushed the *Odyssey* back out into the shallows, climbed in, hoisted the main, raised the jib. The air turned into a slow-moving thickness that matched my somber. I looked at my father, still curled into himself, and I thought he could be a sleeping boy instead of a man so broken and bruised he couldn't raise his head. I took one more look and saw Ruby just at the point of disappearing, a red bead on a string of sand.

Daddy and I turned toward home, the heat of the day dragging the life out of the wind. We trickled south with more fluky air off the starboard bow, but to what end? Daddy could bolt after I hauled him back or Momma could give him the boot. Some part of me wished he had died when his boat flipped over and I had gone on with Ruby to the Klondike. She and I might have seen the world together, the way I thought Catfish and I could have done. Two souls I wanted to be with were now gone into the far away where I couldn't follow, and I was left with another soul I had lost respect for. Nothing seemed right with this consolation prize, and my brain kicked me from one end of Lake Erie to the other. Then the hurt boy stirred from sleep.

"Where is she?"

"Who?"

I let him twist in the stalled air.

"Ruby?"

"You've been through a lot. You must be hallucinating."

"Ruby. Red Hair. French. Ruby Francoeur."

"Now that you mention it, I do remember seeing someone like that."

"Where is she?" Daddy looked to the land.

"She had a card game to make."

Odyssey found a skinny patch of air and slipped through it to the south. Daddy put his head in his hands. Everything about this first day together was unsettled.

"Better start talking, Daddy, or I'll throw you back in the drink."

He canted his head like a dog all done in.

"It's complicated," Daddy said.

"What isn't complicated?" I asked.

"I got into a jam," he said, his face one long wrinkle.

"How much?"

"Lost money in the market. Needed cash to float everything. No way to make it back except by running hooch."

"That's another lie. You lost your money at the casino on Middle Island."

"Who told you that?"

"You wanted to impress Ruby so you placed big bets at her table."

Daddy looked back toward Canada with a lovesick gaze. I wanted no part of it. The slap of sailcloth told me we were out of air. The sweat trickled off Daddy's nose. In the momentary lull, I found more bitter seeds, but none left for Ruby.

"I knew what she was. Tried to let her go, but when I came back to Rye Beach, I couldn't stop thinking about her."

"Call her your siren if it makes you feel better," I said, swallowing my words. "Just like in the *Odyssey*, the book you said was the greatest adventure story ever told."

Daddy said, his hands trembling, "I had no wax for my ears."

In the distance, the wind riffled the water. Like someone flipping through the parchment of the great hero's journey. I knew everything was about to change.

"I struck a deal with the rumrunners."

"What were those terms?"

"I would work for them for free if they would kidnap me out of my own house."

"That's not what happened."

"Damn well is."

"For once, would you stop lying to me? The three men who took you out of our house were not the boys you ran hooch with but the casino boys. They wanted you to help them figure out how Ruby skimmed or they thought you were in on her table. The kidnapping looked real because it was," I jabbed.

"How do you know this?"

"I trust Ruby a lot more than you."

"Breaks my heart to hear you say that."

"About time your heart was broken."

Daddy reached out to slap me. I caught his hand, lowered it to his waist. The world will end not with a bang but with a whimper, or so my father vouched with no volume left in his throat.

"I told the casino boys I knew nothing about how she skimmed. Which is the whole damn truth and nothing but. They only spared my life because I knew how to fix their engines. You have no idea what I've been through."

"That makes two of us," I scoffed.

Daddy reached out to touch my shoulder. I pulled back. The wind kicked up a knot and rattled the sheets in the running blocks.

"You had something they needed and they got it dirt cheap," I said, shocked at the hard flutter of my words and also proud I had them ready to fly.

"I was determined to get out of there," Daddy argued.

"That's another lie. You had no plans for coming back to Rye Beach. You only wanted to be with her."

"Goddamnit, Norah. Can't you—"

"Why did you come north when you did?"

"Some barkeep from Detroit—"

"From the Rusty Nail?"

"He sent word down asking if anyone knew anything about a sporting girl with red hair. Wondered if she was the one the casino boys had been looking for in connection with a missing boat called the *Purple Goose*. He said the redhead had stayed at the Nail and she was with a girl. I knew that was you. I had to find out. A faster boat followed me, and, well, you know the rest."

"Funny thing is, Daddy, you got what you wanted, but you were half dead and didn't know it. The woman who took your money and nearly got you killed, also took off her clothes for you, laid down with you, and brought you back to life. Don't you think there's something strange and funny about all that? It's such a good story maybe you stole it from Homer." Daddy slumped against the combing with his head thrown back. A thin whisper of cool air skimmed us like the whistle of a thrown card.

"It was a terrible thing I did."

"That's one way to describe it."

"I'm a weak man, Norah. Not like you."

"That's hogwash," I snapped. "The man who helped me to build this sailboat knows how to clean up his own mess. You could have asked Momma for a divorce. You could come to me and told me something of your troubles. You could have lived by some other religion than deceit. You could have spared me and your family a world of misery."

"I didn't know what was going to happen on Middle Island."

"Nothing happened there you didn't have a hand in."

"I couldn't face your mother. She loves our cottage in Rye Beach."

"You mean you couldn't tell her about Ruby?"

Again, Daddy lowered his head, pinched his nose like he was sinking back into the river water I fished him out of.

"We don't hang our head in this family. That's what you told me from the time I could use a napkin so at least do me the courtesy of looking me in the eye."

Daddy lifted his head. He looked at me from the distance of the near and far and in that one moment, I almost felt something like fellow feeling for the great unknown he had come to. Like he had no real idea where he had been, how he got there, and how to add up all the squandering he had paid for.

"It's not right you got dragged into this, Norah. I had no idea you'd come looking for me. I knew the sheriff wouldn't come to Canada and it didn't even cross my mind you would set out. That seemed like something not even you could manage."

The air turned thick like a cream soup set off. Inside this layering of unsettled heat, the wind found a new curling from the south. In the direction of our heading, I could sense Lake

Erie gathering sheer under a distant crack of thunder. Nothing this hot and stale could resist explosion. My boat knew this and I knew this. Maybe even Daddy knew our reckoning was at hand and the hurt and hidden parts of him were glad for the impending brawl.

"Let me tell you what sorry looks like," I said, flecks of spit flying out of my mouth. "I'm sorry we mean so little to you that you ran off without saying goodbye."

"That's not true, Norah Bow," he said, putting a little snap into his protest.

"Don't lie to me ever again."

"I know you hate me right now. You have every reason to. But you need to understand everything was closing in. Your mother wanted more children. Wanted more of everything that comes with family. I didn't want two more children. I didn't want one more. I couldn't see my way through. I felt like I was living a lie. I was never meant to be a father. I was never any good at it. You were more than enough for me."

"You can't blame this on Momma."

"Ten years of shooting blanks, coming up empty, then she had twins. Just when I wanted a little freedom, everything—"

"Save your confession for a priest," I said, fighting the need to slap him the way he almost had with me. "Oh, I forgot you don't believe in priests."

"I don't have faith like you," he said.

"We don't have to pull on that old piece of rope."

"You deserve a lot more," Daddy said, his shoulders slumped again.

"Why do you want to live, Daddy? Just answer me that."

"I don't know anymore," he said, with his eyes driven down toward the bright collision of waves sprung from the south.

"Well, I'll tell you why any man wants to go on living. Because there's something he loves more than himself. I thought my father used to love me. And that love was worth all my tomorrows."

I wanted Daddy to say he was sorry for something and for

everything. And that he loved me and his family, more than he craved Ruby. He stammered, sputtered, and twisted in the cockpit like he had mosquitoes dive-bombing his neck and ankles, but he never delivered the one line I was looking to grab and hold on to for dear life. Why couldn't Daddy cough up a simple apology? That's the one question that's been chewing on me since before the flood and now the flood of time is about to sweep me off and my query will fall before it as all things do and then rise inside some other girl as an interrogation that lives on without us.

"We're sailing back to Rye Beach tonight," I announced. "In one shot, no stops. You may not know if you want to return home, but that's where we're headed, due south. Once there, you can either tell the truth or pack your bags, but if you do leave again, you better stand up in front of your family and make your case. You better look us eyeball to eyeball and tell us why our love for you has never been enough."

I said my piece and I felt some better for the swag and stab of it except for one thing. The clouds could have been a mile-thick quilt sandwich stuffed, not with cotton, but with dark wet wool. It was a sky I'd read about in newspapers and books, but never seen before. Most of the devil storms on Lake Erie roared down from the north in November. The summer months brought fast-drenching squalls with straight-line winds and hailstones the size of cherries, but if you reduced sail they weren't that bad to ride out under bare poles. A storm from the south in the summer. That would be something freakish. That meant a possible collision with troubled air that was already parked in the north. This buffeting to come, this thrashing, this jolt and slam coming right at us seemed to fit the far reach of secrets bound to the summer of 1926.

"Do you know what day it is?" I asked.

"No," Daddy said, his voice so quiet I had to lean down to hear it.

"August 20th."

I looked at him slacked-jawed and eyes flickering. He didn't recognize the significance of that day and I was not going to tell him just yet. He didn't even acknowledge that the dark quilt of clouds following us home looked like a shroud sewn with black thread. Death by water never comes twice or does it?

26

Daddy let his sulk do his talking.

I focused on the brisk southwesterly wind throwing off five footers. His frozen stare said, *Who am I now in my forlorn misery?* My grit stare said, *Go ask Blind Danny. Go ask three bootleggers gone up in flame. Go ask Catfish anchored to buoy #4 in the Detroit River. Go ask whiskey and hard water. Go ask Ruby of the golden thighs. On second thought, you will never find her or anyone else who died on this journey to find you.* To the north and south, the sky bulged with black patches, the same color as the bags under Daddy's eyes. Some part of me thought he was still floating in the drink and didn't deserve to know about second chance revivals from the hot shine of a ruby.

"When the boat flipped, I got tangled in line," he said, breaking the silence.

After my ride down into the Detroit River, I had no problem picturing the panic he must have felt, but I didn't give him one inch of slack.

"I was hanging upside down. Harder I tried to get free, the more tangled I became."

The more he talked, all I could think was how clear the punishment fit the crime. On a long boat delivery, I read *Crime and Punishment* and saw the parallel between that story and my father's. How once the deed is done, the imagined liberation from poverty fails to emerge and the doomed hero of that Russian tale finds himself wracked with confusion and disgust, with no way forward but back into the permanent horrors of the deed. Dirt and shovel. Action and consequence. Crime and punishment.

"I got free and kicked toward the light of the surface except it wasn't the surface. I swam toward the bottom on my last breath. I didn't know where I was until I saw the bottom, so I turned around but I was out of air. Then I thought of you. Us. The demon switch. How we know how to do the hard things no one else can."

"Then you died out there?"

"Maybe I did. I don't know how I reached the surface because all I remember was my lungs filling with water. Instead of panic, I felt this quiet. Like everything was happening the way it should. I knew you were close. I knew I had found you."

Daddy continued in the same spirit-talking vein like a man set loose in the rose glow of a gospel tent. I'd seen him inspire a rapt audience of insurance salesmen. I'd heard him rouse and captivate his own family until they were breathless with the twists of his storytelling, but now I sat there unfazed, unconvinced, unavailable.

"My mind went back to Rye Beach and all of us at dinner before the men broke in and took me away. I saw everyone there. How they loved gathering around Momma's food. I wanted to tell you and Momma everything, but I couldn't find the words."

"I said no more lies."

"I'm not lying."

"You were eye-balling Aunt Cora before we all sat down to eat."

He ignored what I said. Just like he ignored the snarl that leapt out of the sky.

"I saw it was a good life even as it was leaving me."

"Could have fooled me," I said, throwing my hands in the air out of disbelief.

"You don't know what it's like—"

"Don't feed me excuses."

"Have it your way," Daddy said, with something between a croak and a whisper. "Have any food?" he asked abruptly.

"There's some peanut butter, maybe an old apple."

"That's all?"

"Nothing for the last month has had a plan."

"We could starve out here," he said.

"My anger should tide me over till we get back."

"It's a long way yet."

"That's North Bass Island," I said, pointing to the southeast off the port bow. "If you hadn't noticed, we're flying home."

"You see those thunderheads?"

"How can I miss them?" Satin clouds crept under a long reach of black tarp.

"You know the 30-30 rule," Daddy said, in a voice I recognized as belonging to a man who taught me. Between the flash of lightning and the bang of thunder, there should be more than thirty seconds. If there is any less time, you had no business being on Lake Erie. I didn't even bother counting. Soon enough, I knew there would be no time between the flash and bang. No time to get off Erie. No way out but through. No hope but of the desperate kind underneath a bruised sky with only a gash for a mouth.

"We're parked on the tracks and there's a runaway train coming at us," Daddy said.

"That suits us, don't you think?"

"Norah, feel the air, the hot is cut with cold, barometer is falling fast."

He made me step back from my own wall of hurt.

"How bad is it?" I asked him, hoping he was wrong about the runaway train.

"Probably a low-pressure system ripping up the Ohio Valley, slamming up against another low-pressure center bearing down from the north."

"Ever seen one of these?"

"Not like this."

Daddy was right, but I didn't give a damn for reason. The hurt part of me wanted to hurt more. I wanted Erie to bite us down to nothing and make us clean. I'd been caught in a dozen Lake Erie squalls with ear-deafening rain and thunder, but I'd never come nose to nose with the fury of something so ragged you can't describe it. Just then, I knew this was exactly where Daddy and I needed to be, inside a two-headed gale with no way out.

"Why are you doing this?"

I let his question hang in the air while I brought *Odyssey* up into the wind so we could reef the main. While Daddy tied off the sail, I changed out the jenny with a spitfire jib that he and I designed and that Momma had sewn with her Singer. As the bow lunged over air, I found the only way to answer him.

"Why are we doing this? Because today, August 20th, is your anniversary."

"Oh my God," he said, spellbound by his own admission. I saw him eyeing the water like a man testing the strength of a hanging beam and I told myself if he threw himself overboard I wouldn't go after him. The keel flexed and shuddered. The tiller quivered my hands. The sails rattled and slurred like telephone wire. To the south, black clouds with skinny waists, broad shoulders and their heads torn off. In thirty-five knots of air, we flew by Middle Island while the wind held out of the southwest. If we could keep the heading, we'd round the Kelly's Island Shoal, and turn south for Rye Beach, my little boat no more than eighteen miles from home. That was the idea, but the weather had a different heading in mind. Hell never came from the south, except on Daddy's anniversary.

In the time it took to make a fist, the wind jumped from thirty-five to forty-five knots and switched from southwest to south to southeast and back to south. The five-foot seas catapulted into eight, then into deep-green ten footers with square shoulders and frosted heads, the thunder and lightning now continuous as if a vindictive army was intent on forcing their advantage from the south. This was how the world must have started and how it would surely end, and now this is where Daddy and I found ourselves scalded with a vexation so aggressive in my throat it felt like incurable disease.

The waves washed over the deck in sheets and the self-bailing scuppers couldn't stay even with the volume. The standing rigging whined. My right arm shook with the strain of holding the tiller. Daddy grabbed harnesses from below and we each strapped ourselves into the combing with Lake Erie all white with gnarled foam and heaven gone by. We had come to a reckoning, but for the first time since Ruby and I plucked Daddy out of the water, he looked alive. There was a splash of red in his cheeks, a glint of gold in his eyes and something other than fear scratching his voice.

"If we can ride this out halfway to Vermilion," he said, with new intention, "maybe we can beat back to the Rye."

"Thinking the same way," I screamed, my voice swallowed by wind and the slap of waves. In the boil, I told myself I got what I wanted: a storm so out of control there was no way to gauge its force. Each trip over a crest, a monster plunge. It took us forever to climb one wave before we dropped into another sucking breach, then climbed again, each time with less strength remaining. While I hung on to the tiller, Daddy pushed, then the other way around, my legs and arms burning through wet clothes. Daddy's face, one long crease with a trickle of blood seeping from his nose. When the waves slammed into the hull, they didn't split apart but rode on like a flame-lit pendulum.

"This was a damn foolish idea," I cried out.

"Yes, it was," Daddy said. "But we'll make it. You're Norah Bow," he said, his voice a blend of shout and whisper. "You were born for a storm like this."

Born for this?

To be sandwiched between a northern front and a southern gale? Was this some divine punishment we both required or an elemental plunge into the demon switch we were both drawn to? The leap, plunge, and stall of my craft was not ready for an answer. With the wind gusting to seventy knots, I didn't think it was possible to beat my sloop into such a force with the heads of smaller waves now torn off so only their black stubs remained. It would only be a matter of time before we snapped the mast or tiller, lost the rigging, shredded the sails, capsized. Only a matter of time before something this ugly, this beautiful, this fierce and unforgiving grabbed us by the throat and dragged us the long way down. I looked at the rail wanting to be sick. Daddy held me back. Then I held him back. Like that, we kept going into a gyration of blackness and blinding flash with no end. Helping each other out there to stay the crooked course.

"Lifejackets?" Daddy shouted.

"They won't fit over the harnesses," I shouted back, long strings of wet slicking my chin. "It's either one or the other."

"One good thing," he said.

"What's that?"

"If we can make any headway south, the waves will get smaller."

"A big if."

The moment we both dreaded arrived.

Dark by hour, dark by sky, dark as the face of all the first untamed water, we were out in some of Erie's deepest hundred-foot water with waves bigger than a house. I had seen the sky blotted out by the pulse of mayflies in heat, watched a man choke on his own blood, and I'd sunk into the whiskey river believing death smarter than life. Had I come this far to sink to the bottom of Lake Erie? On the other hand, could anything that floats outrun the cage of lightning closing in from the north and south? Answer me that, O captain, whoever you are! Doubt had found me and more questions, then more doubt, but I told the quivering animal I'd become I wasn't ready to trade flesh for spirit. I wasn't ready to die even though it seemed clear in that blur of wind and water that no world, not here nor beyond, was strong enough to hold back my disappointment with a man who bore me. Disappointment was hardly the right word, but it would have to suffice until I found another word and then I would use that one against him for some greater punishment than what we found out there that night.

Halfway to Vermilion, we had to tack into the full brunt of the storm or we'd never get back to Rye Beach. There were no freighters out there, no dredgers, no fishing boats, no ferries, no Coast Guard, no other boats anywhere, large or small. Nothing to be seen but the mesmerizing onslaught boiling around us, and the stab of lightning, and no way forward but through the teeth of the south. I studied the waves, waiting, waiting, waiting for a short one that would not fall on top of us. Inside the squeal of wind and breaking water, I screamed the only words that mattered. "Ready about. Hard-a-lee."

Daddy released the spitfire jib on the port side but it whipped against the head stay and didn't catch and fill. *Odyssey* staggered into the climb of the next wave, then disappeared into its trough without finishing her tack. We stalled in wild irons, bobbing fifty degrees up, then the same arc downward. The starboard sheet caught on a mast cleat. Daddy saw the caught line and crawled forward to free it just as another wave dumped into the cockpit and laid us over on our side. Daddy skidded off the cabin, but he caught at the gunwale. I left the helm and reached out for him, but my harness wouldn't let me grab him.

He looked at me with this sorry grin as if to say, *Maybe it's better if I let go.*

"Not losing you after all this."

I unhitched my harness, fought my way through sheeting water, and got back to him. "On three," I shouted. One bought us nothing. Two bought us less. On three, I grabbed him by the seat and hauled him back to the cockpit. We got lucky. The wind sprung the line off the mast cleat and I brought it in on the starboard side. I looked at the mainsail and saw that it was torn along the foot, at the tack, up the luff. Daddy too saw the damage and grabbed a handful of lanyards.

"You can't save it," I said.

"Worth a shot," he muttered.

Watching Daddy in the lightning dark, after nearly vanishing for a second time in the drink, I believed he had a little more life left in him. I told myself he wanted to get back to Rye Beach and reckon with all he had left behind. Daddy cinched the mainsail to the boom and spar so it looked like a crumpled piece of paper, but it filled enough to give us some steady. With each plunge of the bow, the waves raked the deck and swamped the cockpit. With each new wave colder than the last, we took turns filling and dumping a bucket. Capsizing and sinking was no longer our biggest problem. It was the cold water, our own blue skin. Daddy was only a few hours removed from having almost died from the cold. He and I both knew most sailors don't drown. They die of exposure. I saw again the chatter of his teeth. Then, I followed suit and my own front teeth made a short, sharp, grinding sound in my head.

"You want...to be found...floating dead?"

Daddy shook his head with no words coming out of his mouth.

"Then we better get after that demon switch you say we both have."

Daddy's smile was all crook. Made him look a hundred years old. His eyes jiggled, his teeth clacked, half man, half wet skeleton. And then we bailed with new fury. We pounded our chests to keep the blood flowing. We slapped each other on the back. We stomped our feet and screamed to make ourselves heard above the shrieks of wind and water breaking over our sloop as she jiggered up a crest, hung at the top of a wave, then fell like a stone into a black hollow. I would like to say I took control of my boat, but it would be a lie. I had more luck to spend down. Like me, she blundered and groaned and wondered how such falling could be followed by so many perilous climbs. This storm was thrilling in its brute force, but it scared me like no other. No, it wasn't luck out there that kept us afloat and it wasn't the demon switch that allowed for more strength. Out there, it was the bitter seed I planted in the dirt of my soul, the seed that needed more time to grow, it was that small, unruly thing with no quit in it that kept us alive on that night.

No matter the muscle of this storm, we hung on like hell's fingernail. Maybe everything that went wrong, starting with the night Daddy was taken at gunpoint, couldn't stay wrong forever. Maybe the pink strands to the east were enough to grab and ride out. I didn't argue with how the change in weather found us, but it did. It took another five hours for us to sail less than ten miles but the killing blast of the night turned into a new day, and eventually, as we neared the Ohio shoreline, the ten-foot waves fell back to five footers. Shallow and snaggle-toothed Lake Erie, lit up from the south like never before or since, had no more running room to jig and jag and collapse on top of us. The storm weakened just enough for us to escape. Who in the hell can say how it happened this way? And then we were back home: two demons hoping to tie up, dry off, start again.

Many unthinkable, glass darkly things happened in the six weeks after I left Rye Beach and went in search of my father, but none more so than seeing Momma waiting at dawn on the break wall. Like maybe she had seen us in her prayers and she had helped to reel us in from the impossible, jagged edge. There were no lights on in any house. The power lines had to be down. Captain William's house, set back from the harbor's mouth, had been crushed by the sheared limb of a cottonwood believed to have been planted by Scottish fathers who first came to Rye Beach in 1820. Our beachy town was not yet awake after what must have been a night of howling dogs, snapped branches, blown windows, and locked doors. Daddy and I entered Rye Beach lagoon at some speed, but once in, we stood up into the wind and dropped sail. I wanted to laugh or cry, but I was too tired to do either. I couldn't even wave to Momma. Daddy and I each grabbed a paddle and made our way to a dock where she held her vigil.

Daddy threw Momma a bow line, but she missed the catch. She bent down on her knees to retrieve the line. Daddy kept his head bent low. I couldn't raise my right arm. It had turned an ugly blue after we'd made our last big tack. After Momma tied off the line, she covered her eyes. Like maybe she thought we were apparitions from an earlier dream who should not be greeted. When she pulled her hands away, we were still there, the two of us—cut on the face and arm, waterlogged, hair plastered on our scalps, two ghosts no longer, only her sailors tested by a monster storm.

As spent as I was and shivering, I could tell Momma looked different. I figured she would be gaunt from all the page-turning of her King James, but she looked unburdened. I couldn't place what the change was, but then from another angle, I saw it. Like Daddy, she too carried a new color splash. Not from makeup or crying, but from what? Keeping guard, keeping still, keeping faith? The sun and the wind had given her a new sway that stood out against the break wall. On that morning with the clouds still hanging in gray threads, she wore a yellow sundress and stood barefoot with more legginess and poise than I remembered. Imagine, until that day, I had never before seen my mother barefoot.

"Where on earth did you come from, Norah Bow?"

At first I didn't grasp her meaning, then I tasted blood on my lips. I couldn't make words. I pointed back to the inky sheen of Erie still cut open with whitecaps.

"I came from a Lake Erie gale."

"You surely did."

Daddy and I dragged ourselves onto the dock. I could tell by his eyes jumping in his head, he was already at work plying his story, wondering what he should put into it, what he should leave out. Momma hugged Daddy and smiled through tears sheeting off her face which she didn't bother to flick. It was a rare thing to see this watery downpour. Almost as rare as watching a few patches of blue returning to the last tent of slanting rain. Her smile and tears told me she too had been to the ends of the earth and she was not afraid to show the stain of her own travels. Maybe that's where her new equilibrium hailed from. From the place known by some as the back of the far beyond. Where all things begin and end.

"I knew you'd come back," Momma said, looking me over like birthday cake.

"You did?"

"Most nights I just saw you sailing all good water."

"Maybe a little worry is not such a bad thing," I said, wanting to hear a bit about how many flares and prayers she'd launched while I was gone.

"I knew she would protect you," Momma said, pointing to Lake Erie.

"I had my doubts."

"I set your place at the table every night. I thought it was only a matter of time before you got hungry. Bob sat at the front porch door every day since you've been gone. He would hardly look at me, but he never once stopped looking for you."

When she told me about holding a place at the table and then about Bob's keeping one eye peeled toward the lake, I turned into a puddle because I hadn't allowed myself to dwell on Bob since I had left. Momma now took a hard look at Daddy and I wished I could tell you everything I saw: *relief, anger, gratitude, sadness, doubt, resentment, fear.* All of it skidding through her eyes like seven bolts of lightning. She turned back to me, took my hands, held my palms to her face. Her breath warmed my fingers. When she pulled my palms away, her eyes widened.

"You did it, Norah. You brought him back. Only you could do this."

"Will they ever be clean again, Momma?"

"What are you saying?"

"I've been marked by what I've done."

"I see only faint shadow."

"You do?"

I looked at my hands, thinking I would see again the ugly dark stain reminding me of the three men Zane killed on Pelee Island, but the inky bleed had been scoured by wind and water and my grip on the tiller. All that was left was a scrim of shadow and my nails rimmed in black.

"Looks like oil stain," Momma said, squeezing my fingers.

"I was told I might be stained forever."

"Whoever told you that doesn't know anything about salt and lemon."

"Such good news," I said.

I threw my arms around her and squeezed with all my might. Then Momma glanced over at Daddy and drew him into a tight trio and for the first time her arms felt as strong as the wind battering us out of the wild, keening south.

Whatever good feeling set us back on land didn't last long. I took two steps toward our cottage and threw up from the pain shooting up my arm. I waved Momma off and walked off on my own accord to see the pump house, the thick-scrolled border of hollyhocks, and our rain-slicked cottage with half her shingles blown off. And there on the porch where I left him was Bob hammering his tail. For only the third time in my life I cried until there was no more cry left. Once when I left Rye Beach. Once for Catfish. And now once for Bob. There would be other crying jags, many others like something spit out by a storm, but nothing like those three rainfalls when I was fourteen.

27

For the rest of the summer, Daddy looked sobered by what had happened. He was kind to Momma. He spent time with the boys. He took us all to Cedar Point, where we got hung up on the Ferris wheel at the top of its spin, laughed, and ate cotton candy like gravity had not been invented. When our car paused in the upper sphere and swung us gentle for what seemed like an eternity, he and I looked out at the hard water we had traveled, but we said nothing and asked nothing of the other. Maybe he thought I would get busy and forget and, in my forgetting, I would have no call to look back any longer.

I never knew what he said to Momma the first day or the day after, and I never asked. I don't know if he told her more lies or if he dusted off some piece of the truth and sold it to her sad. All I knew was: *He and I would never be close again.* We kept our wary distance. Me as much as him. We each knew too much so maybe what happened was partly because he believed I would eventually tell Momma everything about how he had thrown in his lot with the rumrunners so he could be with a card dealer named Ruby Francouer. Some part of me cried out to tell Momma, but I couldn't bear the thought of turning Ruby into a villain or a tramp. Besides, I didn't want to hurt Momma more or less than she already was. And good lord I never saw this coming, Momma and I became friends. We talked about girl things, laughed over mosquito bites on the nose, and gobbled too many ice cream cones, and went swimming together, and I took her out on the *Odyssey* even though she never learned much more than when to duck her head when the boom swung. I even let her teach me how to sew and cook, and I committed three of her recipes to memory: one for peach pie with lemon juice, cinnamon, nutmeg, butter, and one egg; the one for fried

perch rolled in cornmeal, flour, salt, pepper, and beer, and another for buckwheat cinnamon pancakes made with buttermilk,
cinnamon, and a shot of maple syrup.

While making her famous cakes for dinner one night, Momma asked me about what happened while I was gone and I told
her some things about Pelee Island and even Detroit and Windsor. I told her how a boy named Catfish had saved my life and
I showed her the pearl-handled knife he had given me. I didn't
tell her how he died. Or how I wanted to stay with him. Or that
he was the first boy I kissed, but from the way she smiled she let
me know she understood how much I cared for him.

"What happened between you and your father?"

"I brought him back."

"You two don't talk anymore."

"We said most of what we needed to say out on the lake."

"He's still your father," my mother said, her hands brushed
with oil and flour.

I didn't even try to cover all the breadth and depth. Some
secrets just have to stay where they are. Vital Bow is linked to
me forever by blood, but the water between us would not be
crossed again. Momma took my face in her hands and stared
into my eyes like she was trying to help me come all the way
home, but I didn't give her any tears. The brindled stain on my
hands went away. My arm strength returned. The scratch on
my eye healed. But what I saw hurt just as much as all I hadn't
seen before.

As that summer of 1926 drew near its end, Daddy started
coming home late. He said he was working, but I didn't buy a
biscuit of that story. I figured he still hungered for another life.
The life he had fashioned from great books, ten-cent insurance
policies, and twin boys was just not enough. He never found the
backbone to tell Momma outright what happened or maybe she
knew and turned a blind eye.

At dinner, Daddy and I would pass each other as if we'd

climbed on board separate boats and sailed off, the remoteness between us cut by islands, rivers, and one ragged gale with two heads. We could no longer bring each other clearly into focus, so we faded into an uncharted shipping lane, until finally we fell off the rim of each other's horizon. It went on like that until one day after school started, I pulled from his shelves a book on geology and read about the earth's crust and inner core, how the fires below are as hot as the sun's surface, the entire earth bubbling from the inside out. Then, I read that beneath the earth's crust, there are layers of solid rock of which little is known. And that was how I finally came to see my father, Vital Bow. He was forced as a child to work the coal mines, and even though he left that underground world as soon as he could and taught himself how to read and speak like a prince, some stray piece of him still wandered beneath knotted tunnels of bituminous rock. He found me in his library and asked to see the book I was reading. I handed it over. He held the book for a long time before saying anything.

"What do you want from me?"

"Not sure I know."

"Not everything works out the way you want," he said in a flat voice.

"Sometimes I wish Ruby had never found you in the drink," I said, my voice a braid of sting and agitation.

"I can see all that in your eyes."

"Why don't you just leave again," I said. "You know you want to."

"This is my home, our home."

"Daddy, you'll never be at home."

I took the geology book out of his hands and put it back on the shelf where it belonged, and I left him there, his eyes turning wet and his big ears in a blush. I never again returned to his library where he hatched his dreams. When his late nights became more frequent, I sensed he was not making more money, just spending the money he had, more freely. Sometimes when he didn't come home, I would ring up Aunt Cora's house, always ready to click the phone, but she never answered. When Daddy was home, I called her number and she always picked up. I knew then that the woman he'd kissed while I was under the car was my mother's sister. The flirtations, the kissing, the fondling on the porch—all of that became a regular grab. What Daddy had not been able to consummate with Ruby, he brought home to Aunt Cora. The night I had planned to share my evidence with Momma was the night Sheriff Kelly came to our door with a pinched face as if he'd just clamped down on a lemon.

"Vivian, ma'am, and Norah," he said glumly, "I got bad news, real bad. Vital was in an accident. His car hit a tree and he was thrown from the vehicle."

Momma squeezed my hand and I squeezed back.

"He was killed instantly."

"My sister?" Momma said, shocking me with her first question.

"She will live, Vivian. She was hurt bad, but she will live another day."

"Where?" she asked.

"Over in Huron, near the Sand Bar restaurant. Bartender said they had left around ten."

"Don't say anything more," Momma said to the sheriff. "Not another word."

My great protector, my great deceiver. Two sides of the same man, no wider than the lip of a whiskey bottle: hello, goodbye father, green pastures, hard water, short breach of sun, long pale night, whoever you are. Vital Bow, who lived most of his brief life in the doorway of flirtation and disguise, was buried without fanfare. Daddy would have objected to a preacher at his funeral, but Momma contracted with Reverend Raymond Francis who read from Corinthians, a verse she and I were both drawn to: *For we know in part and we prophesy in part, but when completeness comes, what is in part disappears.* Sometime during the

eulogy, I thought I would swoon and hit the ground because
while the reverend spoke, I thought I heard Daddy making
again his play on words, *Norah Bow, Norah Bow. You are the bow
of the world.*

As pallbearers lowered Daddy to the faraway, I thanked him
for giving me my name, teaching me how to walk again during
the great influenza, offering me the rake of a mast when I needed it most, and telling me of the demon switch and how I might
draw from it when nothing else would do. After my thanking,
I prayed for all the broke in him to be returned to the source
incorruptible, but I did not let him have my tears. For Aunt
Cora, I offered nothing. She stood at the rim of the circle in an
arm and leg cast. No longer a whisper in the dark. No longer
a beauty. I gave her no more than a glance. She and Momma
did not exchange a word that day. It would be another ten years
before they did.

Years before his death at the bright age of forty-seven, Daddy had purchased two plots on a grassy knoll overlooking Lake
Erie. His last perch made me think he chose this spot to ensure
he would gain no rest, even in death. I imagined him feeding
on the shimmer that lies at the horizon line, straddling another
country and another life, both just out of reach.

That night, after the guests had left the house and the con-
dolences had thankfully petered out, Momma and I talked.

"You knew about Aunt Cora?"

"Didn't think it would last," she said.

"Turns out, it didn't," I said, with a touch of snide.

"Your father wasn't always so unhappy," she said.

"I want to believe that."

"You were the light of his world."

My eyes watered some. My head felt heavy with all the un-
said things, but what I needed then was to hear Momma's voice.

"When did things go wrong?"

"He didn't want any more children and I did. You were
enough for him."

"You make it sound like I was——"

"No, no. It's not that. He wanted…"

"What, Momma?"

"I don't know. More lives maybe or some other life."

I saw him again, above ground, below ground, at home, with Ruby—a man always ready to leave for the night and not return, a man who, top dead center, taught me how to enter the wind, unafraid of what I might find there.

"Did you love him?"

"Seems like your father and I both blinked, then one day he was gone."

I put my arms around her and then we cried together—not so much about the Daddy we knew, but about the man we never knew and who was now free to wander anywhere he wanted. The great blessing that emerged from Daddy's death was simply this: For the first time, Momma and I talked openly and easily about the stuck parts in ourselves and in Daddy who we knew only in part. We became confidantes and so I came to tell her my plans. At fourteen, I told Momma if a girl can't hire out on an ocean-going freighter from Toledo, then I would build a bigger sailboat from scratch to take me out from the land. She nodded and said, "Yes, of course you will. You are Norah Bow."

In those days and in that time, we offered each other a sliver of daylight that would only gain volume with more time. But first, there was more hooch, more hurt. Near the end of my senior year, I went down into a deep-traveling sleep of expectation and forgetting. I sailed back to the whiskey river and saw again my friends and my enemies, all of them like so many watery portraits in a shooting gallery. I never heard Bob whining to be let out, so he nosed himself out through the screen door. The sun blinding in its first gleam. Bob was getting on in years and he may not have been wide awake himself. A car rattled by, kicking up dust. Bob must have thought that odd because fast cars didn't come into Rye Beach. This one did and so Bob gave chase.

What Bob didn't know was there was another rumrunner's

car behind the first one and he never saw that big boat of a car before it clipped him in the hindquarters and spun him sideways. I woke then, knowing in my gut something was terribly wrong and so I ran from my bedroom with almost nothing on and found Bob all broken up and gasping. Later that day, I carried him a good ways out onto a bramble spit and buried him behind a dune. If you know "Cry Me a River," written some twenty years later for Ella Fitzgerald, then you know the kind of mournful tune I brought for Bob. Since he was a pup, Bob and I had craved each other's company and reassurance and not a day passed when we didn't take heart from each other's being all in for the other. You could offer me my own private island on Lake Erie or one more day with Bob and my choice would not even be close. What I'm trying to say is, Prohibition just about did me in. I couldn't eat. Couldn't sleep. Couldn't do anything but listen to my heart caught between a hush and a hammer. So what came next was like a key busting me out of jail.

Just a few days before my high school graduation I got a postcard from Victoria, British Columbia, that read simply, *Seventy-foot schooner leaving for Marquesas in July. Thought you might like the cut of the jib. Meet me at the Bent Mast Bar, R.*

That postcard from Ruby arrived in Rye Beach some eighty years ago. I thought I had lost the picture of two flower baskets hanging from a wrought-iron lamppost until a big wind rattled the front window glass and the postcard, tucked behind another picture, slipped from its pocket and landed at my feet, which is what made me think I had to get this story out in the open. I had no choice in the matter. This story had been looking for me for a long time.

Now, after eight decades—or is it nine?—I ask myself how much of what happened was true down to the bone or have I only rearranged events to suit my conclusions? Such is the deviation of memory. Not to be trusted, not ever, and yet our remembrances are all we can carry with us until they too are unremembered and untended by anyone.

That said, I'd like to tell you I know a great many things with certainty but I don't, but I do know this. The world runs on secrets buried in the ocean of the blood. Each vantage point on the compass depicts one degree of truth, so we may all lay claim that our chosen reading of the past is correct. But nobody tells the whole story. Nobody grasps the whole truth cloaked by time and distance, both fickle in their loyalties. And nobody gets to map the bottom of this ocean except when they are scattered there.

What's more, I wish I could say I pegged most everything right about Daddy, but chances are I got just as many things wrong, and I never saw the man as he saw himself. Lick of smoke, molecule of hunger and longing, burst of rose in the shade of an oak, my days are more like his than not, only so many breaths counting down to an unmoored signature. It's probably fair to say Daddy wasn't keen on the vaporous nature of our fate and so he tried, with all motor oil he could stash away, to escape it. No such luck, Vital Bow. No one gets to outrun the feet of smoke we are born with, not even Ruby.

No, I won't give my last word to smoke.

Everything breaks open eventually—the sky, the Great Lake beneath it, the four-chambered pump stuck in the chest, even the earth itself troubled by its own chain of internal fires. I used to think all these broken places were the source of my sadness and the world's, but that's only where the story starts.

The hard part is knowing where to go after the disappointment has blown you down. Do you stay and rebuild from scratch or do you leave? I'll wager the only ones who eke out any measure of happiness are those who wrestle or pray all night for answers, then in the morning they settle for more questions. When you get a sign, even a faint electrical pulse of how to proceed, you don't hesitate to act because weak signals from the horizon may be the most explicit orders you'll ever receive.

That blast of air, that swept my long-ago postcard from behind a picture, was the leading edge of a low-pressure system that swept down the North Carolina coast and rattled my windows. Maybe the big wind aimed to wash out Topsail Beach in North Carolina where I live alone, but my cottage stood up to this storm. There are many times when I thought I've had enough difficulty here, more than enough, but now I can't seem to die.

Every moment I can't seem to die is coupled with every other moment and all of this coupling is less understood than the dark blue veins on the back of my hands. My veins tell me I am losing volume as my blood pressure spikes. Sooner than later and maybe in just a few hours, these bulging rivers will join the one great river, so what more must I tell you about the river of time my father and I made with our moments?

I never knew the origin of his unhappiness or if the broken in him was given away at birth and he had no say in the matter. I do know it's always been a scandal to say, *I love you. How can we fix this? Please forgive me.* I never heard him say those words, so now I say those words for him, thinking maybe he still needs help in this department and anyway, I'm the only one left on earth who knows his name. I'm the only one who can say, let's go out on the water, Vital Bow, and hoist sail and see if we can sort out those parts of ourselves we never understood.

And, yes, Ruby and I island-hopped across the South Pacific before we parted company again in Fiji where sailboats from all over the globe are abandoned because the enormity of the Pacific suddenly comes into view from there and even the most intrepid skippers think, *What more must I prove to the gods of adventure?* Others arrive looking for a bargain, for a cook, for a last-minute savior, for weather-tested crew. Ruby left on a boat called the *Yellow Jacket* with an Italian skipper who promised a grove of olive trees and a hilltop villa. Maybe she stayed with him. Maybe not. Either way, I'm sure she held tight to the lightning bolt of her life song. That's what a ruby can do.

I caught another boat to New Zealand, but no matter where I went, no matter how many Panamas, Argentinas, and Tristan da Cunhas I reached, the cottage on Rye Beach was how my heart could always lay down a new heading. Rye Beach, within spitting distance of a tempting arc of Lake Erie islands, home of the untamable wisteria keen on prying apart any window with its vines, and Bob, the best beach hound in the world who never failed to make me laugh. Rye Beach, gathered for Sunday dinner where I trust the fat jade crickets still bivouac in the swale beside Johnny's penny candy store. Rye Beach, where my barefoot mother in a yellow sundress waits on the break wall with open arms. Rye Beach, a summer cottage place not far from a whiskey river that caused so much pain and pushed me toward the many sweet things I claimed for myself after the pain was gone.

ACKNOWLEDGEMENTS:

I want to thank my fearless readers who weighed in on this novel as it evolved over many years. I asked so much of you and you all gave even more: Ann Ryan, screenwriters and story consultants Allan Katz and Joe Gilford, Bill Tremblay, Pat Francisco, Sally King, Mary Logue, and most of all, Lynne Armstrong who read multiple versions of this story without reservation. I also want to thank my father who told me stories of his days at Rye Beach, Ohio, where he first learned to build sailboats from scraps of lumber that washed up on shore.